The Guardians:

Richard Austin is the pseudonym of a popular science fiction adventure writer.

Also by Richard Austin
in Pan Books

The Guardians

Richard Austin _____

THE GUARDIANS
Trial by Fire

PAN BOOKS
London, Sydney and Auckland

Acknowledgments:

Thanks to Robert Pruden and John Brooks
for advice and technical information.

First published in USA 1985 by the
Berkley Publishing Group, New York
This edition published 1990 by Pan Books Ltd,
Cavaye Place, London SW10 9PG

9 8 7 6 5 4 3 2 1

© Richard Austin 1985

ISBN 0 330 31254 5

Printed by Clays Ltd, St Ives plc

For Joseph Reichert,
Senior Prophet

PROLOGUE —————————————

It is two weeks since the Third World War wiped out a third of humanity at a stroke. The good news is that the lethal zones of radioactive fallout have significantly shrunk back to the craters left by the groundbursts that gave the fallout birth. The bad news is that millions have already received a lethal cumulative dose—and that's only the beginning. Now the true devastation has begun: the grinding attrition of famine, disease, disorder. Around the globe, those nations not stricken by thermonuclear warheads are locked in death struggles with neighbors, paying off old grudges or seeking new expansion—or merely desperate to seize the resources to feed populations cut off from the breadbaskets of Australia and the Americas.

And in America, everything worth having—food, clothing, shelter, medicine, fuel, and, increasingly, ammunition—is running out.

In Oregon, mobs of refugees streaming away from Portland overrun a survivalist retreat near Mount Hood. While state patrolmen look on, the refugees loot the retreaters' food and medical supplies, while those defenders who weren't killed in the storming of their retreat are systematically beaten to

1

death. They attracted the mob's attention by attempting to set up an aid station along a nearby highway.

A rat pack of sixty bikers overwhelms a convoy carrying medical supplies to a displaced-persons camp in Ohio. Six National Guardsmen and three paramedics are killed. A dozen student-nurse volunteers from Kent State are raped so savagely that five die.

A people's court in Massachusetts sentences a hundred "hoarders"—people who have stockpiled goods against catastrophe—to death. Confiscated goods are appropriated by the court's specially empowered police squads. Somehow few of the expropriated supplies find their way to the suffering masses in whose name the court is acting.

Right-wing paramilitary death squads travel in a caravan across Virginia, executing "traitors" in drumhead courts-martial. Victims include antiwar activists, union officials, a popular network newswoman who had escaped the bombing of Washington, D.C., alleged draft resisters, and a prominent child psychologist.

In California's San Joaquin Valley a truckload of former union enforcers surrounds an abandoned farmhouse in which a family of Hispanic migrant workers are squatting, trying to harvest crops rotting in the fields north of Tulare. The would-be farmer's brother is gunned down, his wife and fifteen-year-old daughter raped before his eyes, which are then gouged out. The marauders geld him, sew his severed genitals in his mouth, and for good measure chop off his hands. They then set the farmhouse afire and leave. The squatter had been the ringleader of a group of squatters resisting the union's demand that they turn over fifty percent of anything they managed to glean.

Whole towns along the shattered Eastern seaboard are overrun by locust swarms of refugees, who loot stores and homes and warehouses and kill anyone who gets in their way. In the South, armed bands of citizens in rural areas patrol the highways, turning back people fleeing from devastated cities who are seeking refuge in their communities. In Arkansas a camp full of fugitives from the saturation bombing of the Little Rock area is attacked by locals who claim the DPs have been raiding their homes and fields. Over three hundred are killed.

For the foreseeable future, this will be the normal course of things in the formerly United States of America.

The heat of early summer sun lay like a leaden plate on a derelict field forty kilometers south of Enid, Oklahoma. The last driving prairie thunderstorm had turned it into an ocean of black mud. The feet of hundreds of the lost, the hungry, the stricken, the homeless, the hopeless had churned it into a mass of ripples and wavelets, and the sun had baked the mess hard. The water that had cascaded down like a new Deluge from the black, distended clouds was coming back out of the earth in hot, humid coils to clutch at the throat like strangler's hands.

Tents sprouted like exotic fungus on the sea of hardened mud—some the drab of military surplus, others modern synthetic shells, dome shaped and incongruously colorful. Most were makeshift affairs, cobbled together of tarpaulins, plastic sheeting, scraps of cloth, anything to make a gesture at keeping off the rain and the killer sun that alternated like beasts chasing each other across the broad midwestern sky. Off to one side, near the highway, stood a brightly colored pavilion that in another life had been the bingo tent at the Kingfisher County fair. Its bright plastic fringes flapped noisily in the desultory breeze as from its muggy shade came moans, small cries, occasional screams. A pair of haggard medics—a young man and woman in fatigues and Red Cross armbands—moved to and fro in the pavilion, doing their pathetic best to ease the wounded, sick, and dying that lay there.

On the far side of the pavilion, forty or fifty meters away, a truck was parked. Corpses lay stacked like firewood on its wooden bed. The ones on the bottom had begun to balloon in the humid June heat. Some bore marks of the thermonuclear blasts that had smashed Enid in the enemy's attempt to take out Vance Air Force Base on its western fringe. Others had been maimed by the pair of airbursts that had gone off over Oklahoma City to the south. Burned, battered, broken, these survivors had staggered here to die—or had died and been dragged or driven here by kinfolk pathetically hopeful or simply unwilling to face the fact of death even when it was staring them in the face. Others showed signs of violence of the more personal, down-home type—bullet holes, knife slashes, livid bruises left by the proverbial blunt instrument. These were victims who had tried to resist when the new breed of predator took their food or cars or whatever they'd managed to escape with. Some of the more recent corpses, hairless and discolored, their shrunken legs smeared with dried shit, had obviously died of acute radiation poisoning. Others, more traditionally, had shit themselves to death, compliments of man's old companion, cholera, which had been enjoying a renaissance these last two weeks. In fact, more than half the bodies bloating on the truckbed had come there through the agency of one disease or another. Rumor had it that some of the diseases had arrived from space—*Yup, saw one of them biologic rockets myself, big silver nosecone layin' there in the dirt with CCCP painted all over it in red.* As of now, the overworked medics had no reason to believe that was any more than talk. Take the total breakdown of medical care and a few million bodies lying around to act as cultures, and what you had was a brave new world for bacteria.

Stacking the stiffs on the truck like that wasn't the best way to keep pestilence in its place, but there was no fuel to burn them with, no dozers to scrape mass graves in the dirt. The Red Cross team had some disinfectants, but they were needed to keep the Kingfisher County Bingo Pavilion and Hardscrabble Clinic in some degree sanitary. The best they could do was put the corpses a distance from camp in what they hoped was a generally downwind direction. When enough bodies accumulated, one of the medics would try to round up enough displaced persons with strength to wield a shovel and dig a pit for them. As of now, the Red Cross people had even given up trying to cover the bodies with plastic. The DPs kept swiping it to make shelters with.

Back among the dumpy mushrooms of tents and lean-tos were collected representatives of America's most underprivileged group: the living, who were rapidly on their way to achieving minority status. Some of them kept prudently to the doubtful comfort of their shelters. Others stayed put because the next move they'd be making was to the back of the truck on the other side of the pavilion. A lot of patch-balding borderline cases sat or lay slumped in the bone-deep torpor that so often attended rad poisoning. Others slouched before their tents or perched on rumpled blankets, keeping careful watch over the handfuls of possessions they'd brought out with them. A few filthy children, their ragged jeans and smocks and T-shirts hanging on their skinny bodies, played in a desultory way. But mostly, this time of day everybody just stayed put.

"Thank you, Jesus!" A half-dozen survivors clustered alongside the right-of-way of U.S. 81, watching the dead-car-clogged highway that stretched like a ribbon of steel toward Enid to the north and Okie City to the south. They were looking for the relief trucks they knew were coming, bearing food and medicine. It'd been two days since any of them had eaten, and they were hoping awfully hard.

"Praise God!" The pious outbursts rang out intermittently, like sparrows startled out of a bush, from a woman in a white dress with flowers printed on it and huge crusted sweat stains under the arms. She had rigged an awning of old blankets to the side of a tractor trailer and sat in its shadow, knitting, in a frayed yellow lawn chair. She hadn't eaten any more recently than the others keeping sunken-eyed vigil along the highway; only, she showed it less. Her bulk almost overflowed the flimsy chair. Her arms and legs were sausage-fat, the translucent white of uncooked dough. Colorless hair was knotted any which way on the top of her kidney-bean head. "Hallelujah!"

"Shut the fuck up," growled a big man in a cap with Peterbilt written on the front. His heavy face was burned almost the shade of the brick-colored hair cut close under the hat—burned by the sun, fortunately for him. His left arm was strapped across his chest. Brandishing a tire iron, he'd tried to defend his load of Del Monte canned foods from a gang of hijackers a couple of days after the war. He was lucky; they'd shot him in the shoulder with a .38 and tossed him in a ditch.

A farmer with a narrow, balding skull, whose farm had lain downwind of Vance AFB, scowled and squared skinny shoulders. "Watch your mouth," he said. "Oughtn't to talk that way in front of no lady."

The trucker rounded on him. "You shut up too. She ain't no lady. She's a crazy old bitch."

"Mighty big talk for a man can't even hang on to his own rig," another watcher said.

The brick-haired trucker waved a scarred right fist. "I can sure as shit take care of you miserable sodbusters!"

The woman raised her head. Thick rolls of fat bulged at the back of her neck as she squinted north. A figure had materialized out of the heat shimmer. "Someone coming," she said in her high, froggy voice. "Praise the Lord."

Heads swiveled hopefully. They saw the single man on foot, his shoulders sagging as he walked along the row of deserted cars. "Damn," the trucker said. "Just another goddamn stumblebum refugee."

But the fat lady had laid her knitting in her voluminous lap. "No," she said. "He been sent to us. I can tell. It's a miracle, praise Jesus!"

"Only miracle round here is that that friggin' chair don't collapse under your fat butt," the trucker muttered under his breath. But the others were watching the man intently. The trucker hiked his cap up his sweaty, freckle-dotted forehead and studied the newcomer while the wind punched the makeshift awning like a great slow fist, and hooted mournfully down and around and through the carcasses of cars and trucks and men.

He was a long, shambling scarecrow of a man, got up like an undertaker in black trousers, a white shirt without a tie, and a black coat. He stalked down the asphalt like some huge bird. His head was surrounded by a black ragged halo of hair and beard. Eyes like black gemstones stared out of a face the white of polished bone despite the fact the man went bareheaded in the merciless sun. The impact of his eyes was physical, even at thirty meters.

"Where you come from, cousin?" called the man who'd mocked the truck driver. He was a stocky blond man who'd worked in a machine shop in Oklahoma City.

The stranger strode closer, and the trucker could see that his black shoes were held together by electrician's tape. They had been expensive shoes, but he'd plumb walked them out. "I have come from Enid," the man announced in a ringing voice, and stopped twenty or thirty feet from the watchers.

"Bullshit," the trucker said. "Enid's still hot."

The black eyes turned to him. The trucker quailed. The other's look seemed to suck the heat from his body.

"I have been in Enid," the tall man said again. "I have seen the wrath of the Lord visited on many sinners—men such as you, brother. But I am immune to the poison of wormwood. The Lord has chosen me as His messenger."

"Hallelujah!" the fat woman exclaimed. She slid forward onto her knees in an avalanche of pallid flesh. Her knitting dropped to the asphalt with a clicking of needles. She knotted her vast hands under her jowls. "I told you it was a miracle. I told you I could feel it!"

"Blessed are you, sister," the man intoned, "for you have eyes wherewith to see. You are a burning and a shining light; ye bare witness unto the truth!"

"Now, wait a minute," the sturdy machinist said. "You mean to tell me you've been in Enid since—since the war?"

The man nodded grandly. "I was summoned there by the will of God. I have passed through the unseen fire and the dust that kills, and emerged unscathed, though the very clothes I wear are now death to the unpurified."

He held out one arm, pivoted to address the camp as well as the watchers by the road. The young Red Cross woman, curious, stepped out of the shadow of the aid tent, brushing a straw-colored lock from her eyes with the back of a blood-stained hand. The refugees looked up, some curious, some hostile, but most just blank. "I bring you a message, my children," he announced, speaking with the exaggerated diction of an evangelist and the Plains-Texas drawl of Oklahoma. "A message of hope, of redemption for ye who are ready to receive it."

"Tell us, brother, tell us," sobbed the mountainous woman.

"The hand of God is laid upon the world. Great is his wrath and stark his judgment. Hear me: the punishment has just begun!"

A gasp went up from the crowd. Looking right and left, the trucker saw that the others who had held vigil with him by the road were watching the man in rapt amazement. "Yea, the Four Horsemen ride, and the suffering of mankind has just begun. But you need suffer no more, my children. The Way lies clear before you.

"Consecrate yourselves to the great task at hand. Follow

me, and I shall lead you to cooling waters where you may have to drink; follow, and I shall lead you to a land of milk and honey. The sinners hoard their earthly goods while you have not to eat. Do you wait for relief, for supplies to succor you in your time of need? I tell ye, you wait in vain. For the sinners will not share of their bounty. But you shall know a treasure greater than they can imagine.

"Follow me, and ye shall be delivered!"

"Hallelujah!" screamed a woman in the camp, falling to her knees on a dried mud wavelet. "Hallelujah!" chorused a hundred throats. The refugees were all coming forward, genuflecting before the magnetic stranger. The skinny, bald farmer knelt, and the machinist and the other watchers as well.

As if in a trance, the trucker lowered himself to his knees. "God have mercy on me," he said hoarsely. "Dear God, have mercy."

"Gentlemen," the heavyset man said in English as he stepped up to the elevated podium. A spotlight beam high and behind turned his grizzled dark hair to a cloud around his massive head. "Ladies. The Internationalist Council is now in session."

The thirty-odd men and women assembled in comfortably padded swivel chairs around the vast white oblong oval table at the center of the meeting hall murmured quietly among themselves. Maximov waited on the dais which rose like a small stage at the head of the large room, and smiled beatifically behind his dense but well-trimmed beard. High overhead the ceiling of the chamber slanted downward from left to right. The mellow afternoon sunlight of the Bernese Alps spilled in through a line of tall windows, splashing the big white rectangular-sectioned roofbeams and the gallery over-looking the hall. The effect was of a Bauhaus cathedral, all geometric shapes and muted neutral hues.

"I have much good news to impart," the big man said, his richly rolling bass a sonorous counterpoint to the subtle hum-ming of the climate-control system. "Though the world lies in ruins, much of what we have worked and struggled for over the years has come to pass, bringing new hope for humankind. Recognizing—after the brutal lesson of a fortnight ago—that the anarchic order of the world would have to be dispensed with for humanity to survive, the nations and peoples of Europe have at last acknowledged the need for unity. They have placed themselves and their destiny under the benign and centralized stewardship of the Internationalist Council, which is now the governing body of the new Federated States of Europe."

He paused for polite applause. The surviving members of the forty-member council—a gathering of industrialists, statesmen, editors, and intellectuals, all brought together under his aegis in the early seventies to work for a new world order—knew all this already. Nonetheless, he rehearsed the facts of the situation for them. He liked to hear himself talk, and wanted, this one last time, to observe the effect of his words on the faces of his colleagues. *Few empty seats,* he thought. His intelligence network had reported that every member of the council who had survived the holocaust had managed to reach his stronghold for this convocation. *Splendid.*

"Further, the commanders of the armies of NATO and the Warsaw Pact, which so recently were making a shambles of Germany, have rendered their submission to the authority of the FSE as master of a united Europe. The Soviet Union has been shattered, and the surviving subject peoples battle to complete the overthrow of their former masters. What little we can learn from the United States of America indicates that that nation is in little better state. No great nation of the world escaped the violence of the Third World War. And the lesser-developed countries are fearful, uncertain of what the new age holds for them.

"Much as we men—and women—of goodwill must deplore these fearsome events, it would be irresponsible of us not to acknowledge the opportunity with which we find ourselves presented. For years you and I have worked toward a time when a responsible, professional hand might be placed upon the rudder of world affairs. And what better hand than that of this council, comprised as it is of those experienced in the management of states and great corporations, the molders and shapers of Western opinion?

"The time has come, ladies and gentlemen. The world floats

adrift on a sea of turbulent disorder. It remains for us to seize the tiller."

This time the applause was sustained, sincere. Beneath the humanitarian rhetoric of the council lay the raw fact that these men and women had been scuffling for years to rearrange the world for their personal power, privilege, and profit. Personal animosity, national rivalries, or ideology had never been permitted to interfere with the master plan. The wiser among the council realized that even the One-Day War had been an instrument of the council's policy. Of course, even they didn't necessarily realize the war hadn't quite turned out according to plan.

Nor would they ever learn.

As the clapping died down, a red light glowed on the podium before Maximov. It indicated that one of the members wished to speak from the floor. The signal was so much more refined and civilized than shouting and waving one's hand. "Yes, Mrs. Coyningham," he said, addressing the pinch-mouthed woman with elaborately coiffed silver hair who, as a Labourite prime minister of the United Kingdom, had presided over the resurrection of the welfare state that had suffered under Maggie Thatcher.

"When will we learn the specific positions we shall occupy in this new order, Mr. Chairman?" she asked in her well-bred, supercilious, slightly nasal voice.

Maximov gazed down upon her. He reflected on the way her watery gray eyes swam in magnification behind the lenses of her ridiculous batwing glasses. A majestic smile spread across his face. "At once, Mrs. Coyningham. At once. The part you shall play in the new order may be simply summed up: none."

A beat of silence, then an outbreak of outrage, disbelief, and sheer confusion. "The logic is quite impeccable, my friends," Maximov said matter-of-factly. "We have all devoted outselves to the principle of centralization. It is only rational, now that we find actual power in our hands, to carry that principle to its natural conclusion.

"Therefore, I am assuming absolute power as sole executive of the FSE. This council is dissolved."

Across the table and down from Mrs. Coyningham, a lanky, tanned man in a brown suit sprang to his feet like an angry stork. He had a prominent nose and a shock of chestnut hair, touched with distinguished Grecian Formula gray at the temples. His eyes were furious slits in a network of weathered wrinkles. His name was Dr. Joseph Bryce, and his narrow fanny had until recently occupied the Henry Kissinger Chair of Political Science at Harvard. He shook a twiglike finger in the air. "Do you actually expect us to sit still for this egregious usurpation, Maximov?" he shouted.

Maximov's smile broadened. "Why, no, Doctor. I don't."

He pressed a button on the console set in the podium. Instantly a transparent sheet slammed down from above, blocking off the dais from the floor of the meeting hall. Through the smoky metallic shimmer of armored glass, Maximov saw the faces of the council members go slack and stupid with alarm.

Along the catwalk above, doors burst open. A squad of men dressed in black, with black ski masks over their faces, burst in. They held stubby KG-9 machine pistols in their hands.

The screams and the yammer of the machine pistols floated through the shield as though from a great distance. Maximov punched another button. Speakers on the dais began to relay the sounds of the slaughter from audio pickups in the chamber. The volume was damped by computer so that the noise of the guns would not be painful to Maximov's ears.

He sensed a presence at his side. His peripheral vision registered a tall, slender man in a white pullover. He was narrow headed, with a snow-bird tan, broad shoulders, and blond hair that swept back from a high forehead. "Chief Zeeman at least is displaying a certain clumsy panache, Ivan Vissarionovich," he remarked. The hang-bellied former chief of the Los Angeles Police Department, now a politician and a tub-thumper for law 'n' order on American network television, had whipped out a snub-nosed revolver from a concealment holster in the back of his waistband, assumed an isosceles firing stance, and begun blazing away at the masked gunmen. One dropped his machine pistol and pitched forward over the guardrail. A second stitched the chief from his crotch to the lower of his chins with black-scarlet holes.

Maximov shook his head and clucked with mock reproof. "For a man who campaigned so vigorously for firearms control, he was certainly quick to smuggle one of those new graphite-composite pistols past our metal detectors."

The classic features of the man at his side twisted in a brief grimace of distaste. "You've created a grotesque scene, Yevgeny."

On the other side of the metallized glass, the council members performed spastic dances as metal-clad slugs tore through them. Dr. Bryce of Harvard lay with his back on the table and his arms outflung in a crucifixion posture. Mrs. Coyningham had managed to crawl under the table, which did her little good, since the killers were crisscrossing it with their fire—and the surface had been specially designed to offer no undue resistance to the passage of bullets. Maximov nodded.

"What Goya did with paint on canvas, I do with reality," he said, not without smugness.

Colonel Ivan Vesensky of the KGB snorted through sculpted nostrils. "It looks more like something out of a James Bond movie. Bourgeois decadence writ large."

"Actually, I got the idea from a Robert Ludlum novel. If I were attempting to achieve Bondian high camp, I would have arranged to have them electrocuted in their chairs. Which would be absurd, to say nothing of expensive."

The last member of the council had fallen under the copper-jacketed rain of fire, to lie moaning or motionless on the blood-soaked carpet. Several of the death squad came down the steps to make sure their victims were dead while two kept watch from above. "You could have arranged accidents for them, something more surreptitious."

A bushy brow cocked. "*All* of them?"

The colonel shrugged. "Against the backdrop of the war, not impossible. Who would sort their deaths out of millions?"

"Bah." Maximov waved his hand expressively as the killers went among the fallen, firing shots into the backs of necks. "You've grown too much like your masters in the Kremlin, too staid, too prudish. I am reminded of the way those withered old men dissolved SMERSH after Ian Fleming used the name in his novels. No sense of humor."

Vesensky grinned. "I've never been called prudish before."

"You've managed to conceal your streak of primness hitherto, I confess." The thud of another pistol shot pulsed from the speakers on the dais. "Besides, this way I got to see the looks on their sheeplike faces when they realized their fate and saw the way they had been finessed." Maximov punched yet another button. In a moment an acknowledgment crackled from a speaker in the console. "You filmed that?"

"Yes, Excellency," came a feminine voice.

"Very well. Begin editing."

As the slayers made their way around the table administering coups de grace, Emma Coyningham burst from beneath it like a frightened pheasant. Her shoeless, nyloned feet scrambling madly, she ran straight at the podium and hurled herself against the glass wall, scratching desperately at its impervious surface, eyes glaring madly at Maximov and Vesensky, who stood not three meters from her.

With a shout, one of the men on the catwalk turned and fired from the hip. Steel-nerved as he was, Vesensky shrank back reflexively at the jarring impact of bullets on the glass. Maximov watched, motionless, as Coyningham's body slammed against the shield, her face contorting in agony. Then she seemed to deflate slightly, and her watery eyes rolled up. She slid slowly down, leaving diffuse red smears on the glass.

"Begin editing the film for tonight's Euronews broadcast," he finished, as if nothing had happened.

"Yes, Excellency," said the voice on the communicator.

He broke contact and turned to Vesensky. "You see, there's method to my madness, Ivan Vissarionovich. Appropriately edited, with the aid of computers—marvelous machines, I never cease to wonder at their potential—this vignette becomes an attack by terrorists on the Internationalist Council, legitimate government of the Federated States of Europe. An almost totally successful attempt, but fortunately the council's chairman was hustled to safety by his aides before harm could come to him—we taped that earlier today, by the way. A pity your cover wouldn't permit you to participate. You missed your chance at television stardom."

Maximov gestured at the carnage beyond the glass. "This bit of theater will confirm my absolute rule over the FSE. If such vile terrorist acts can still take place, it's obvious measures must be taken. A police state must be established in

Europe—for the protection of its citizens, of course."

"A not unfamiliar phenomenon," Vesensky remarked dryly.

"Indeed. Democratic government was a joke in most of Europe even before the war, thanks to terrorists and the countermeasures they provoked. Why do you think the council secretly provided the ETA, the IRA, the Red Army Faction and all those other quaint special-interest groups with funds so they could pay the outrageous tariffs you Soviets charged for your outmoded arms?"

Vesensky twisted his mouth impatiently and turned away as Maximov continued, "All that remains is to secure the Blueprint for Renewal." He held up his large hand. "And then I shall hold the world . . ." Maximov's hand clenched with convulsive power. *"Here."*

"America and Europe aren't the whole world, Yevgeny."

A bushy black eyebrow rose. "Aren't they?" He laid his hand on his aide's shoulder. "Come, let us drink to today's success—and my emancipation from those narrow-minded, backbiting, mewling hypocrites." He glanced down at Mrs. Coyningham, who lay in her blood like a broken mannequin at the foot of the dais. "Pity we can't broadcast Madam Prime Minister's final performance without giving the show away. It was really quite dramatic."

CHAPTER
ONE ————————————————————

The Backfire bomber ran straight and true. Bombs spilled from its belly like the deadly roe of some fantastic fish while from overhead missiles arced down, MIRVing into lightning branches. Countermissiles leaped from ground bases, exploding in the path of the incoming weapons. But their efforts were in vain; three warheads found their marks, and three cities vanished in brief domes of light.

Casey Wilson gave the trackball a final fruitless spin as the other missiles exploded harmlessly on the rocky landscape etched in light on the screen. "Shit," he said.

"Christ on a crutch," said ex-Marine Lieutenant William McKay from over Wilson's left shoulder. "You're the hottest American ace in forty years, and you can't beat 'Missile Command'?"

Casey slumped back in the form-fitting rec area chair. "I never played video games before," he explained, his quiet southern California-accented voice half apologetic. "This is, like, all new to me."

McKay shook his crew-cut blond head. Six foot three, with a linebacker's build and the ice-blue eyes of a Siberian husky, Billy McKay was leader of the special four-man team to which

Casey Wilson belonged. "And a fuckin' grunt like me was Pac-Man champion of West Beirut before they blew up our barracks back in 'eighty-three. Goes to show, you just can't tell."

It was a late-June afternoon, hot and sticky, but you couldn't tell that either here in the rigorously climate-controlled confines of the Delta-level recreation area, 250 feet beneath the parched farmland of Iowa. Like every cubic meter of the vast subterranean warren that was Heartland Complex, the rec area had been ergonomically designed to reduce stress on its occupants to a theoretical minimum. Ergonomics had been a big word before the One-Day War, very popular with the government-academic crowd who were always talking about things like "human factors" and "optimization" and "modularization" and "computerized structural simulation." It wasn't a word that meant a lot to Billy McKay. What the ringing, sterile emptiness of Heartland mostly put McKay in mind of was a dentist's waiting room.

Leaning forward, boyish-looking Casey Wilson shook blond hair from his eyes and hit the START button on the computer console. The letters MISSILE COMMAND appeared on the screen, white and glaring and huge. As they were replaced by a rocky landscape dotted with white cities, a change came over Casey. The laid-back, easy California kid was replaced by a large, predatory animal, wiry muscles wound tight, hunching over the rolling controller like a leopard getting ready to spring. Grinning, McKay shook his head. Working and living with Wilson for almost two years had taught him that there were several different entities residing under the ex-pilot's smooth, tanned hide, and the transition from one to the next could still be just a bit jarring.

The two men wore fatigues of a silver-sheened dull gray unlike those of any branch of the American armed forces. That was because they—and their two teammates—did not belong to any branch of the traditional services. They were the Guardians, the elite of the elite, and they existed apart from the normal chain of command.

For weeks they'd been cooling their heels in the fluorolit womb of Heartland. At first they'd been constantly on edge. The impenetrable calm of the immense secret facility, its stillness disturbed only by the subdued hum of the air conditioners that maintained an eternal denatured springtime in the suites and labs and corridors, contrasted with the fear and fury of the world above in a way that was downright eerie. McKay and the others had fought their way across a thousand miles of hell, an America devastated by the thermonuclear flames of the Third World War, to bring the President of the United States to safety in this secret subterranean redoubt. Once they'd gotten here, once they'd learned the details of their new assignment—the one for which, unwittingly, they had been selected and groomed all along for almost two years now—once they'd slept off the mind-numbing fatigue of their hell ride, they had been wary as white-collar workers trapped on foot in some inner city by the dark of the moon and a busted streetlamp. This apparent peace and quiet *had* to conceal lurking dangers.

But the sanctuary of Heartland stayed sacrosanct, at least for now. Combat-zone nerves began to be replaced by rising impatience to be up and doing, to launch themselves at the throat of their new job. And by plain, old-fashioned boredom.

A door hissed open as Casey spun the trackball and laid a screen of missiles between his cities and a fresh flight of attackers. Engrossed in the action onscreen, McKay didn't turn his head, didn't even hunch his huge shoulders in the reflexive clearing-for-action that had become second nature in the course of a decade of combat. And realizing his lack of response, he thought, *This isn't good. We're losing our edge.*

"Afternoon," said the soft voice of Tom Rogers, formerly of the U.S. Army Special Forces.

McKay glanced around and said, "Afternoon, Tom." Casey just grunted. Normally he was the picture of open-faced amiability. Now he was locked into single-combat mode.

A stocky, square-shouldered man of medium height and quiet manner, Rogers was dressed the same as the other two. His short brown hair was damped down on his head, sticking up here and there in spikes. He had obviously just been to his quarters for a shower after loosening up from the day's training with a good workout in one of the gyms. McKay himself had just showered away the odor of sweat, busted caps, and burned powder from a good hour on the pistol range and an hour before that working out on free weights. The four of them had spent the day in classroom work, part of the intense maintenance program laid out for them by their team's creator, the scar-faced Major Crenna, to keep them as sharp as possible during the down period before they went out again. For McKay and Rogers especially, the classroom was an alien environment. Man-killing physical exertion was their way of relaxing after concentrated mental effort.

Rogers sauntered over and stood behind Casey's other shoulder, gazing down at the color-filled screen with eyes as steel-gray and inscrutable as those of a shark. A moment later the rec area door slid open again and a lanky specimen who could have passed for Jim Garner's kid brother strolled in wearing a gray sweat suit with a big hardbound book tucked under his arm. He paused as the door shut behind him. "Looks like the gang's all here," he drawled in an easy, ironic down-home-Missouri voice.

Casey didn't even grunt. He was on the fifth board and in a world of hurt, down to one city and a half-dozen ABMs as a fresh wave of bombers, missiles, and satellites hove in for the kill. Rogers nodded and grinned absently. "Running in circles again, Sloan?" McKay asked.

Sloan grinned his slow grin. "Only managed twenty miles. I'll sure be glad when we're out of this rabbit warren. Just isn't the same, pounding around a rubberized track down in the Lambda-level gym. Can't wait to feel the sun on my face and the wind in my hair and the dirt and grass under my feet again."

McKay shook his head. He ran every day, ran hard and far, because that was what you had to do to keep in maximum fighting trim. But he never could work up Sam Sloan's enthusiasm for roadwork. Not that that was surprising; the ex-Navy officer was a fitness nut and marathon runner. In spite of having the most sedentary service job of the four—line officer on a cruiser in the Med—before joining the Guardians, he was perhaps in the best physical shape of the four. And none of them could be called soft by any stretch of the imagination.

"Darn." Casey's last city went out in a blaze of glory as he frantically punched the fire button, as if that would bring more missiles up out of his depleted fire bases. "Can't get the hang of this mother."

Sloan wandered over to a table and pulled out a chair with a red and white Nike. "Don't know how you can waste your time with those silly video games, Case," he said.

Tight-lipped, Casey shook his head. "I'll get it sooner or later," he insisted, ignoring Sloan's question—if he'd even heard it. Casey Wilson was single-minded when presented with a challenge. Unless pried away from the console, he'd be up all night trying to beat the damned game. In all probability he'd found the sardonic question meaningless; it simply hadn't registered. No challenge was silly to Casey. If some cagey five-year-old suckered him into a game of jacks, he'd stick with it until he either won or keeled over from exhaustion.

"What're you readin' now?" McKay asked Sloan, jerking his big chin at the book the former Navy man laid on the Formica tabletop.

"*The Concept of Dread*, by Sören Kierkegaard," Sloan said. "It's a philosophical work," he added with a touch of condescension.

McKay knew perfectly well what it was, though he'd never read Kierkegaard himself. Though his tastes didn't exactly run to Existentialism, he was a compulsive reader; it was his secret vice. For the beer-guzzling, bare-knuckled, brawling son of a Pittsburgh steelworker, a young man who had made a career in the U.S. Marine Corps—which even through the eighties and into the nineties held anyone who read more than the occasional *Sgt. Rock* comic under suspicion of being a pantywaist and possible fellow traveler—that was akin to being a chronic masturbator.

He and Sloan had worked and trained together for almost two years; they had run through the fire of thermonuclear war together and were joined by the bonds that battle forges between comrades. Before they'd met, each had distinguished himself for bravery, initiative, and cool-headed thinking under fire. Each regarded the fraternity of arms as the most righteous of human societies, though Sloan would never have admitted it aloud, and by being chosen as Guardians they felt they had achieved the pinnacle of their calling as warriors. Yet the two had never become friends. Their attitudes and backgrounds were light-years apart. Between them yawned the gulf of mutual disdain that separated the white-collar technicians of the Navy and the dirty-necked grunts of its sister service, the Corps. Finally, neither could fully forget the ranks they'd held in prior service. Sloan was an Annapolis man who'd finished his Navy tour with the rank of Commander, equivalent to a Marine rank of Lieutenant Colonel. McKay was a high school dropout and mustang second lieutenant. Like Rogers and Wilson, Sloan had agreed that with his experience in Force Recon and the dirty-tricks teams of SOG-SWAC, McKay was the logical choice to command the Guardians. But still, the hint of tension was there.

McKay jutted his massive jaw and nodded thoughtfully. "Phi-los-o-phy," he said, drawing the word out as if each syllable were a word of its own. "Yeah. And you were saying *Casey* was wastin' his time. . . ."

As intended, Sloan rose to the bait. "Now, just a minute," he said, darkening to the hairline. "How can you—"

The strident beep-bong of the intercom cut him off. McKay wheeled and punched the answer button on the wall above the computer console. "McKay."

"Crenna," a gravelly voice said. "The others with you?"

McKay felt his heart beat faster. "Affirmative."

"Then if you can tear yourselves away from your four-handed Old Maid game, I'd appreciate your presence in briefing theater Epsilon twenty-three, two minutes ago."

McKay turned a big grin on his teammates. They met it with wide bright eyes. "Roger that," he told the wall. "We're on our way."

CHAPTER
TWO ──────────────

The Oklahoma City air was cleaner than it had been for upward of half a century. Almost two weeks of virtual shut-down of vehicular traffic in the city, along with the savage driving rainstorms that had blasted the city daily since the One Day War, had scoured most of the syrupy petrochemical smog from the sky. Once the season of storms had passed, and the derelict cars, trucks, and buses that clotted the city's veins and arteries had been cleared away, it would probably start building right back up. Oklahoma City had a number of pro-ducing oil fields actually inside its limits, with derricks on the grounds of the State Capitol itself; and the airbursts directed at taking out the country's biggest supply and repair depot at Tinker AFB in the southeastern quadrant of town had left most of the city's refineries intact. Whatever the state of the rest of the nation, Okie City would not soon starve for fuel.

It was raining again. No flashing, crashing, gully-washing thunderstorm this time, but a slow gray drizzle, chill as prema-ture October, washing down from a sky the color of boiled beef. It fell on the just and the unjust alike, and certainly one or the other category would encompass the fantastic com-pound Oklahoma citizens called "The Citadel," as well as the silent, shabby multitude thronged before its battlemented walls.

Nathan Bedford Forrest Smith had been the child prodigy of the revivalist circuit. He'd begun in the tents at the tender age of four, back in the early seventies, and had been the darling of hordes of the fundamentalist faithful. As a teenager in the eighties, he was already a multiple millionaire who had hosted a television program featuring a blend of show business personalities and upbeat electric country-and-western-style inspirational music which was one of the biggest draws on the Christian cable networks. By the turn of the decade, with riches requiring the awesome number-crunching capacity of a Cray Nine supercomputer to manage, the youthful evangelist had embarked on fulfillment of his great dream: construction of Nathan Bedford Forrest Smith University.

A keen student of survivalism as well as of apocalyptic writers and prophets of the Late Great Planetary school, Forrie Smith intended his university to be a literal bastion of the faith as well as a figurative one. On a sizable tract of land—originally zoned for a shopping mall—in an affluent, comfortable suburb named the Village, Smith had built a fortress of massive slope-sided cement structures faced in red glazed brick that looked as if it had already been baked by a nuclear blast. Surrounding the buildings were walls twenty feet tall and twenty feet thick, complete with guard towers which lent the university a prisonlike air that had been the cause of much civic controversy. Looming over the lecture halls and dormitories—sexually segregated, of course—was a tower that was like a cross between a Norman keep and a skyscraper. It was this structure that housed the nerve center of Smith's empire.

But the huddle of modernistic Maginot Line architecture that had caused the press to pillory the City Zoning Commission was merely the tip of a reinforced-concrete iceberg. Under it lay a huge complex of well-hardened airtight bunkers, containing classrooms, computers, communications centers, generators, a complete small hospital with one of the best burn and trauma units in the hemisphere, a fleet of vehicles including small helicopters and collapsible canard-style airplanes; an alternate broadcast facility for Smith's radio station, KFSU; living quarters for several thousand faithful and food supplies to last them over a year; an arsenal containing a highly illegal assortment of heavy weapons, automatic rifles, and explosives; and the world's most complete collection of doomsday prophecies in manuscript form, from John of Patmos through Nostradamus and Goody Shipton to Hal Lindsey and Howard Ruff, all sealed under glass in neutral nitrogen.

Neither the urban setting nor the university's proximity to the Missile Belt that spanned the central U.S. or to the secondary target of Tinker was optimal from a purely survivalist point of view. But famed survival havens like the Northwest were, to young Smith's mind, full of dopers and commies, and were already growing crowded with other holocaust buffs. Smith knew the wellspring of his strength and where it bubbled to the surface. Bible Belt and Missile Belt were close to being the same thing. Unlike many survivalists, Smith wasn't obsessive enough to bet to lose. He built his fortress where it would be best served before things went, as it were, to hell. In any event, it would have taken a megaton warhead dropped smack in the middle of the quad to affect Smith and his believing elite, snug in their blast bunkers underground. And just in case the whole awesome array of fortifications, firing ports, and stockpiled food proved insufficient to withstand the coming storm—be it fire, flood, disorder, or hard radiation—FSU had branches on or near retreat sites in Colorado, northern Saskatchewan, and (reluctantly) northern California that were miniatures of the Citadel, to which Smith and a hard core of followers could repair at need.

Boy wonder Smith was a power to be reckoned with not just in Oklahoma City but in the nation at large because of both his wealth and the influence his TV and radio programs and his newspaper chain gave him with the public. He had weathered a storm of not just local indignation over the building of his Citadel, but also state and federal heat over the fact that the university was built by companies of which Smith was a major stockholder and whose employees, to the fury of the Departments of Justice and Labor, were required to be fundamental Christians. Locally he had led a campaign, unsuccessful to date, to change the name of nearby Lake Hefner on the grounds that it glorified a pornographer, though in fact it

predated the *Playboy* publisher by years. On the nationwide
scene he had spearheaded a drive in the late eighties to ban a
revival of *I Love Lucy* from the airwaves, on the basis that it
promoted interracial romance. That move had alienated certain of Smith's supporters with ties to anticommunist Cuban
émigrés.

Yet this vastly wealthy and powerful man, not yet thirty,
whose word was gospel to millions of Americans and against
whose will even the dinosaurian wrath of the United States
government had failed to prevail, now walked along an
asphalt drive between swatches of immaculate lawn, bareheaded in the rain. He was on his way to meet with the ragged
prophet who had walked out of the radioactive kill zone to the
north three days before.

As he approached the iron gates of his stronghold, he could
see the throng assembled on Hoover Boulevard and packed so
tightly into the park across the way that they threatened to
spill into the broad pond on which swans still sailed, serenely
unaware that the time was fast approaching when some starving poacher would bag them for his pot. He could feel tremendous power here. It throbbed in the uncanny stillness with
which the ragged, hungry, homeless crowd awaited him, a
potent silence broken by the faint thud of gunfire and
whump-crump of mortars to the south, where municipal and
state authorities were contesting ownership of the city's oil
fields. It shone in the shiny faces turned toward him in unspeaking expectation, many of them mottled and ravaged by
radiation sickness. Most of all power seemed to emanate from
the tall, wild-haired figure, clad all in black, which stood in
the center of the thirty-meter semicircle the crowd had left
clear before the gates.

"They're mighty close, sir," the voice of Woodcock, captain of the gate guards, crackled in the induction speaker
pressed to the mastoid bone behind his right ear. "Want we
should move 'em back a little with the water cannon?"

Smith's handsome face, deeply etched with premature
worry lines not even TV makeup could completely mask,
grimaced briefly. On this north wall alone there was sufficient
firepower to repel a battalion. But Woodcock apparently
sensed the power swelling within the crowd, and feared it.

Rightly, perhaps. Hearing the day before of the approach of Josiah Coffin and his Children of the New Dispensation, Bedford Forrest Smith had spent last night in prayer, asking for guidance. Now he knew what his course was to be.

"No, thank you," he said softly to the mike sewn into the lapel of his $2,000 coat.

"He's got some pretty funny-lookin' hardcases with him."

Smith frowned. He could see the men the guard captain referred to—a dozen men at Coffin's back, all dressed in black. A couple, like the burly redheaded man with one arm in a sling, looked like solid workingmen, men who might listen to the country gospel of KFSU on the radios of their big rigs. But there were several whose shaved pates and tattooed faces identified them as members of road-gypsy or cycle gangs, and even one or two self-mutilated zombis—the very scum of the earth in the eyes of most fundamentalists, if not most Americans. To Smith it was an indication of the true nature of Coffin's ministry.

"The Lord will protect me, Darrel," Smith said. "Now, open the gates if you will."

A pause. The rain tickled his face with cold fingers. From the direction of the Capitol sounded the slow-march pounding of a .50-caliber machine gun. The crowd waited with that eerie utter silence. Then: "Yes, sir," Woodcock mumbled, and Smith wondered how long it had been since an underling had dared wait so long before obeying an order of his.

Electric motors drew back the heavy barred gates into slots in the walls. The crowd drew in its collective breath. Coffin stood immobile as a statue, the Lincolnesque planes of his face composed above the tangle of his beard.

Nathan Bedford Forrest Smith stepped through the gate, walked forward, stopped before Josiah Coffin, self-proclaimed Prophet of the New Dispensation. On the wall behind Smith, fingers tightened on triggers. He was a tall man, just over six feet, but he had to tilt his head back to meet the blazing black eyes of the preacher.

For a long moment their gazes held each other. Then Forrie Smith, God's own boy wonder in his expensively tailored garments, dropped to his knees and prostrated himself on the wet blacktop before the black-taped shoes of Josiah Coffin.

"You are mightier than I, Father," he gasped, his well-modulated voice choked with passion. "Your shoes I am not worthy to bear. Truly you shall baptize your children with the Holy Ghost. *And with fire!*"

And Josiah Coffin bent to lift the sobbing man to his feet. And with him rose the multitude, crying out, "*Hallelujah!*" in a voice that shamed cannons.

One week later and eight hundred kilometers away, four men sat facing a fifth in an air-conditioned womb buried deep in another, similar fortress. It had been taken for granted by most of the press and public that Heartland Agricultural Research Center was nothing more than a pork-barrel project dreamed up by a former junior Senator from Iowa who found himself President of the United States. Of course, certain keen eyes noted that the complex was being dug awfully deep, and that the excavation was swallowing a huge amount of concrete and steel. To those who pointed this out USDA spokespersons blandly explained that the center was being constructed wholly underground, both to conserve heat and thereby energy and to preserve the appearance of the rolling green farmland surrounding it.

Skeptics, unconvinced, chewed over rumors that Heartland was meant to house unpopular recombinant-DNA researches, possibly for biowar purposes. Nonsense, said the more cynical. It was meant to house political prisoners, dissenters against William Lowell's activist policies at home and abroad.

It was all twenty-four-carat bullshit.

What William Lowell was building underneath the fertile black soil of Iowa was his personal fallout shelter. Heartland was to be the nerve center for America in case Lowell's foot slipped during one of his exercises in brinkmanship, a nerve center which would not be compromised the way the Raven Rock and Mount Weather facilities near Washington had been, one which would not attract Soviet missiles by being taken for a target of some other strategic import, and one which would be too far from Washington for the armies of bureaucrats and Congresspersons Lowell so heartily despised to come banging at the massive concrete doors. As government projects go, it had been a smashing success.

No one guessed the true purpose of Heartland. The Soviets understood pork-barrel projects quite well, since that was the only way anything ever got done in the workers' paradise. And of the alternate stories deep-cover KGB agents sent back concerning the complex's nature, the one analysts liked best was the secret prison yarn. The Politburo could get behind that too. In any event, it was nothing they'd care to waste a missile on when there were all those nasty MX and Minuteman silos to worry about. And, indeed, even if any of the selfless public servants inhabiting Washington had guessed at the secret of Heartland, not one of them had a prayer in hell of reaching it when the balloon went up.

The only catch was, President William Lowell hadn't either.

When the CIA, the NSA, and the DIA all concurred that the Soviets—their offensive in Europe stalled and in places collapsing, their subject republics beginning to flare into revolt—were about to push the button, Lowell had climbed into a helicopter and flown off to Andrews Air Force Base, there to board the converted 747 that would theoretically bear him above the holocaust. Behind him he left a thoroughly disgruntled Billy McKay and team to hunker down in the new War Room beneath the White House with Lowell's Vice President, the young and handsome Jeffrey MacGregor, and the Chief Justice of the Supreme Court, in case things went amiss. And they had. President Lowell and his National Emergency Airborne Command Post had disappeared without a trace, leaving MacGregor President—and the Guardians with the task of getting him to Heartland.

"Since you found out what your real assignment was, gentlemen," the man with half a face was now saying, "you've been pawing at the gate, ready to go. It's been an uncomfortable situation, I know. You're trained and keyed to a fighting pitch, with nothing to expend your energies on except largely redundant training and occasional bouts of baiting one another." At this, McKay and Sloan guiltily avoided the sudden stab of his gaze. "And though your mission is as urgent as any in the history of the Republic, we haven't been able to let you go, because we haven't had a single damned idea where to send you."

He paused. "Now we have."

"You mean you've got the key to the Blueprint for Renewal?" Sam Sloan asked, sitting up straighter in the plastic chair in the small briefing theater. It felt as if an electric charge were jolting through his bloodstream.

Major Crenna shook his head. "Sorry, Mr. Sloan. We're a hell of a long way from having that."

In consternation, the Guardians stared at the compact man in the immaculate Special Forces uniform. He gazed back at them, his single eye imperturbable and inscrutable as always. They looked at one another, shifting in their desk seats like impatient schoolchildren. Like the rec areas, briefing theater Epsilon 23 had been ergonomically designed, though with an almost opposite intent: by means of uncomfortable design to focus alert concentration on the briefer who stood on a small raised platform at the head of the room. The main effect of the red-orange-yellow decor and stark molded plastic furnishings was to remind all four Guardians of a McDonald's. At any rate, it wasn't that restful.

"Excuse me, Major," McKay said hesitantly. Major Crenna was the only man he'd ever met who had such an effect on him. "But the technicians have had *two weeks*—"

Crenna nodded briskly. "They've had their work cut out for them too. You know the story as well as I do, McKay. The list of scientists and caches that make up the Blueprint were loaded into the memory banks of the NEACP-2 when President Lowell took off in it. They were supposed to be tight-beamed straight into the main memory here at Heartland—and they weren't. Which means they were lost when the President's plane went down."

"Any idea yet where that was, Major?" Sloan asked.

"We've been studying satellite photos of half of North America since the war. No shortage of crashed aircraft, as you might guess, but none we've spotted had the proper characteristics. The EA-4Bs are equipped with disaster-proof transmitters and transponders, and we haven't heard a peep. Our best guess is that NEACP-2—and Lowell—flew into the fireball of an airburst somewhere over the northeastern U.S."

He paused a moment, then rolled on in the manner his Guardians knew so well—unhurried but relentless. "What we've been doing is running an analysis of the probable scientific and technical personnel involved with the Blueprint. It's eaten huge amounts of computer time, even though we need all the capacity we've got and then some to try and get the situation on the outside under control. If the Blueprint weren't so absolutely vital, we'd never have been able to devote this much energy to the search.

"What we have, gentlemen, is a list of names. Four names, to be exact, of individuals deemed mathematically most likely to fulfill the criteria: one, they're part of the Blueprint, and two, our computer projections give a better than eighty percent chance they're still alive."

The Guardians stared at one another. *Four names?* Out of the hundreds that had gone into the Blueprint for Renewal, the master plan meant to pull America back from the devastation of thermonuclear war. Sam Sloan felt a descending-elevator sensation in the pit of his stomach.

Major Crenna punched buttons on the console of the podium at his side. The lights in the room dimmed, and the blank white wall at his back suddenly glowed to life, revealing its secret identity as an outsized high-res video screen. On it amber letters appeared.

Dr. James M. Okeda. Research biophysicist, J. Robert Oppenheimer Particle Accelerator Facility, Kansas City, Kansas.

Gerald Matz. Chief Engineer, Nova Robotics Corp., Houston, Texas.

T. Nolan Perkins, Ph.D. Systems Analyst, Dept. of Energy, Denver Federal Center, Denver, Colorado.

Marguerite St. C. Connoly, Ph.D. Professor of Economics, Yale University, New Haven, Connecticut. NOTE: Last known location (5/5): vacationing at survivalist retreat called The Freehold, southern Colorado.

"The names are listed in order of our itinerary for you. Getting Okeda shouldn't be hard; our intelligence indicates Major White of Kansas City has things pretty much in hand. The others . . ." He shrugged. "Expect those pickups to be moderately hairy to worse."

Sloan rubbed his jaw. "Dr. Connoly's supposed to be the guiding light of the Keynesian revival," he said. "What's she doing with a bunch of kooks in Colorado?"

Crenna gestured with his chin toward the plastic folders on the writing surface of each Guardian's desk. "You have digests of all the information we've got on your objectives, dealing with both the personnel and likely conditions on the ground. Read them. In answer to your question, Mr. Sloan, she's visiting her daughter for the summer."

He touched another button on the console. The lights came up, and the screen faded back to nondescript off-whiteness. For a moment he stood unspeaking, the intact half of his face regarding his handpicked team with grim appraisal. He was a mystery man. Both McKay and Tom Rogers had put out feelers among their old contacts in the shadow world of covert operations. They hadn't learned anything concrete.

One rumor said Crenna'd lost part of his face in Nam while emplacing a faulty Claymore mine that was triggered accidentally by a static discharge. Beyond that, scuttlebutt put him at every corner of the globe, sometimes in Special Forces, sometimes as "civilian" operative for CIA, DIA, NSA, sometimes, apparently, on his own. He was a manipulator, a puppet master who deliberately cloaked himself in obscurity, and the hints McKay's contacts whispered about him at clandestine meetings in waterfront bars and four-star hotels, in the shadows of derelict barracks, and in the rat maze of the Pentagon itself, raised the close-cropped hair at the back of McKay's neck—even though Billy McKay was veteran of some of the dirtiest missions in the history of secret warfare. The apparent suicide of a West German minister of defense, the deposition of a "friendly" African head of state, the disappearance of a Soviet premier, allegedly removed for "ill health"—all suggested Crenna's superhuman effectiveness.

What Major Crenna's official title was now—if any—none of the Guardians knew. He was the originator of Project Guardian and, it now developed, an architect of the Blueprint for Renewal as well. As far as McKay could tell, he was answerable only to President MacGregor.

At least as far as he was answerable to anything or anyone outside his scarred and shrapnel-furrowed skull.

"The time you've spent since arriving at Heartland has been a prime example of 'hurry up and wait,' " Crenna said. "Nothing to be done about that. Now you have to act, and act fast. The Federated States of Europe are getting their act together rapidly, and a lot of the developments there look troubling to us. If we don't get *our* act together soon, we just might be looking at an attempt to impose a 'protective occupation' on us."

"You can't be serious!" Sloan exclaimed. Even taciturn Tom Rogers was shocked into uttering a quiet "Shit." Much as they would have liked to, none of the Guardians could dismiss the notion of America's former allies invading her—for her own good, of course.

"We also have intelligence reports of a Soviet combat team on the ground in Alaska, of either brigade or regimental size. Our intelligence network is not operating at peak efficiency, to say the least, but it seems certain that the Russians have men on American soil."

"Do you think they'll attempt a full-scale invasion?" Sloan asked.

Crenna grinned. The scar tissue that formed the left side of his face was a gargoyle mask. "The Union of Soviet Socialist Republics has closed up shop for the time being, and if fifty or sixty million of her former subjects have much to say about it, she won't be doing business again for quite a while. There seems to be a well-equipped Soviet force on the ground in Alaska, but that doesn't mean they'll get much support from home."

He shook his head. "What that situation will lead to, we can't tell. The Canadians might deal with the problem for us, though they were hit just about as hard as we were, and they seem to have full-scale civil wars going on in Quebec and the western provinces. For now, whatever happens will happen a long way off. What you need to concern yourselves with is getting the scientists on your list to Heartland so we can start to piece together the Blueprint for Renewal."

He regarded each man in turn with his single gray eye. "It may sound corny as hell, but the future of the United States of

America depends on this mission.''

A clatter like a tubercular cough rattled through the vent ducts. While a barrage of groundbursts was plastering the Virginia landscape a few klicks to the west—aimed at collapsing underground facilities much like this one—another battle had raged in the very hallways of the huge Langley complex that was the nerve center and cerebral cortex of the Central Intelligence Agency: a savage struggle for control over what was—propaganda about the KGB notwithstanding—the largest intelligence establishment in the world. A burst of gunfire had damaged the main ventilation unit; the backups had been blown up by the losing faction. It had taken a very uncomfortable thirteen hours for technicians in the service of the winners to restore fresh-air circulation to much of the rabbit warren of offices, dormitories, and communications facilities buried near Quantico.

Now the shirt-sleeved leader of the victorious faction sat in his well-appointed office. His collar open, he leaned back in his swivel chair with his immaculately polished shoes propped on an equally well-polished hardwood desk on which were neatly stacked reports from both overseas and domestic agents. It was a casual posture that didn't mesh at all with the man's well-known public persona. Then again, there was a lot that the public didn't know about him. Publicly he acknowledged having worked briefly for the Company during his student days at Princeton. He hadn't found it necessary to add that not only was he still affiliated with the Agency, but was in fact an important figure within it. And he certainly never let it be bruited about that he was—in the shadow of a suitable figurehead, of course—the dominant force behind a faction of the Company dubbed ''the Romans,'' by others in-house. The Romans felt that the CIA could do a far better job of administering the United States than its duly elected government.

With the One-Day War, the Romans had acted. They seized Langley, in the course of which their apparent leader unfortunately perished. And now the man code-named Trajan was head of the CIA—and determined to be imperator of America.

Even now, however, he was not his own boss.

He turned a page of the latest précis on conditions within the wreckage of the United States of America and cursed the day he had ever heard of Yevgeny Maximov, let alone hitched his destiny to that of the mysterious Russian émigré financier. *The madman does nothing but harp about his precious Blueprint for Renewal,* he thought sourly, *when we're presented with a perfect opportunity to reconsolidate the country under our control without having to invoke any pie-in-the-sky secret projects!*

In irritation he snapped the dossier shut. It was all there in black and white. A disheveled, self-proclaimed messiah staggering out of the fallout belt north of Oklahoma City may have seemed no more than a ridiculous incidental to Maximov, but to Trajan he was a pearl beyond price—potentially the key to power in postwar America. If Europe's new master didn't understand America's historic penchant for religious revivalism, Trajan did. And when the raw fundamentalist appeal of this strange hayseed mystic—Coffin, his name was—was coupled with the tremendous resources of multimillionaire television evangelist N.B.F. Smith, a tremendous opportunity lay to hand.

Better even than capturing or canceling that callow fool MacGregor, he forcibly reminded himself. The memory of *that* debacle still rankled. An Agency air base leveled, a Hercules gunship destroyed, more than a score of operatives compromised or killed—and nothing to show for the whole catastrophe but a blistering reprimand from Maximov, delivered with a heavy Slavic undertone of threat. In terms of grand strategy, it was a minor setback; possession of the nominal head of a shattered government was a trifle in comparison to the hearts and minds of a sizable chunk of the One-Day War's American survivors. *If only Maximov could acknowledge the opportunity with which we're presented!*

Still, if Trajan were given the opportunity to avenge the destruction of the CIA's assets and the humiliation his agency and he had suffered at the hands of MacGregor's damned bodyguards, he wouldn't let it pass. Not by any means. He smiled at the thought, and it was not a pleasant smile.

His desk communicator requested his attention with a respectfully muted chime. He sighed. It was probably Maximov again, or one of his minions, calling to prod him about the pursuit of the elusive Blueprint. "Accept," he said wearily. A microchip in the communications unit verified that the voice was his, accepted the command keyword, and completed the call circuit. "What is it?"

If his caller was Maximov, his bluntness, and its tone of much-tried patience, would have been a daring impertinence indeed. Instead, a deferential voice said, "Domestic Division analysis department, sir. We have results on your Code Blue search."

The gleaming Guccis swung off the desk. The pleats in Trajan's tailored gray trousers snapped to sharpness like memory plastic. "Code Blue" was the in-house name for the Blueprint for Renewal. *At last, something to assuage Maximov's monomania!* "Yes? Out with it, man!"

"We have a name, sir. With eighty-seven percent chance of corresponding with Code Blue personnel."

Trajan seemed to deflate inside his expensive clothes. "One name? That's *all*?"

"Y-Yes, sir. But we're continuing our analysis of available data and project a future rate of point seven correspondences per week, given—"

"Seventy percent of a name will hardly prove productive," Trajan said waspishly. "What name *do* you have? And what fraction might it be? A middle name, perhaps?"

"Oh, no sir. It's a whole name."

"Splendid." What an incredible passel of literal-minded dolts he was saddled with! He supposed their plaster-of-paris mind-set helped in dealing with the cybernetic *idiots-savants* on which the Company so heavily depended. "What is it?"

"A Professor Perkins," the voice said. "He's on our records as a systems analyst at the Denver Federal Center in Colorado."

"A federal employee?"

"Yes sir. A special administrator with DOE."

Trajan was smiling again. "Excellent. Carry on. Trajan out." The communicator obediently broke the link. "Get me Germanicus in Domestic Ops."

A moment while his cybernetic secretary queried that of the head of Domestic Operations. "Germanicus," grumbled a deep voice from the desktop speaker.

"Trajan here. Who's our asset at the Federal Center in Denver?"

CHAPTER
THREE ─────────────────

Like a panorama from an after-the-holocaust adventure flick, it all unfurled before their eyes as they boomed over a rise in the rolling land south of Osceola, Iowa. One moment Mobile One was making good time along the usual back-country road, hatches closed against the intermittent spatters of rain spitting down from patchy slate-colored clouds. The next they were looking at an isolated farmhouse that was surrounded by a score or more of bizarre vehicles.

The huge car swung around on the wet red clay road as Tom Rogers jammed down the brakes. In the electronic-systems operator's chair at his side, McKay leaned abruptly forward, clamping down hard on the stub of cigar between his jaws. "Shit," he said under his breath, staring through the forward vision block.

It was a two-story whitewashed frame house, with a line of box elders planted to the west for shade and as a break against the wind off the plains, and with a real old-timey storybook red barn out back. A green John Deere tractor was snuggled up against the side of the house like an elephant scratching its side on a baobab tree. An ancient Ford Apache pickup, red sun-faded to a dusty pink, sat up on cinder blocks in the yard.

Next to it lay a dead dalmation, as much red as white from the short-range shotgun blast that had killed it. The lady of the house, or so McKay gathered, was the pile of drab clothing slumped beside the front porch at the foot of a broad scarlet smear. A daughter of the household was out in the yard near the dead dog. She was clad only in a T-shirt and was being raped by a half-dozen burly dudes in Mohawks and black leather.

"Road gypsies," Sloan said from the turret.

Since the dwindling of the eighties, nomad gangs in their stripped-down cars, vans, and dune buggies had plagued the nation's highways. Like the bikers of the fifties and sixties, they had drawn inspiration from the movies: the Australian *Mad Max* movies, the New Zealand *Battle Truck*, and a raft of imitation after-the-holocaust highway flicks. Now it *was* after the holocaust, and the marauders of the open road were getting the chance to live out their Road Warrior fantasies for real.

Of course, in *Road Warrior* the gangs' opponents had only been armed with crossbows and scavenged sidearms.

"Fire 'em up," McKay growled. "And don't shoot too near the house or the girl." Miraculously, no one had noticed the presence of Mobile One on the hill four hundred meters away. The road gypsies were making enough noise to cover the growling of the car's big diesel. As McKay watched, a pair of the nomads led a bay horse out of the barn and slapped it in the ass. It bolted into a cultivated field filled with some low plants McKay didn't recognize. One of the gypsies raised an FN assault rifle and began spraying full-auto fire after the fleeing animal. His third burst brought it down kicking in anguish on the furrows.

"*Bastards!*" Sam Sloan shouted. Mobile One rocked with the recoil of its turret machine gun. The long .50-caliber burst picked up the two road gypsies and threw them, trailing streams of blood like pennants, fifteen meters into the field. They didn't even have time to scream as the 700-grain slugs had their way with them.

Not even the world's loudest heavy-metal group in full throat could drown out the roar of a Browning M-2HB less than a half klick away. The outlaws looked up in open-

mouthed amazement, then broke for their vehicles. Afraid of
igniting the frame farmhouse with a stray white phosphorus
round, Sloan didn't open up with the M-19 automatic grenade
launcher. He didn't need to. With a little luck, the .50-cal
could take out an armored car. The chopped gypsy offroad
vehicles were nothing to it.

The hood of a dune buggy erupted in debris as the M-2
blasted chunks out of the engine block. Firing in short bursts
the way the instructors in Arizona had taught, Sloan walked
his fire along a line of half a dozen cars to a black van painted
with red flames. A gypsy dove frantically out the rear as
machine gun fire exploded the windshield. An instant later the
van vomited real flames out the windows. Apparently gas
siphoned out of the tractor and the other farm vehicles had
been stored in the back. A dragon's belch of orange fire
engulfed the fleeing nomad. He ran mindlessly into the fields,
wrapped in flame. His screams carried clearly to the V-450 in
the gaps between bursts of fire from the turret gun.

"Drive on, Tom," McKay said. "We got the fuckers on the
run. Sloan, keep 'em movin'." Tom straightened the big armored car's angular snout on the road and drove down the
gradual slope at about forty klicks. Sloan sprayed bullets to
either side of the farmhouse.

As they reached their cars, the gypsies peeled out. The half-
naked farm girl struggled to sit up. A bearded outlaw racing
into the house snapped two shots from a big handgun into her,
and she went down writhing. From the second-story windows
a half-dozen of the nomads opened fire on Mobile One as it
approached.

With a jackhammer noise, bullets ricocheted off Mobile
One's alloy hide. "Motherfuck," McKay said. Somebody was
shooting a 7.62-mm weapon at them full automatic—a G-3 or
maybe another FN. It wasn't likely to do them much damage.
Even the tires, honeycombs of plastic and steel that were virtually impossible to flatten, weren't vulnerable. But McKay
believed in making sure. "Take those shitbirds out."

The machine gun fell silent. "There may be people in there,
McKay."

"Then they gotta take their chances." The car bumped
down the road. Muzzle flashes flickered frantically from the

house, now a mere sixty meters away. "Might be doin' them a favor if you hit them."

A pause and then the big fifty roared again, rocking the V-450 back on its massive suspension and raking the second story of the farmhouse. The bullets knocked meter-long splinters off the front of the building, punching through both wooden walls—and any intervening nomads—and barely slowing down.

"Billy." Casey Wilson, minus his shooting glasses but with his inevitable baseball cap jammed down on his head, had come forward from the air mattress aft of the turret root and was hanging on to the back of McKay's seat. He pointed out the passenger-side vision block. "The road gypsies, man—they're coming back!"

McKay looked around. *Those fuckers're harder-core than I thought.* A dozen or more of the gaudy vehicles were circling in on Mobile One and the farmhouse like a pack of sharks stalking a killer whale.

A road gypsy broke from the front door, clearing the stoop in a leap and lining out for the trees. He held a chrome-plated .44 Magnum in one hand. "That's the same one shot the girl," McKay said.

Without a flicker of expression on his tan face or in his gray eyes, Tom Rogers hauled the huge car around in a turn, its wheels tearing chunks of sod out of the lawn, and rolled past the dead girl in pursuit of her killer. Hearing the hunting-lion growl of its engine, the outlaw cast a look back over his bare shoulder. McKay saw the purest look of terror he'd ever run across—eyes bulging from a grimy, sweat-streaked face, tongue protruding from the taut ring of the mouth, neck tendons standing out in relief like hoses. Then Mobile One's snout hit him low in the back and he disappeared.

The ten metric tons of the car barely bounced as they rolled over him.

McKay almost went facefirst into the blinky lights on the electronic systems' console as Rogers slammed on the brakes. The turret motor whined as Sloan brought his guns to bear on the wolf pack closing in. The M-19 coughed. A high-explosive dual-purpose round hit a buggy right on the nose. It was built around a Volkswagen of some sort, with the engine in the back. The grenade exploded against the fire wall. The blast of superheated gas from its shaped-charge warhead vaporized the driver's legs and blew the car in two. The front tires pivoted off to the right, and the rear half of the vehicle blew up.

Bullets whanged off Mobile One's carapace. The attackers behind the wrecked dune buggy veered abruptly and disappeared behind the farmhouse. Then Casey shouted, "Behind us!" from the rear of the car.

There was a loud *whoosh!* and suddenly it got a lot hotter inside Mobile One.

"Molotov!" Casey hollered. McKay fell back against his seat as Rogers goosed the 450.

"Fire on the rear deck!" Sloan shouted down. Casey snatched a fire extinguisher from the bulkhead, popped the top hatch behind the turret, and climbed half out to try to douse the flames before burning gas seeped down into the engine compartment.

Gunfire popped from outside the V-450. There were gypsy cars all around, harassing Mobile One like wolves bringing down a moose. Casey gave a choked cry and fell back down through the hatch.

With a single leap McKay was out of his seat and scrambling to the ex-fighter jock's side. Casey's face was white, his lips a thin line. He rubbed at his left shoulder. "Take it easy, Case," McKay said, easing his hand away. A bullet had punched through his cammie blouse and been stopped by the Kevlar of Casey's Second Chance vest.

"I-I'm okay," Casey said, struggling to sit up. "Arm's like, numb, though."

"No shit." McKay dug a deformed blob of lead and copper from the fabric at Casey's shoulder. It looked like a jacketed hollowpoint from a .357 Magnum—a potent mother—and while the vest had stopped the round from penetrating, Casey Wilson's shoulder and chest had absorbed most of its considerable energy.

"Got the fire out," Casey said stubbornly. If his words hadn't been coming over the intercom to the bone-conduction speaker behind McKay's ear, he never would have heard him, so loud was the yammer of the turret guns through the open hatch. McKay felt an impact on the hull and glanced up—straight into the wild eyes of a road gypsy with a yellow Mohawk who was crouching on the rear deck.

The Mohawker swung up a sawed-off shotgun. Moving faster than he ever had before, McKay swept his right hand back, snapping open the flap of the Kevlar field holster that held his sidearm. He snatched the .45 free, pivoted his hand while his thumb snicked off the safety, and snapped two quick shots from the hip.

It was a desperate move. Under any other circumstances it would have been a damn fool stunt—trying to get the rounds out the small hatch without aiming while the armored car bucked and pitched below his boots like a small boat caught in a squall. But no copper-jacketed ricochets whined past his ears. For a heart-stopping millisecond McKay stared straight up the yawning bores of the sawed-off. Then his two slugs knocked the road gypsy up and away. The shotgun discharged uselessly against the impervious rear of the turret, and the nomad was gone.

McKay stuck his head out. The wind whipped at his face. The V-450 was thundering along the road past the farmhouse now while the gypsies pursued along the graded strip and through the fields to either side. McKay saw a snarling outlaw standing in the bed of a pickup cock his arm back to throw a Molotov. McKay snapped a shot at him, missed, and ducked, slamming the hatch shut. The bomb sailed over the car and filled a ditch with brief fire.

The gypsies were smart. Sloan could only depress the muzzles of his turret guns so far. The gypsies were crowding close so he couldn't get them or were maneuvering to stay away from the front of the turret as he traversed it left and right. Glancing out the rear view slit, McKay saw several black columns of smoke rising into the gray sky behind. He grinned. Not all the attackers had been successful at keeping out of Sam Sloan's way.

On the other hand, if the bad guys stayed close, it was only a matter of time before one got a Molotov aboard.

"Hold tight, everybody." Tom Rogers sounded as calm as if he were out for a fishing expedition with his two kids. McKay rammed his Colt back in its holster, grabbed a hand-hold, and clung.

It was a good thing. A stripped Maverick had gotten a little ahead of Mobile One. A nomad leaped from the back of it onto the front of Mobile One and caught hold of the left-hand headlight. Rogers cranked the wheel hard to the left.

The impact of the V-450's snout knocked the Maverick onto its side. It skidded along in a shower of sparks and dirt. Rogers put the pedal to the metal, and the huge car surged ahead, up, onto, *over* the stricken gypsy wagon. McKay was thrown into the bulkhead, and then Rogers had control of the 450 again, leaving the Maverick a twisted ruin across the road behind. Another nomad swerved a heartbeat too late to avoid the wreck.

McKay shook himself and pushed off. He grabbed his Maremont, a lightweight version of the 7.62-mm M-60 machine gun, out of the clips that held it to the hull. It was his pet long arm, a heavy, hard-hitting piece of ordnance. The fuckers thought they were safe, snuggling up to Mobile One. They were about to find out what the firing ports let into the hull on all four sides were for.

He felt more impacts through the soles of his boots. "Billy," Sloan called, "I can't see!"

"Shit." The outlaws had gotten smart. Some of them had climbed up on top and flung a burlap bag over the turret vision block. The servos that moved the turret whined abruptly. There was a shriek, fading instantly behind. Sloan had swung the turret unexpectedly and knocked an unwary nomad off with the muzzles.

Rogers hit the brakes hard. McKay went flying forward. So did two more road gypsies. Rogers rolled them into red jelly and drove on.

Untangling himself from the systems operator's seat, McKay wondered if any of his ribs weren't cracked. The top hatch cracked aft of the turret. McKay swung up the Maremont's muzzle and fired a single shot into the face that peered in.

Not even the earsplitting bark of a 7.62 next to his ear was enough to flap Tom Rogers. He was so hard-core he damn near frightened even McKay sometimes. McKay jumped up and ran to the hatch.

A burly gypsy in Foreign Legion pants stood prying at the

turret hatch with a crowbar. McKay prodded him in the left butt cheek with the barrel of the Maremont. He turned with a curse.

The machine gun's muzzle was six inches from the man's crotch. McKay triggered a short burst.

Road gypsies were all over the V-450 like baby opossums on their mother's back. Firing the big chopper one-handed, McKay peeled another outlaw off the right-hand headlight. Then he pulled himself up out of the hatch.

The turret was facing to the side. McKay faced a pair of startled nomads across it. He grabbed a metal rung let into the turret and fired from the hip, sweeping the light machine gun from left to right. The big slugs tore the two to pieces.

A weight descended on his back. He felt a pang in his right side as the outlaw tried to jam a knife through his Kevlar vest. He let the M-60 drop on its sling, reached back with one hand, grabbed, and jackknifed forward. The gypsy went over his head—without letting go of his handful of McKay's blouse. His momentum tore the former Marine's grip free of the handhold.

Desperately, McKay grabbed. He grimaced as his left hand closed around the red-hot barrel of the M-2. "Whatever you do, Sam," he said through gritted teeth, "*don't shoot.*"

He was dangling from the turret with the gypsy hanging off him. He smelled the man's foul breath as McKay put an elbow in his eye. The gypsy's grip slipped down McKay's body, and the gypsy clawed madly for a grip as his boots hit the ground racing by underneath. His face a mask of agony and determination as the hard earth ground at his legs, he hung on to McKay's right leg with fingers like steel talons.

McKay kicked him hard in the face. He let go. For a moment McKay hung off the side of the car, the ground rushing along centimeters below his feet. Then he swung his legs up onto the rear deck and hauled himself back aboard.

Ignoring the pain in his seared palm, McKay grabbed another rung and blasted at a gypsy lunging for him. The man spun sideways, a greasy gray-purple coil of intestine spilling from his bare belly, and rolled off the rear deck. Still shooting the ponderous weapon one-handed, McKay sprayed the V-450 with fire. The three outlaws still aboard went away quickly. He pulled himself upright.

The pickup truck was alongside, the rail-thin outlaw in back gearing up for yet another try with a Molotov. "You never give up, do you, asshole?" McKay said, but the wind whipped his words away.

It didn't affect the flight of the bullets he sent hosing toward the beige truck, however. Three red flowers blossomed from the gypsy's bare chest. He dropped the bottle and went over the side.

McKay flung up a hand to shield his face from the sudden savage wash of heat as the other bombs in crates in the rear of the truck went off.

The explosion of the pickup was the signal for the surviving road gypsies to break off the engagement and flee up the dirt track. The bare-boned vehicles were a lot faster than the ponderous V-450. The Guardians were content to let them go, though Sloan picked off another pair of dune buggies after McKay cleared his view slit for him.

Back at the farmhouse, three outlaws staggered out, weeping and choking, after McKay fired a few 40-mm tear gas rounds through the ground-floor windows from an M-79, a single-shot grenade launcher that broke open like a shotgun to reload. Reluctantly, Sam Sloan cut them down with bursts from the .50-caliber. He hated to kill them in cold blood, but the Guardians weren't equipped to take prisoners. And not much inclined to.

They were even less inclined to do so after McKay and Rogers went inside the farmhouse—cautiously, gas masks in place and shotguns in hand—to search for survivors. In the kitchen they found the man of the house pinned to the wall with a pitchfork beneath a knitted sampler that said, "There's No Place like Home." He was coughing feebly, drooling blood down the front of his overalls. McKay glanced at Rogers, the team medic. Rogers raised his Smith & Wesson 3000 riot gun and blew the man's head apart. It was the kindest thing they could have done.

They found a boy lying in the hallway leading to the stairs.

He must have been about twelve years old. He'd been killed with an axe.

The house had been torn to pieces—furniture chopped up, pictures knocked from the walls, TV set blown in with a shotgun. Upstairs was no better. To the mindless vandalism had been added the effect of Sloan's .50-caliber bullets.

They'd caught a half dozen of the road gypsies. Two were still alive. But not for long.

They parked in the shade of the box elders while Tom Rogers looked at their injuries. Each responded in his own way to the letdown that followed the hot blood of battle. McKay grumbled and stomped around, Casey sat babbling to a thoughtful-looking Sam Sloan about some science fiction book he'd read, while Rogers, impassive as always, wrapped an Ace bandage around his bruised shoulder.

They were very different types, these four Guardians, from very different backgrounds. Yet each had proven himself on the field of battle.

Sam Sloan, the farmboy from Missouri, had been a gunnery officer on the U.S.S. *Winston-Salem* on station in the Gulf of Sidra almost three years before, when an attack by Libyan missile boats had blasted the cruiser's bridge into oblivion—and him into command. From an auxiliary bridge he had fought the stricken ship clear of savage surface and air attacks. His bravery and skill had won him nationwide fame and a Silver Star. A nuclear engineer by training, he was a whiz with computers and anything electronic. He was communications officer for the Guardians; on patrol he carried an Israeli-made Galil short assault rifle modified to carry an American M-203 40-mm grenade launcher beneath its barrel.

On a summer morning, Lieutenant Kenneth C. Wilson had lifted his F-16D into a blazing sky from an airfield in the south of the Rub al-Khali, the Empty Quarter, most evil desert in the world. He was flying MiGCAP on a strike against Aden, capital and deepwater port of the troublesome People's Democratic Republic of Yemen. With two kills to his credit, he was considered quite an up-and-comer—a natural born stick-and-rudder man with a marksman's eye. When a Sea Stallion rescue chopper fished him from the Gulf of Aden where he'd ditched the riddled ruin of his Fighting Falcon, he was a hero, too, with the United States' first five-kill mission since the Second World War. Mellow-speaking California Kid from affluent Silicon Valley and a graduate of USC, Casey was an expert mechanic and aficionado of Eastern philosophy. He was the group's driver and sniper.

Tom Rogers was a war hero too, but not the kind you read about in the papers. He had a decade's experience on active duty with the Green Berets, fighting unheralded battles from the jungles of Central America and Southeast Asia to the deserts of the Mideast and the rocky plateaus of Iran. Some said he had even operated behind the Iron Curtain, raising Muslim guerrillas against the Soviet empire. Others said he had been instrumental in the assassination of one of the Ayatollah Khomeini's favorites by means of a bomb concealed in a tape recorder on the dais from which he was speaking. His comrades knew he had a wife somewhere who'd divorced him and taken their two kids with her because he could never devote to them a fraction of the attention he poured into his work. Beyond that, and the fact that he was an Army brat who'd grown up all over the world, they knew nothing of his background. A demo expert and team medic, the taciturn, balding Rogers was a jack of all trades. In the field he carried an unadorned Galil as well as his two pet knives.

Machine gunner, past master of urban and desert combat, and leader of the Guardians, Billy McKay was the brawling, beer-swilling, cigar-chewing, skirt-chasing son of a Pittsburgh steelworker. Beginning his career with the Marine peacekeeping force in Beirut, he had gone on to see combat with the Corps's elite Force Recon. Subsequently he'd fought his own war in the shadows with the dirty-tricks teams of the innocuously named Studies and Observations Group, Southwest Asia Command. Major Crenna had found him in a hospital in Haifa and tapped him to head the new ultra-elite team he was putting together: the Guardians.

Now these four men were on the trail of the Blueprint for Renewal, a compendium of high-tech and high-powered experts whose knowledge was vital to the reconstruction of a war-ravaged America.

• • •

The sun had swollen up like a rotting peach as it dropped behind the trees. McKay eyed the white zinc-oxide ointment smeared on his palm with distaste. He took a long pull from his canteen, which he'd refilled from the hand pump next to the now-abandoned farmhouse. "Let's drive on," he said, wiping his mouth with the back of his hand. "We got a civilization to save."

CHAPTER
FOUR

"If it's all this easy," Casey Wilson remarked as he drove over the big highway 635 bridge across the Missouri River into the Kansas half of Kansas City, "then we'll be back at Heartland to celebrate the Fourth of July."

"Looks as if Major Crenna's intelligence boys gave us the straight scoop," Sam Sloan drawled from the electronics-systems operator's chair next to Casey's.

Riding in the passenger compartment of Mobile One, hanging on to a strap, and peering out a rain-streaked vision block, Billy McKay had to agree. Whatever Crenna's intelligence consisted of, whether it was merely monitoring radio traffic that had survived the electromagnetic pulse associated with high-level thermonuclear blasts, or reports tendered by a network of agents and contacts abroad in a ruined America, it indicated that their K.C. assignment should be a breeze.

The first name on their list was that of Dr. James Okeda, a researcher in nuclear medicine at the new joint University of Kansas/University of Missouri particle accelerator facility in Shawnee, a suburb of K.C. on the Kansas side. The Guardians had had virtually a straight shot down from Heartland. After passing the still-hot spattering of craters that was what was left of Omaha, Casey had steered the V-450 armored car onto Interstate 29 and driven on. Not only was Kansas City the nearest of the cities where the four probable participants in the Renewal Project were located, but the précis they'd been given concerning conditions they'd be facing on this trip claimed that Mayor White of Kansas City, Missouri, had both sides of the city under firm control and that reconstruction had already begun.

And so far it looked as if their mission briefing was holding up. The fallout sensors in the vehicle's hull registered a safely low count, and not only was the highway bridge intact enough to bear the V-450's ten-ton weight, but it had been cleared of stalled vehicles. Most thoroughfares, from back alleys on up to superhighways that were anywhere near cities, were still packed tight with derelict cars, trucks, buses. Casey was right; it was a good sign, even though the rain was hammering on Mobile One's iron skin like a million goblin fists.

A decade before, thermonuclear war had devastated Kansas City in a much-heralded TV movie. By all rights the real thing should have done no less—though perhaps not so comprehensively. On the screen, two blasts had knocked the whole damn city into jumbles of rubble that looked as if most of Rome had been dropped on the downtown area from about a kilometer up. In fact, it would have taken a much more sustained pounding even with megaton-range weapons to make a modern city into that kind of a mess. On the other hand, K.C. might easily have received just such a *Götterdämmerung* smashing, with attendant levels of radiation sufficiently high to sterilize the rubble of everything but cockroaches. The city sat pretty much in the middle of the Whiteman complex of missile silos—and downwind from a goodly chunk of the country's potential groundburst targets. Had anyone been offering insurance in case of nuclear war, Kansas City residents would have been paying high premiums.

But Fate, with its usual broadly ironic sense of humor, intervened. A single one-megatonner had airburst over the eastern suburb of Independence, wiping out about a quarter of the metroplex. Most of the Soviet missiles aimed over a circumpolar trajectory at Whiteman overshot and blasted much of southwestern Missouri and southeastern Kansas into slag.

And even though Forbes AFB and the McConnel complex around Wichita had been well-plastered with fallout-spawning groundbursts, Kansas City, down the prevailing wind, came out with a cumulative dosage of about a hundred and fifty rems—high, but not so high as to produce clinical effects of any sort in more than about thirty percent of the population —with minuscule incidence of fatalities. Between three and four hundred thousand people out of a population of 1.2 million had died as a direct result of the bombing.

As the One-Day War went, it was a glancing blow.

"Checkpoint up ahead, Billy," Casey said as they neared the southern end of the bridge. "Looks like they're getting ready for us." A pair of police cars had been parked nose-to-nose across the four southbound lanes. A blue riot squad van with wire mesh windows and topped by pintle-mounted water cannon was parked behind. Pushing himself from the fold-down seat and swaying forward to peer over Sam Sloan's shoulder through a forward vision block, McKay saw a squad of police auxiliaries piling out of the back of the van, hauling bulky armored vests on over light blue shirts and fumbling with their clear-visored riot helmets. Right behind the barricade stood two regular cops in Kevlar vests and powder-blue helmets, one holding a shotgun, the other an M-16. Their faces were hidden by shadow and by the condensation on their rain-streaked visors, but their attitude didn't look too calm.

They had a good reason to be uneasy. In the best of times, the approach of a squat green armored car, with the blunt muzzles of an automatic grenade launcher and a .50-caliber machine gun protruding from the turret, wasn't the most reassuring sight in the world. This time the V-450 fairly throbbed with menace. If there had been bad guys in the olive-drab behemoth, the whole squad of auxies, forming up behind the riot cops with their shotguns and assault rifles held nervously at the ready, stood about as much chance of driving them back as a platoon of Girl Scouts armed with spit wads.

On their part, the four Guardians quietly readied themselves for action. Sam Sloan unlimbered a stubby shotgunlike M-79 grenade launcher from clips beside his elaborate console, broke it open to confirm that a 40-mm tear gas grenade was loaded and ready inside. McKay slid back to a side port, work-

ing the action of an MP-5 submachine gun. In the one-man
turret above, Tom Rogers kept the barrels of his two automatic weapons carefully averted from the approaching roadblock—and his feet on the pedals, ready to traverse the turret
and open fire in an instant. Grinning at the obvious unease of
the waiting cops, Casey braked the bulky machine to a stop,
ready at the first hint of trouble to accelerate its ten metric
tons right on over the two cruisers, and anything or anyone
else foolish enough to get in the way. The four men did so
naturally, automatically, without the need for orders or a lot
of chatter. They had trained a long time together to function
as a team, and they did.

Not that they were expecting trouble. Probably the blue-
uniformed cops at the roadblock were on their side. But none
of them had been accustomed to take things for granted, even
before becoming Guardians by grace of a secret act of Con-
gress.

The angular snout of Mobile One stopped a reassuring ten
meters short of the patrol cars. Sloan glanced over his shoulder at McKay, who nodded. The ex-Navy officer's fingers
pressed keys on his console. "Afternoon," he said, his words
picked up by a flesh-colored mike taped to his Adam's apple
and spewed out by the car's PA system. Several of the auxiliaries flinched. The two cops in front stood their ground.
"We're on official United States government business. Could
you please clear us to pass?"

The two regular cops exchanged glances and muttered to
one another. "Didn't know there was a United States government anymore," the taller, leaner one shouted, his words
picked up by Mobile One's sensors and relayed over the bone-
conduction speakers each Guardian wore behind his ear.

McKay felt a quick flash of anger. *What the hell did you
expect?* he thought. "We're under the personal direction of
President Jeffrey MacGregor," Sloan said. "We have an
urgent assignment. Please clear us to pass."

More muttered consultation. "MacGregor? Ain't he Vice
President?"

A nod, a frown. "I always thought he was kind of left wing
myself."

The shorter and stockier of the pair laid his Atchisson 12-

gauge assault shotgun over his shoulder and said, "What about William Lowell? He was President last time I heard."

"He was killed. His plane went down."

"Well now, shit," the stocky one said. "If I'da known that commie MacGregor was gonna wind up President, I never woulda voted for old Wild Bill."

Irritably, McKay moved forward, nudged Sloan's shoulder. Hiding a grin, Sloan patched his colleague's throat mike through the PA. "I spent a week in this goddamned tin can with Jeff MacGregor," McKay said through the loudspeaker, "and he's no more of a fucking Communist than you are. Now clear us through this damn checkpoint before I come out there and ram that riot gun up your fat ass!"

The lower, visible half of the man's face reddened. From the phalanx at his back came muffled sounds of laughter. "Wow, Billy," Casey said. "That's really winning their hearts and minds."

McKay grinned. He signaled Sloan to cut him out of the loudspeaker circuit. "Figured we'd be here all day debating if I didn't shake the fuckers up," he said.

The two regular cops were arguing heatedly in lower voices. The rain was picking up, and that and a muted growling of thunder ate most of their words. Inside Mobile One, the Guardians managed to make out the skinny one's voice saying, ". . . roll right over us if they'd a mind to . . ." and the fat one grumbling what *he'd* do if that smartass son of a bitch would just climb out of his fucking tin can.

As if his words were the open sesame of Ali Baba, a hatch opened in front of Mobile One's low turret and Billy McKay hoisted himself out into the rain. He got his combat boots under him on the wet deck and rose to his full height. The 450's deck stood higher than a tall man. With his own six foot three added to that, tree-trunk arms folded across his bull chest, McKay looked like a not-so-jolly Green Giant who'd gotten an all-over bleach job and traded his leafy loincloth for urban-warfare camouflage fatigues. He'd laid aside the machine gun, and the flap of the Kevlar holster at his right hip was closed over the butt of his combat-modified .45.

"Here I am," he announced, "out of my tin can."

The fat cop swallowed and took a step back. The skinny one

bit his lip and began reflexively to bring his M-16 up. Almost at once he thought better of it. The big mother who had just emerged from the hatch was contemptuously unarmed, but he didn't need to be. If one of the weapons mounted at the stranger's back so much as cleared its throat, there wouldn't be anything left of the roadblock but a few bloody smears and a black spume of smoke.

"Now that we've got that out of the way," McKay said, grinning, "how about letting us pass?"

"Gotta—better call the chief," the skinny one said. He shouted something at the van.

McKay waited. Though the rain was coming down at a pretty good clip, the air was thick with smoke—and the sick, sweetish odor of rotting human meat. They were familiar smells to an ex-Marine who'd started his combat career with the peacekeeping contingent in embattled Beirut. *But I never expected to smell them here in the good old US of A,* he thought.

In a few moments somebody shouted from the van. The skinny cop looked up at McKay. "Can you come down a moment and talk on the radiophone?"

"I've got their freek, McKay," Sloan's voice said in his ear. "I can patch it through your personal communicator."

"Roger that. Put it on PA too."

The tall cop had pushed up his visor, revealing a long, pale face deeply etched with lines of fatigue and worry. He was rubbing a lumpy tuber of a nose and looking curious when a mellifluous voice said, "To whom am I speaking?" from Mobile One's exterior speaker. He jumped.

"The Mayor!" startled voices whispered from behind him.

"William McKay, commander of this operation." He carefully left off the honorific. Plenty of that when he was sure he was hooked up to someone who rated it. He was fucked if he'd *sir* some big-bellied dispatcher at the K.C. cop shop.

"Yes, I've heard of you. Your reputation in the Corps is quite distinguished," the voice said. Even distorted by the loudspeakers, it was deep and rich, the voice of a man in command of himself and his situation—a well-educated black man who was surprisingly young for the responsibilities he'd assumed even before catastrophe had made him arbiter of the destinies of more than three-quarters of a million survivors. The voice flowed like honey through McKay's earphone. "And you're on orders from the President, are you not?"

"Yes, sir." No dispatcher talked like that. "We're on special assignment."

"I understand. I'm pleased to make your acquaintance, Mr. McKay. Or do you have a rank by which I should address you?"

" 'Mister' will do fine." McKay commanded the Guardians by right of ability, and didn't need a fancy title to remind everybody of the fact.

"Very well, Mr. McKay. I'm Mayor Dexter White."

"I'm honored, sir." It wasn't strictly courtesy—something that was never McKay's strong suit, especially when speaking to civilian wheels. He'd heard that Dex White was an okay guy. "If you could give us clearance to enter Kansas City, we'd appreciate it. We're kinda in a hurry."

"I understand. If you could provide some form of written identification to the officers at the checkpoint? You understand the necessity for caution."

"Yes sir." The electronics officer's side firing port opened and Sam Sloan handed out a zippered Cordura portfolio. The skinny cop slung his M-16 and came forward to inspect the Guardians' bona fides. Crenna had supplied them with an impressive-looking set of papers for this trip: ID cards, clearances, even a suitably vague and stirring "Personal Message from President MacGregor," addressed to whomever the Guardians presented it to. It was all happy horseshit; it said not word one about the nature of their mission—which was top-drawer secret—and of course there wasn't a whole lot right on hand to prevent Mobile One's just driving on, with or without permission. But it wasn't part of their mission briefing to go looking for trouble, especially with those doing their damnedest to restore order to a shattered America.

Riffling through the stamped and official-looking documents, the tall cop wandered back to where an arm stuck a telephone handset out the window of the van. With his usual efficiency Sam Sloan cut the conversation out of the PA circuit, both to avoid feedback and to avoid reminding the cop his confab with the Mayor was being overheard.

In a moment the cop handed the phone back into the van and came forward. "Mayor says it's okay."

"Thank you, Your Honor," said McKay, who knew it already.

"If you could give me some idea of what you're doing, Mr. McKay?" White's voice said. "I'm not asking you to compromise yourselves. But if you could at least let me know what part of town you'll be operating in, I might be able to give you some information."

McKay shook his head as if White could see him. "Sorry, sir. I'll be happy to tell the officer here about where we're headed." *Hard to sneak around in an armored car.* "But I'd just as soon not announce it over the open air."

"Very well. I wish the best of success to you and your men. White out."

Whether they'd gotten an order or merely gotten bored, the auxiliary cops behind the barricade had relaxed, some grounding their weapons to lean with gloved hands folded on the muzzles, others to slouch against the battered blue flank of the van. McKay murmured into his throat mike and jumped down off Mobile One, to the wet pavement. The ease with which he did, unconsciously sinuous and graceful as a panther, mightily impressed the onlookers.

As did the sight that met their eyes when the driver's-side hatch popped open and Casey Wilson emerged. The drab lethality of his camo blouse didn't quite jibe with the easygoing expression of the green eyes blinking behind yellow Zeiss shooting glasses at the glare of the outside light, or the blond hair worn long beneath a Bruce Springsteen *Born to Run* tour souvenir cap—itself an item any self-respecting seventies nostalgia buff would kill for.

Unfolding a Triple-A map of K.C., McKay walked over to meet the taller cop. The man's pale, homely face split into a grin. "Pleased to meet you, McKay." The other regular, standing aside with his broad butt propped against the door of one of the cruisers, grumbled something beneath his breath. "My name's Logan. Don't mind my partner there. Slocum's always pissed off about something."

McKay shook hands with the man, then held up the map.

"We're headed for Shawnee. The university particle-accelerator facility. Should we be lookin' out for anything special on the way?"

It seemed the man's face turned a shade paler for a hairbreadth of time. "The nuke plant? They got a crowd down there. Whole buncha people."

"There a DP center near there or what?" McKay asked, frowning.

"No. They're—they're like, uh, protesters."

McKay grimaced. "Jesus fucking Christ. After all that's gone down, people *still* got the energy to demonstrate?" He shook his head.

"It ain't— Well, you'll have to see." He took over the map. "This route here's about the clearest," he said, tracing a path with a blunt, black-clad finger. "Mayor's got crews out all over town, cleanin' up. They're makin' some progress, but it's one hell of a job."

McKay nodded. "This Mayor White's quite an hombre, I guess."

Thin lips compressed out of sight. "Yeah. Yeah, he is. Just keep that in mind. He's doin' the best he can. An' he's got the worst job of all." He handed the map back to McKay. "Good luck. And—keep your eyes open."

"Always." He turned away. Something had been eating at the cop, but the man didn't seem willing to talk about it. *Fuck it,* McKay thought.

Some of the auxies had drifted forward to inspect Mobile One, listening with interest as Casey held forth about the monstrosity with the enthusiasm of a teenager with a new hot rod. He knew every bolt, circuit, and chip of the V-450, from the huge honeycomb-construction flatproof, up through the heavy suspension, the husky V-8 diesel engine and state-of-the-art electronics packed into the amphibious and NBC-resistant foamed-alloy hull. With the belt-fed 40-mm M-19 automatic grenade launcher and Browning M-2HB .50-caliber machine gun mounted in the low, sharp-faced turret, and an assortment of weapons within that could fire through ports beneath Goodyear no-spall vision blocks of tough glass-plastic laminate, the Cadillac Gage V-450 was a fine-tuned, highly mobile high-tech instrument of destruction. When he got worked up like this, Casey Wilson could almost pretend to himself he was as satisfied driving it as he would have been in the cockpit of his old F-16.

Logan climbed into one of the cars blocking the bridge. The engine whined and coughed in protest before turning over. "Let's roll," McKay called to Casey, who nodded and grinned a farewell to the admiring auxiliaries and disappeared back down his hatch like a long, lean prairie dog. McKay started back toward the armored car.

"Smartass," he heard the fat cop—Slocum, was it?—say behind him. He turned back to face the man, who stood in the open door of the other cruiser. "Think you're hot shit, don't you? Well, you can just try me any time you want to. Any time at all."

McKay gave him the slow Irish grin that had infuriated legions of teachers, probation officers, drill sergeants, and officers of every stripe. "You said you'd take care of me if I climbed out of my tin can," he said. "What do you want me to do *now*—drop 'em and spread 'em?"

Amid hoots of laughter from the auxies, he clambered back up onto Mobile One's deck and let himself down the hatch.

CHAPTER
FIVE ─────────────────────

Mayor White's doin' the best he can. Patrolman Logan's words replayed themselves unbidden in Billy McKay's brain as Mobile One rumbled into the suburb of Shawnee. *Just keep that in mind.* He shook his head. The skinny cop's speech, the troubled, hooded look in his eyes, had held some mysterious import. McKay hated mysteries.

He did have to admit that White was a hell of a man. On the drive through Kansas City proper to the suburb of Shawnee in the southwest quadrant of town, they had seen repeated evidence of an orderly attempt at reconstruction. They passed work gangs manhandling stalled vehicles aside to clear traffic lanes on clogged streets, while others followed behind to salvage gas from the tanks. Once they passed a burning apartment block, with, unbelievably, a crew of uniformed firefighters battling it with hoses under full pressure. To have repaired broken water mains and gotten pressure up in the system, even if it was only in this part of town, must have required a prodigious effort in the chaotic aftermath of war.

In this part of Kansas City, the wrath of the Independence airburst had mostly expressed itself in broken windows and flash fires. But blast waves are fickle beasts, bouncing at ran-

dom. In southern Iowa the Guardians had passed a small
town, hundreds of klicks from the nearest blast hypocenter,
that had been smashed flat by an invisible hammer from the
sky. The blast wave had been focused by some lens created by
unimaginable forces at the core of a thermonuclear maelstrom
and been reflected off the upper atmosphere to strike home far
from its point of origin. The same freakish quality had been
at work here. Mobile One cruised along whole blocks that
showed no sign of damage at all, and then come on a patch of
rubble where a shockwave finger had poked a building or a
block to pieces.

Often the Guardians saw people among the ruins—not
desperate, huddled survivors, but disciplined workers picking
through the debris, men and women both. The fortunate
among them wore gas masks, the rest rags, which McKay
guessed were steeped in gasoline, tied around their faces.
Anything to cut the thick stench of death, the decay of three
weeks of alternating heat and torrential, almost tropical rain.
The charred or bloated forms being hauled out on makeshift
stretchers—or sometimes in big galvanized tubs, depending on
the state they were in—and loaded on trucks were long past
rescue. The frantic effort here was meant to rescue
others—the living—from contagion, the plagues that bred in
corrupting human flesh. According to the briefings the Guardians had gotten during training from experts on the effects of
thermonuclear war, disease and starvation would almost certainly kill as many as the bombs themselves. Mayor White and
his people were doing what they could to contain at least the
former threat.

They were working on the problem of hunger too, though
that was trickier. McKay had glimpsed other groups apparently out scavenging for food, usually escorted by armed
police or, occasionally, National Guardsmen. Once, just after
being waved through a second roadblock on the south end of
the I-635 bridge over the roiling, rain-swollen Kansas River
that split the city in two, McKay spotted a crowd of people
standing in the drizzle in front of a former supermarket.
Policemen and women staffed a table in front of doors and big
windows that no doubt had been blown in by the blast and

were boarded over with warped sheets of plywood. The people were calmly waiting their turn to step forward, present a card, and receive a few cans in return. Overall, the situation in K.C. was much more in hand than anybody had the right to expect. It very much looked as if Mayor Dexter White was accomplishing the impossible.

But now they'd entered a residential district, whose streets were lined with trees stripped of their leaves by blast and heat, to find fires burning unheeded and the bodies of humans and dogs lying in streets and yards, swelling into obscene parodies of their former shapes as the gases of decay bubbled within them. "Welcome to Shawnee," Casey murmured, scratching at the bridge of his nose where his shooting glasses chafed him.

Back in a fold-down seat, Billy McKay peered out through the glass-plastic laminate of a vision block. He felt a growing sense of unease. Maybe the suburb of Shawnee was being neglected because Mayor White's people had so much work to do in the city proper. An itching of his street fighter's instincts, like sandpaper rubbed along nerve endings, told him that wasn't it. Something was wrong here, something beyond the obvious devastation.

He took his Maremont from the clips set into the hull and cradled it in his lap. It had been a favorite of McKay's when he was with SOG—SWAC, and he still felt it was the finest weapon in its class.

Most of the armed forces were converting to the M-249 Minimi, a Belgian-designed machine gun that fired the same NATO standard 5.56-mm round as the U.S.'s M-16 and the new European generation of disposable plastic battle rifles. The Minimi was a fine weapon, light and flexible. It could fire from box magazines as well as linked ammo, meaning it could be deployed in combat in a true automatic rifle role, like the old BAR, without the necessity of messing with long belts of ammunition that liked to get twisted or hung up on the underbrush and generally required the services of an assistant gunner to keep feeding. It could also be set up on a bipod with an A-gunner, belted 5.56 rounds, and the whole nine yards, to act as a full-dress sustained-fire machine gun. Fine, but McKay didn't see a whole hell of a lot of sense in an infantry support weapon that wouldn't reliably kill soft-skinned vehicles at any kind of range. 5.56 bullets just didn't have the penetration of 7.62.

Granted, even the "lightweight" M60 weighed almost nine kilos—a shitload more than the M249. But back in boot camp McKay had taken perverse pride in his ability to carry the full-size M60, an eleven-kilogram beast universally known as a "pig," on the longest march, though common practice was to rotate the monster among the members of a platoon. And the four and a half pounds' weight differential between the M60 and the Maremont LMG made a real difference. Besides, McKay carried Australian-designed half-moon ammo boxes that held fifty rounds of linked 7.62, and worked almost the same way as the box magazines of the BAR or the Minimi—removing the need for an A-gunner—and if you needed to use the chopper in sustained-fire mode you could break the box free and clip a belt to the links in the gun in a matter of seconds. That made a lot more sense to McKay than saddling the grunts with inadequate firepower, but for some reason the brass had neglected to ask his opinion before adopting the M249. He was used to that by now.

In response to the pricklings of instinct at the back of his mind, he was ready at need to fire the Maremont out a firing port—or bail out of the V-450 and fight on the ground if that seemed called for. He was not an armored-cav trooper either by training or inclination. When the shit hit the fan, his reflex was to get into the open.

Following the promptings of the maps stored in Mobile One's vast computer memory, they turned west into what seemed to be the suburb's business-administrative district. It had consisted of mostly low commercial buildings and the normal locally-owned shops interspersed with franchise food joints, all clustered around a core of taller glass-box municipal buildings. In calmer times it had probably been a typical midwestern suburb, enjoying moderate bustle in the daytime until the sun went down and they rolled up the sidewalks. Now it was a ghost town. At this distance from the Independence airburst, there was little visible structural damage other than that all the east-facing windows were blown out and most large windows on the north and south sides of streets too, knocked out by eddying gusts of overpressure. The thermal flash had had a more pronounced effect; the top sections of the taller buildings were all burned out.

But from the looks of things, damage hadn't stopped with the passing of the heat pulse and shockwave. Debris scattered on sidewalks in front of stores and restaurants showed they'd been thoroughly looted before being torched. In front of the blackened husk of a Wendy's hamburger stand lay what had probably been the body of a teenage girl. The sun had faded the orange and brown of her uniform, which was beginning to give at the seams as her body ballooned inside it. The skirt was rumpled up around bare hips gone pale and translucent with decay. She'd obviously been raped before being killed, though, swollen as the body was, there was no telling the cause of death without a lot closer examination than the Guardians were going to give the poor girl.

Sam Sloan glanced at Casey Wilson. The boy—hard to think of him any other way, even after all the time they'd known each other—was distinctly green under the tan he maintained from hours under the ultraviolet lamps at Heartland. *Reckon I'm about the same shade,* Sloan thought. He and Wilson were both seasoned warriors; they'd killed men in the course of their military service. They'd even caused destruction not much different from this. Casey had flown bombing missions and Sloan had directed naval bombardments against civilian targets in the Med. But their wars had been detached wars of distance where you never looked your enemy in the eye—or saw what became of his dead body after a few hours in the sun.

Sloan frowned suddenly and adjusted the earphones on his head. "Hull pickups are getting some crowd noises from up ahead," he announced.

They were reaching the western border between the business district and more residential zones. Casey drove the V-450 up to the top of a hill and abruptly halted.

Setting his machine gun back in its clips beneath the vision port, McKay came forward. "What is it?"

Tapping his fingers on the top of the wheel, Casey just nodded. At the foot of the hill stood the J. Robert Oppenheimer Particle Accelerator Facility. A milling mass of humanity surrounded the cluster of brick and cinder-block buildings.

"Pull back, Casey," McKay said. "Sloan, get on the horn and see if you can get in touch with the people inside. This don't look good."

Mobile One lurched once and rolled back down the slope toward the center of Shawnee until only Rogers' low turret protruded above the paved hilltop. McKay took his light machine gun and a big pair of binoculars and let himself out a side hatch. He wanted a closer look at what was going on below.

He lay down on his belly a few meters to the side of the car and crawled forward. The wet pavement was chill beneath him. The air was sour with burning and corruption. Mobile One's powerful diesel idled, farting softly. At the crest he propped arms on elbows and raised the glasses to his eyes.

The Oppenheimer facility lay at the bottom of the hill, about two hundred meters away. It had been built in the late eighties, during a resurgence of public interest in science unmatched since the days of the space race. Though its purposes were peaceful—it was devoted to subatomic physics research as well as a few biomedical experiments—it hadn't gone unopposed. As popular fascination with technology grew, public opinion branched in two different directions. A majority of the public thought that the rapid expansion of technology was great, while a vocal minority recoiled in fear. Protest marches had attended the building of the facility at every stage. Matters hadn't been helped by the fact that several residential blocks had been razed to build the center.

Popular ambivalence toward science was expressed in the architecture of the facility. The grounds had been landscaped into a green park. The one-story structures were designed with the contours of the land in mind. One end of the central building, a long low brick hemicylinder McKay guessed housed a linear accelerator of some sort, disappeared into a hill crowned with a stand of walnut and oak. It was all very low-key and inviting.

But in '91 the facility had been invaded by a group of activists armed with sledgehammers, and since then the compound had been surrounded by a three-meter chain-link fence topped with a helix of barbed wire.

Now the park and the streets around it were thronged with an incredible crowd, a thousand or more men and women, even a few children. They were ragged and filthy, and many sported balding, discolored heads, signs of exposure to radiation. Some sat about in listless clumps, seemingly indifferent whether it was soft turf beneath them or hard, clammy pavement—another symptom of radiation sickness. Others milled about in larger groups, listening to orators standing on overturned cars, and some were crowding right up against the wire, shouting and shaking their fists at the facility. A handful of men and women in tan uniforms McKay guessed were those of the university police, lay behind sandbags on the rooftops. They seemed to be armed with shotguns and M-16s, though these wouldn't do them much good if the crowd got really serious about taking the place down.

McKay frowned. These people were obviously pissed off, and from the looks of them they seemed to figure they had nothing to lose. He didn't guess they'd let the Guardians just walk in and walk out with one of the hated scientists. Vivid images flashed in his mind, of the desperate battle against the mob storming the White House in the hours after the bombs fell on Washington. He knew all too well how dangerous a mob could be when its members gave themselves up for dead.

Just look at that fuckin' hill, he told himself. *If these bastards get bright enough to put snipers up there, they'll sweep the guards right off the roofs.*

"McKay," Sloan's voice said in his earphone. "We have Dr. Mason on the radio. She's head of the facility, and—"

He never heard the rest. With a roar, a huge knot of people broke forward and rushed the fence.

CHAPTER
SIX ─────────────────────────────

Every fiber of Billy McKay's being urged him to swing down the black muzzle of the Maremont and open fire on the mob. *They'll go through that fuckin' fence like it's boiled spaghetti,* he thought. He longed to order Rogers to open fire with the turret guns, to rake the ravening horde with .50-caliber slugs, blow them away with high-explosive and white phosphorus grenades. Had it been a younger Billy McKay who lay on his belly in the street of that Kansas suburb, he would have given the order without hesitation.

But he was no longer a brawling leatherneck, nor an ace gunslinger with an SOG killer team. He was commander of the Guardians, and in a very real way he had the fate of the country in his hands.

"Sloan!" he shouted. "Pop the hatch and drop some grenades on those bastards. Rogers—range in on those buildings across the park!" He put down the binocs and snugged the buttstock of the M-60 against his shoulder.

The crowd had reached the fence. Even as the barrier bowed under the weight of a hundred bodies, screaming men and women began scrambling up on the shoulders of those in front, tearing at the barbed-wire coils with their bare hands.

Behind the sandbags on the roofs, the pitiful few defenders
tensed. They had obviously been ordered not to open fire
unless people actually broke into the compound, and McKay
couldn't help admiring their discipline in actually refraining
from shooting. Even up here he could feel the raw hatred
beating from the mob like heat waves from a desert highway.

He heard the clatter of a hatch opening and then the heavy
thump of an M-4 grenade launcher. An instant later a dense
white cloud burst among the crowd scaling the fence. "Okay,
Tom—*rock and roll!*" McKay shouted. He tipped the machine gun's barrel to the sky and held down the trigger.

Coughing and weeping people began to reel back out of the
tear gas. Across the park stood a number of two- and three-
story buildings, their windows gaping empty. Abruptly their
facades erupted in smoke and dust and fire and a tremendous
concussion that drowned out the howling of the mob. McKay
could actually feel the combined muzzle blasts of the .50-cal
and the automatic grenade launcher in Rogers' turret. Their
enormous recoil was enough to rock the car slightly but
perceptibly on its mammoth suspension. Next to them, the
yammer of his 7.62 juddered in their ears.

The effect on the crowd was electric, scattering them in
every direction. Those brave souls who managed to press
against the fence with their eyes streaming from the CS gas
Sam Sloan was dropping on them with metronomic regularity
freaked out as the hurricane of noise broke over them. Even
the ones caught in the doldrums of rad-poisoning lethargy lit
out for cover like coyotes caught raiding a chicken coop.
"Hold your fire," McKay said.

The silence was deafening. Down on the greensward, people
were running in circles, choking and gagging and holding their
hands over their ears, lying curled in fetal positions or hugging
the sod for dear life, screaming and shouting and pointing in
all directions. Some of them probably thought the Soviets
were lobbing missiles at them again.

"Good job, guys," McKay said. Even though he wore
special earplugs designed to bugger his eardrums against the
damaging clamor of gunfire, he felt his words in his skull more
than heard them. "Sam, patch me over the PA system."

As he waited for the ex-Navy officer to lower himself back

into his seat, McKay was asking himself, *Where the hell are White's people? They ought to be doing something about this shit.* Permitting an army of crazies to overrun a bunch of virtually defenseless scientists just didn't square with the control White seemed to be exerting elsewhere over his stricken city.

In any event he was glad his spur-of-the-moment plan had worked. He'd aborted the attack on the facility without anybody getting killed. Thank God the drizzle had petered out. If it had been raining, Sloan's tear gas might well not have worked.

Their brief as Guardians was clear: they had the right to use deadly force at their discretion. This new, older Billy McKay was reluctant to use it until he knew what the situation was, knew that it was the only way to go.

"You got it, Billy," Sloan said.

He stood up on the rise above the facility, feeling like the Humongous in *Road Warrior*. "This is Billy McKay," he said. Heads turned as his voice boomed out from speakers mounted on the car's hull. "I'm an official representative of the government of the United States of America, and I'm telling you people to disperse now. There must be displaced-persons centers you can go to but get the hell away from the particle accelerator facility before someone gets hurt."

People were pointing at him now. A man with a thin fringe of hair—who knew what the hell age he was?—shook his fist at McKay. Then somebody screamed, "It's a pig! It's another fucking technocrat!"

A wave of jeers and curses washed up the slope at McKay. He had to fight down the impulse to scoop up the Maremont and show them just who the fuck they were yelling at.

"Jesus, Billy," Casey said over the communicator, "these people sure don't give up easy."

"Dr. Mason's back on the radio, McKay," Sloan said.

"Put him through," McKay said, shaking his head. The world had sure gone bad crazy. People used to have respect for things like machine guns, even when they didn't give squat for duly constituted authority.

If nothing else, K.C. had gone to cellular telephones like a civilized city, and obviously they'd been adequately protected against electromagnetic pulse. That meant the Guardians didn't have to rely on the facility personnel to have CBs or anything to talk to them. They could just tune their radio into one of the frequencies the cellular system used, and talk to them on the phone.

"Mr. McKay?" a woman's voice said in his ear.

"Uh, yeah. Lemme talk to Dr. Mason, please."

"You *are* talking to Dr. Mason."

He winced. The scientist lady could have gotten royally frosted at him. Instead, she just sounded amused.

"Beg your pardon, ma'am."

"Think nothing of it. I don't know if there's anything you *could* do to offend me after what you've just done for us."

"Uh, yeah, well— What the hell's goin' on down there anyway?"

"We seem to be the target of a spirited protest demonstration."

"It's a shitload— Uh, excuse me, it's a whole lot more than that. Those people were gonna tear down your perimeter and then do God knows what."

She sighed. "We've been hoping they'd realize we had nothing to do with their present predicament and leave us alone. Instead, they've been growing more hostile with every day. That was their worst outburst yet."

"I know. If they'd tried for you that hard before, I'm afraid there wouldn't be much left." He hesitated. "Look, you know we've got some pretty potent firepower up here. You want, we could try to clear 'em away from you."

"No!" Her voice was shocked. "Please, please—you mustn't! These are helpless people, people who've lost everything, homes, loved ones, perhaps even the chance of survival. They're Americans just like you and—" She broke off abruptly. "You *are* an American, aren't you?"

He roared with laughter. "American as pizza, Doc. You think we're Russkies or something? The Sovies have got more important things to worry about than invading us. Like tryin' to keep a couple hundred million Muslims from skinnin' 'em for prayer rugs."

Remembering what Crenna had told them at their briefing about the possibility that the new Federated States of Europe might make a move for the U.S., he frowned. It came back to him with renewed force how vital his and the Guardians' mission was to America.

"We're a special team, Doctor," he said. "on an urgent mission from the President. Is there a Dr. James Okeda there?"

"Why, yes. Would you like to talk to him?"

"Sure would."

"Just a moment, please."

"Like, what's the crowd up to down there?" asked Casey Wilson. He couldn't see what was going on down by the facility.

"They scattered pretty good when we cut loose with the sound-and-light show," McKay said. "Now they're kinda clumping again. Doing a lot of pointing and yelling my way."

"McKay." It was Sam Sloan. "I've cut us out of the phone link. I'll let you know when Dr. Mason gets back."

"What's on your mind?"

"You aren't thinking of us trying to shoot our way down there, are you?"

"Only if we have to."

"Good God, there are thousands of people down there."

"You're not going soft on me, are you, Sloan? You got a glimpse of what was going down. They'll tear those scientists apart if they get their hands on 'em."

"There must be some other way to do this!"

"I hope to hell you're right, Sloan."

"Billy? This is Tom. I ain't sure we *can* shoot our way down. Not and get clear again. Those people are mighty determined."

For the soft-spoken Rogers, it was a lengthy speech. And as usual it was worth listening to. Sloan was right; opening up on the mob with the full fury of Mobile One's armament would kill hundreds.

The trouble was, there were at least a thousand of the bastards. Enough to overturn even a ten-ton armored car if they were sufficiently determined. They hadn't been determined enough to bust down the fence and get at the Oppenheimer accelerator—yet. But it looked as if that situation was changing. The thunder of Mobile One's guns had taken them by surprise, distracted them from the charge against the wire. They wouldn't be surprised again. If the Guardians started cutting them down, would their rage be enough to overcome the V-450's guns and thick metal skin?

It wouldn't be the first time, McKay thought. *Hell, all it'd take would be a few bottles of gasoline.* None of the Guardians were afraid of death. But getting broiled alive before they even achieved their first objective wasn't going to get the Blueprint for Renewal together.

"Yeah," McKay said. "You're right, Tom. We'll just hope—"

"Mr. McKay?" It was a man this time, speaking in a calm, quiet voice. "This is Dr. Okeda."

"Doctor, we've come from President MacGregor. We're to recover the blueprints."

Did he hear static or was it a hissing intake of breath at the other end? Okeda replied, "Do you have the proper recognition codes?"

McKay would have cursed under his breath if the mike hadn't been taped to his larynx. Crenna had authorized them to use the introductory code phrase, *We've come to recover the blueprints*—and no more. McKay knew the need for security, but sometimes it seemed to work against you as much as it did for you. "They were lost with President Lowell when his plane went down, Doctor. We have bona fides from President MacGregor."

"I understand. I'll want to see them, of course."

"We'll bring them when we come to take you out."

"And how are you planning to do that?"

"I'll get back to you."

He asked to be connected to Dr. Mason again. When she came back on, he asked, "Why hasn't the Mayor provided you a police guard?"

The pause was like a necklace strung with beads of static. "Perhaps he doesn't have enough people." There was a hint of bitterness in her tone.

"That's bullshit—excuse me, Doctor. But he's got people sifting through wreckage all over town. He could sure as hell spare a few men for an emergency like this."

"I don't know that Mayor White regards our situation as an

emergency, Mr. McKay. Research scientists don't have much of a constituency these days."

McKay looked down the hill at the crowd. A number of them were swarming around a tall young man whose hair had turned white and was falling out. It looked as if they were trying to nerve themselves to rush the V-450. McKay half hoped they did. Meantime, he decided to keep a sharp eye out in case some of them tried to circle and sneak in on their flank.

"I'll talk to the Mayor and see what he can do about clearing these scumbag—these turkeys out of here." He paused a moment, scratching his stubble of crinkly blond hair. "If he won't go along with that, I'll talk to him about arranging to have you folks evacuated."

"Oh, no. I'm sorry, but we couldn't do that."

McKay shook his head. "Beg pardon?" He was stunned. He could barely believe he'd heard right.

"We won't leave. Our work is here. We have our notes, our research materials. And it may be years before facilities such as this one are built again." More pregnant popping of static. "You see how important it is that we stay by our posts, don't you? Dr. Okeda—he's involved in vital research into treatment of radiation disorders. Humankind desperately needs that information."

He filled his bull chest with a long intake of foul air, then let it out again in a sigh. He said simply, "We'll get back to you," and rang off.

Down at the foot of the hill, the crowd had started cussing him out more heatedly, and were even pitching a few chunks of rubble and empty Coke bottles in his general direction. He decided he'd established enough moral ascendancy, scooped up the big machine gun and cradled it suggestively in his arms.

He walked over to the car and rapped his knuckles on Sloan's hatch, which the former Navy man had closed when he dropped back to his seat. "You guys can unbutton and get some fresh air—fresh as there is anyhow," he said. "Tom, keep a special lookout in case any of 'em get cute ideas about creepin' up and poppin' a Molotov in on us."

Leaning with an elbow propped on the deck, he gazed back down. A bottle arched up, glittering dully in the gray light, to explode in shards on the blacktop halfway up the slope. "Bold cocksuckers, ain't they? Ring up Hizzoner, Sloan. I may want to chew on his ass some."

Glancing through the vision block, McKay saw Sloan's brow crease in a frown as he started punching buttons on his console. "You don't seriously think Mayor White's deliberately neglecting those people?"

"Don't think nothin' yet." He reached into a pocket of his camo blouse and took out a cigar and a Bic lighter. "Don't get paid enough to speculate."

He stuck the cigar in his mouth and flicked the Bic. *Sure hell hope they got a lot of these things stockpiled at Heartland,* he thought as he lit up. *Fucking matches are always getting wet in weather like this.*

Sloan had punched McKay's throat mike out of the intercom net. McKay watched him arguing with somebody, presumably at the Mayor's headquarters. His face had undergone a sudden transformation—from its usual look of easy, Missouri farmboy amiability to an icy mask of command. Sloan had learned his lessons well at the Naval Academy. McKay had never had much use for officers, especially starched-collar Navy men with the black shoes of the surface fleet. But right now he was especially glad to have a man with Sloan's background on his team. Sloan had a lot more experience dealing with the standard bureaucratic pissant than McKay did. For all his awshucks manner, he could rip somebody a new asshole without ever using language strong enough to make a nun raise her eyebrows.

In a moment Sloan looked out at McKay, gave his best James Garner grin, and nodded. "McKay," White said into his ear, "what can I do for you?"

McKay was in no mood to go through bullshit about how he knew the Mayor was a busy man and all that. "Listen, Mayor, why don't you have people out here protecting the particle accelerator? There's a mob out here howling for blood, and if something ain't done soon, they're gonna get it."

"A regrettable situation, but we're terrifically shorthanded. I'm sure you understand the tremendous task we're faced with, trying to feed and shelter hundreds of thousands of survivors, trying to keep some semblance of order and do a million things at once."

"Yeah, but there're lives at stake out here."

"There are lives at stake all over Kansas City." For the first time White's tone stiffened.

"Okay. But you got lots of men guarding the approaches into town. Couldn't you spare some for a while to run off this crowd?"

"Guarding the approaches is a very important task. Unfortunately, we've had a lot of difficulty with people who had a mind to help themselves to what we've scraped together with our own blood and sweat. We need to keep marauders out. And besides, what could we do to this mob that would keep them from returning as soon as our men pulled out? Every man and woman is urgently needed for the task of reconstruction. We simply cannot divert our efforts to safeguard people who insist on remaining in such vulnerable circumstances."

"They claim their work's important, Your Honor."

White made a disgusted sound. "Ivory tower anchorites! They think their intellectual passions override all other considerations."

McKay didn't think that was exactly fair. He could understand devotion to duty. And what Dr. Mason said about their work being important—that made some sense too. But McKay wasn't going to accomplish anything standing here arguing. "Listen, if you don't get people down here, there's going to be a bloodbath. You're doin' such a hell of a job with this city—why fuck up your record with something like that?"

White said nothing for a moment. No doubt he wasn't accustomed to being talked to like this. Well, diplomacy had never been McKay's strong suit.

"Mr. McKay," White said deliberately, "you are proving very difficult. If you feel the security of these—*scientists* is so all-important, why don't you and your men remain there and guard them yourselves?"

"We got a mission."

"You're not the only ones, Mr. McKay."

McKay felt his upper lip curling. He wanted to spit to clear his mouth of the bad taste. *Shit, what he says makes sense,* he thought. *But something about it just don't sound right.* "I'll talk to you later, Mr. Mayor," he said. "McKay out."

The Mayor started to say something. A stab of Sloan's finger cut him off. *Good man,* McKay thought. A moment later Sloan opened the side hatch and looked at McKay, a troubled expression on his face. "What do we do now?"

McKay turned his ice-blue gaze back down the slope. "Talk to those fuckers down there."

CHAPTER
SEVEN ――――――――――――

Slowly Mobile One rolled forward. In the streets around the Oppenheimer Particle Accelerator Facility, bonfires burned, throwing diffuse clouds of yellow light into the mist-shrouded nighttime sky. The glare flickered fitfully on the silent, sullen faces of those who lined the path the crowd had opened to the gates of the beleaguered facility.

The V-450 was buttoned up tight. But as a show of strength, and for reasons of his own, Billy McKay sat defiantly on the front deck of the armored car, his booted feet braced on hand-holds, his Maremont cradled in his lap, rain dripping from his poncho, and the brim of a boonie hat pulled low over his face to protect the ember of the cigar clenched between his jaws. McConnachie had promised them safe conduct in and out of the compound. McKay didn't for a moment trust the gangly young fanatic with the old man's hair and the face discolored by radiation poisoning, so he'd ordered the Guardians to keep the hatches closed for safety.

On the other hand, he was damned if he'd let these goof-balls think he and his men were afraid.

Choking back his distaste, that afternoon he had called for

negotiations over Mobile One's loudspeaker after his unsatisfactory exchange with Mayor White. At first his request was met with a chorus of obscenities and hurled trash. The crowd calmed down a little when he ordered Rogers to put a few more .50-caliber rounds into the much-abused fronts of the buildings across the park to underscore the fact that the Guardians didn't *have* to talk.

A little while later McKay had walked alone down the hill to meet a party of the demonstrators, if you could call them that. He'd left the M-60 behind, and before setting out had unbuckled his pistol belt and let it fall in plain view of the crowd so they'd know he was coming down unarmed, as agreed. When he'd moved out, Mobile One had rolled back out of sight behind the hill so that its two turret guns no longer bore on the mob. Sloan had protested vigorously against that order, and even Tom Rogers had spoken out against it, but McKay was adamant. If he had to deal with these scumbags, by God he was going to display good faith.

Besides, he didn't think he had that much to worry about. Unarmed, he was easily the equal of any five of the rioters. Though he hadn't seen any firearms in the crowd, it would've been silly to assume nobody had one. On the other hand, he had a Second Chance Kevlar vest with steel inserts under his battle-dress blouse. And the mob's leaders had only stipulated that they wouldn't talk under the guns of the V-450; it'd take no more than a single word to bring Mobile One back up to the crest with the M-2 and the 40-mm M-19 grenade launcher blazing.

Besides, McKay had an ace up his sleeve. Sam Sloan was currently manning the wheel of the big car while Casey Wilson took his ultramodified Remington 700 sniper's rifle with the computerized scope and faded into the buildings north of the facility. McKay had lingering doubts about Wilson as an infantryman—his training and instincts were wrong for war on the ground and he didn't have the well-honed senses and reactions McKay and Rogers did. He had the fastest reflexes of any Guardian, but they weren't necessarily the right ones for patrolling or street fighting. On the other hand, McKay had no doubts at all about Wilson's marksmanship.

Conventional wisdom held that the requirements for a good

sniper and a good fighter jock were mutually exclusive. Sniping called for deliberation, an almost inhuman patience, while air-to-air combat depended on instantaneous reactions and the go-for-the-throat aggressiveness of a mongoose. Yet Casey was the most successful American fighter pilot since Korea, and also the finest sniper McKay had ever met. The apparent contradiction didn't faze the youthful-looking Guardian a bit, so McKay didn't raise any fuss.

McKay was going to talk in good faith. But he wasn't a fool.

He stood, feet spread, hands on hips, as a half dozen of the ragged refugees trudged up the hill toward him. The others stood at the bottom of the slope, silent now, a sea of blank hostility. Over their heads he could see the handful of university cops—augmented, he now knew, by a few Shawnee city police—as they watched the scenario with a nervousness he could sense from here. He'd requested by radio that they not intervene no matter what happened. They had agreed but made it pretty apparent they thought he was picking a messy way to commit suicide.

The delegation stopped a few meters away. Their gangly spokesman stepped forward. "Greetings in the Lord's name. I call on you to give up your futile and sinful defense of the technocrats. Their works are an abomination in the eyes of the Lord. They must be purged."

It took McKay by surprise. What hair the young man had left was long, and his work shirt and jeans were so caked with filth their original color was long lost. His clothing seemed ready to rot off his frame from constant weeks of wear—it was about what any well-dressed survivor of nuclear war could be expected to wear for an informal occasion. But McKay wasn't used to longhairs spouting such fundamentalist-sounding stuff.

"My name's McKay. I'm on a special mission from the President, and I'm calling on *you* to clear out and leave these people be." *Sound just like John Wayne,* he thought, not displeased with the comparison.

"I'm McConnachie." He waved a hand at the still, surly multitude. "And these are the saved, the Children of the New Dispensation. I tell you, we shall not be moved."

That's a little more like it, McKay reflected. *Another minute and I expected him to quote Pete Seeger at me.* "We need to bring somebody out of this facility. I want you to promise me you won't interfere."

"Never!" shouted several of the delegates at once. An old man screeched, "They all have to pay for what they've done to the world!"

Reining in his Irish temper by sheer force of will, McKay said through gritted teeth, "What is it you *want*?"

A young woman standing behind McConnachie spoke out. "These—scientists—almost destroyed humanity with their dabbling. They have to be stopped before they finish the job!"

He stared at her. She was well-built, willowy, with black hair tied back in a scrap of an Army blanket. She showed no signs of rad exposure. Her face would have been lovely if it hadn't been set permanently in a bitter scowl. "You're crazy," he growled. "These people are just theoretical types, harmless. Don't have nothin' to do with weapons work."

"They're blasphemers!" shouted a redheaded youth. "They're prying into the Lord's secrets!"

"Now, if that's the case, why isn't the Lord doin' somethin' about it? I'd guess He's big enough to look out for Himself."

McConnachie tipped back his head and regarded McKay disdainfully along the length of his finely sculpted nose. "The Lord is doing something about it. He's sent His prophet, Josiah Coffin, to show us the truth, the light, and the way."

The others' eyes glowed like coals. "Coffin!" the black-haired woman breathed. "He walks through the fallout, and the dragon's breath of corruption touches him not!"

These people are fucking nuts, McKay thought. Coffin's name took him back; Crenna's briefing had mentioned the sudden rise of an evangelist by that name in the Bible Belt but hadn't said anything at all about this other weird shit. Hell, the Heartland analysts seemed to think Coffin might provide a "beneficent centralizing influence," whatever that meant. McKay knew quite well what it meant and was disturbed by the naiveté of the analysts. "Has this prophet spoken to you in person?" he asked.

"He's addressed his flocks over the radio," McConnachie said. "Forrest Smith, the infamous bigot and capitalist pig, had his eyes opened by the Lord, and devoted his resources to doing God's true bidding.''

McKay blinked his eyes quickly, as if to clear them. This was making his head spin. He wasn't fool enough to think that every American of fundamentalist Christian bent was either an ultra-right-winger or a racist—but not that many of them were given to denouncing both bigotry and capitalism in the same breath. "So Coffin told you on the radio to tear up every goddamn lab in the country?"

"Make fun of us if you want to!" the redheaded boy shouted. McConnachie raised a hand, and he subsided.

"He called us to God over the radio. But his ministers have come among us, denouncing the Christ-less deeds of the technocrats."

"He's coming!" the brunette said. "He's flying here soon, to bring all of Kansas City to God. We'll give him this nest of sin as a gift."

"Maybe you will," McKay said levelly, "and maybe you won't. What I think will happen is Dexter White'll send a few platoons of riot cops, and them and us'll run your ragged asses to Wichita."

McConnachie laughed, a cracked, grating caw. "Not Mayor White! He knows Coffin is coming and fears to anger him. Too many have heeded the Prophet's words, and White loves power too much to risk alienating them."

McKay looked away, hoping they wouldn't be able to read the disgust on his face. He suddenly had altogether too good an idea of why White was waffling about sending help to the Oppenheimer laboratory.

"What's wrong with you people?" he shouted. "Those scientists in there aren't hurting anybody. Shit—some of 'em are working round the clock to find ways to help people like you, people who've been exposed to radiation. You think God's against *that*?"

" 'Vanity of vanities, saith the Preacher, all is vanity,' " McConnachie quoted. "You're playing back falsehoods spread by the technocrats. Many of my flock show signs of the poison. Some of us—I myself—were given medicines the technocrats said would help us."

"We got better for a while," said someone behind McConnachie's left shoulder. McKay stared. He'd thought it was a wizened old man, but the voice, though harsh and ragged edged, was that of a teenager. Like McConnachie, he had thinning white hair and skin that looked liver-spotted from subcutaneous hemorrhaging. But the dehydration and exhaustion of severe diarrhea had wasted his flesh on his bones, aging his appearance by decades. The insides of the boy's mouth showed the shocking bright red of blood when he spoke. He was showing the effects of an acute, probably lethal dose of radiation, and McKay was amazed he had the energy for such vehemence. "But that didn't last. After a little while we were as bad off as before."

"Many of us have been stricken by the science-spawned filth," McConnachie intoned. "Only in faith do we have hope."

McKay knew what the young-old man was talking about. The False Hope, as lecturers at the Guardian training camp in Arizona had dubbed it: an ugly tendency of signs of radiation poisoning to appear, then go into apparent remission for a period ranging from a few days to about two weeks. Then they all came back again.

"Look, some people are going to be too bad off to be helped," he said, carefully avoiding looking at the shrunken youth. "That's a real sorry state of affairs, but there's been a war, and that's what happens in war. But it's not like you don't have any chance at all. You can get a dose that'll make your hair fall out without having any long-term effects. Lots of people are sufferin'. You just got to try to pull through."

But McConnachie was shaking his head and smiling with the infinitely superior sadness of someone dealing with a hopelessly retarded child. "We've all heard these lies before. The technocrats have poisoned our lives. Now they're squirming to avoid their just deserts."

"Leave them." The lovely young woman leaned forward intently, eyes fixed on McKay's. Under other circumstances he would have taken her intensity as a sign of interest. And so it was, but not of the sort he would have liked. "Join us. Throw away your war toys, your futile, poisoned tools. God will forgive you all your sins. He'll accept you if you'll accept Him."

McKay felt anger bubbling into a quick boil inside him. *Shoulda let Tom do the talkin'*, he told himself. *He's trained in this liaison shit.* "Listen, we got to get into that facility. We're gonna do it—one way or another."

"Your threats mean nothing to us," McConnachie said.

McKay thrust himself forward till his face was inches from the tall fanatic's. The man stank like a corpse; maybe he was in worse shape than he permitted himself to show. "Listen to me, Mac, and listen up good. Up on that hill we got the firepower to put your people in a world of hurt. And I'll tell you, had it been up to me, we'd have done just that once the people in the facility let us know what was happenin'. But those *technocrats* you fuckin' hate so much insisted they didn't want us hurtin' you. I think they're just as goddamn crazy as you, but I'll respect their wishes—unless you try to fuck with us. You can have it easy, or you can have it hard. You just make the choice."

After a certain amount of heated debate, they'd made their choice: Mobile One could move in and out of the facility with impunity. "I hate like shit to negotiate with those assholes," McKay had said back in the car while McConnachie gave the word to his people. "And I hate to leave those poor scientists stuck inside there."

"They want to stay," Casey pointed out in a careful voice.

Of the four Guardians, Sloan was the most agitated by the situation. A trained scientist and engineer, he empathized most strongly with the personnel of the Oppenheimer Particle Accelerator Facility. But now he looked thoughtful and said, "We can't save the world, McKay. We're trying to save the whole darn country, and I reckon that means we're going to have to let some of the details go."

"Yeah," McKay grunted. "You're right."

"But that don't mean I have to like it."

"Mr. McKay, how nice to meet you. I'm Dr. Sonia Mason."

After a pair of nervous-looking university cops had let them in the front gate, Casey Wilson had pulled Mobile One to a spot between the low brick administration building and the linear accelerator lab where they were at least partially screened from the mob. A figure beckoned from a darkened doorway. McKay had dropped down and ducked inside, with Sam Sloan right behind. Wilson and Rogers would stay in the vehicle, ready to battle or boogie if the crowd got out of hand.

Hand outstretched, a tall black woman in a lab coat and a beige skirt walked down a corridor lit by kerosene lamps to meet them. She was into her middle years and not particularly attractive. Her yellowish complexion was liberally scattered with dark freckles, and her hair was a tangle of burnt orange, but her smile radiated genuine warmth, and her large chocolate eyes, surrounded with laugh lines, glowed with intelligence and good humor.

A trifle hesitantly, McKay took her hand. Maybe he was way out of date, but shaking hands with a woman was another thing he'd never quite got used to. "My pleasure, Doctor. This is Commander Sam Sloan."

Sam grinned. "It's quite an honor to meet you. I read all your papers on W-particles when I was at Annapolis. 'Fraid I haven't been able to keep up with your work since I graduated, though."

"Why, thank you, Mr. Sloan. Or should I call you 'Commander'?"

"Whatever you like, ma'am." McKay felt a quick stab of envy at Sloan's effortless way with women. Even if Mason wasn't much to look at, Sloan couldn't have been more charming if she were Merith Tobias, sex superstar of the nineties.

"I understand you're taking Jim away from us on some special assignment." She smiled at the expressions of concern neither man could wholly suppress. "Don't worry. He's been properly mysterious. But we will miss him. Come along, gentlemen, and I'll take you to him."

She led them along the corridor, past darkened rooms in which McKay glimpsed stacks of boxes and sandbags piled under windows, and finally to a stair leading down.

Downstairs opened on to a surprisingly spacious basement area. McKay and Sloan saw cots, more stacks of supplies, and a knot of people in lab coats gathered at a table off to the side. They were arguing vehemently by the glare of a lantern.

Dr. Mason saw their looks of surprise. "The facility was

built during the nuclear scares of the late eighties," she said. "It didn't prove terribly hard to convince the regents of both universities to vote funds to build in a fallout shelter. I believe the television movies helped in that regard." She gestured with a slender, graceful hand. "For our own state of preparedness, we can thank Jim Okeda."

"—can't do science in the dark," a squat, beetle-browed man was shouting. "Why in God's name can't we start up the generators for just a little while?"

A trim man with thinning black hair and Oriental eyes sipped steaming coffee calmly from a Styrofoam cup. "We must conserve our fuel for the present, Berthold."

"Hah!" The stocky man chopped air with his hand. "We will simply demand that Mayor White supply us with additional fuel. Our work must go on!" He spoke with an undefinable Eastern European accent.

"Excuse me, Doctor," the smaller man said. Setting down his coffee cup, he rose and came to meet Dr. Mason and the two uniformed men.

"Jim badgered us to begin stocking up on food, water, and medical supplies a month before the balloon actually went up," Mason told the Guardians. "We'd be able to survive almost a year on what we have now, except . . ." She let her words trail off. Unless something drastic was done, the vengeful mob outside wouldn't give them more than a few hours.

"Jim, this is Mr. McKay and Mr. Sloan. Gentlemen, Dr. James Matsuo Okeda." Okeda stuck out his hand. McKay took it; the scientist's grip was firm and dry. In the uneven lamplight McKay had thought him to be on the young side of middle age. Now he saw the gray streaking the straight black hair, the wrinkles on the high-cheekboned face, and realized that the man must be in his sixties.

Sloan shook his hand. "Good to meet you, Doctor. Looks as if you've done a lot for the people in this lab."

Okeda dropped his eyes and inclined his head forward. "It's no great deal." Smiling, he gestured with his head back toward the table, where Berthold was haranguing the other scientists and technicians about intolerable interruptions. "Many of my colleagues are somewhat other-worldly. Someone needed to keep his feet on the ground."

"Jim's *nisei*," Mason said with surprising bitterness. "He spent several years of his childhood in a concentration camp outside of Santa Fe during the Second World War. The government said he and his family were enemy aliens, even though he'd been born in this country and his parents were as loyal as anybody. Jim knows firsthand it *can* happen here." She shook her head. "They say physical scientists often have trouble understanding people. Sometimes I'm not so sure I want to."

In the embarrassed silence, McKay held out a thick manila envelope stamped with the Presidential seal. "You asked to see our bona fides, Doctor."

Okeda waved the packet away. "The fact that you know of the—blueprints—and my connection with them, and that you're willing to offer identification is sufficient for me."

"Well then, if you'll just say your good-byes, Doctor, we'll be on our way," Sam Sloan said.

He shook his head. "Not so quickly. I cannot leave my colleagues until I know they'll be taken care of."

McKay and Sloan looked at each other for a long moment. Then McKay jutted out his jaw belligerently. "You're fucking-A right you're not, Doctor. Excuse me, ma'am. You got a telephone around here?"

The conversation with White was short and to the point. McKay sat sipping coffee, turning the radiophone monitor on so everyone clustered around could hear the conversation. "Mayor," he said after an underling had gone to rouse White from bed under threat of having Mobile One roll across the state line and fire on city hall, "you're as close to a duly constituted authority as K.C.'s got. But one day the U.S. government's going to be back in commission. And then you're gonna have to answer for everything that went down around here.

"You gotta protect these people here at the particle accelerator, Mayor. I'm holdin' you accountable for their safety —both as a representative of the U.S. government and as William Kosciusko McKay."

In the ensuing pause, McKay wondered if the connection

had broken. Then White said, "I don't like being threat-ened." His voice was like a fist with the velvet glove stripped off.

"I never make threats, Mr. Mayor," McKay said quietly.

A heavy expulsion of breath came from the other end. "Well, I suppose you've got a point. You can tell Dr. Mason I'm sending a detachment of riot police and auxiliaries to form a cordon around the facility."

The lab personnel cheered, all except for Berthold. In his Henry Kissinger accent, he said, "You should have insisted on their sending us more fuel for our generators." But he was smiling.

Dr. Okeda had few personal effects: a small briefcase hold-ing his toilet kit, notebook computer, and a sheaf of micro-floppies containing his research notes. Back aboveground in the now-darkened admin building, Mason embraced him tear-fully. "Good luck, Jim. I wish you didn't have to go. We'll miss you terribly."

Diffidently, he patted her upper arm. "I shall miss you as well. But I know the people of the facility are in the best pos-sible hands."

Turning from him, she kissed Sloan on the cheek, then stood on tiptoe and kissed McKay's stubbly cheek as well. "I've never cared much for the military way, I have to admit. But I can tell you two are fine men. God bless you, and take good care of Jim for all of us."

McKay blushed clear to the sodden stump of his cigar. "We'll do our best, ma'am."

They ducked out into the rain. The smell of burning oil and trash clutched at their nostrils. "This way, Doc," McKay said, nodding toward the armored car. As they started forward, he said to Sloan, "I know we're in a hurry, but I still hate to go off and leave these people flappin' in the breeze."

"They'll be fine. White's police are on their way." He pulled open the starboard door just forward of the rear wheel. The soft red glow of the console lights spilled into the night.

From the copse of trees at the top of the hill that loomed just beyond the fence ripped the quick, unmistakable stutter of an M-16 on full automatic.

CHAPTER
EIGHT _____

A couple of steps behind Sloan and the doctor, McKay pivoted on his heel and swung up the Maremont. There was no time to take cover, even to flop on his belly. He just clamped the M-60's stock under his elbow and held back the trigger. The machine gun roared and bucked, bruising his ribs.

Something tugged at his right biceps. From the corner of his eye he saw Sloan bundling Okeda into the V-450. "Button her up!" he shouted. The M-60's clamor drowned his bellow; but his throat mike carried his words to his teammates all the same. Blazing away from the assault position, he walked his fire across the bright muzzle flash whipping at him from the trees.

Another instant and the car's one-man turret traversed the area, the stubby barrel of the M-19 rising. The Maremont jammed and McKay threw himself on his belly as the grenade launcher boomed a four-shot burst.

The top of the hill erupted in a sheet of blinding white fire. Two of the grenades had been high explosive, dual purpose, the other two white phosphorus; the vegetation was too wet to catch fire, but thick, poisonous white smoke crowned the hilltop. McKay heard desperate shrieking as he worked the action of his machine gun to clear it. A WP round scattered hundreds of flakes of white phosphorus that clung to clothing and skin and burned inexorably at a temperature of hundreds of degrees centigrade, and were virtually impossible to extinguish. It was an ugly way to die, but McKay's heart wasn't bleeding for whoever was shrieking his life away up there.

He heard a many-voiced shout and the twanging of heavy impacts on metal under tension. A bent round popped out of the receiver of the M-60. McKay bounced up, dove to the corner of the building, and went down behind the 450 again, throwing down the machine gun's bipod. Wriggling forward, he saw the gate bowing inward under the weight of a score of bodies. The guards on the roof were shouting at the mob to keep its distance.

Fuck that, he thought, and fired.

Short bursts of 7.62 ripped into the crowd even as the gate popped off its hinges. "They're comin' through the wire," he grunted into his throat mike. "Let the fuckers have it, Tom!"

The people at the gate staggered. They weren't twenty meters from McKay, and his slugs were slashing through them at waist height. A dozen squirmed on the ground as the others fell back in momentary confusion. Mobile One's engine snarled and the car lunged back a few meters so its rapidly turning turret could bear on the mob.

A comet blazed a flaming arc through the night and burst inside the gate, spreading a small lake of fire on the well-manicured grass. The V-450's two turret weapons opened up. McKay had a glimpse of the forerunners of the mob, blown away like tumbleweeds in the teeth of a blue norther by the hellstorm of .50-caliber slugs. Then a wall of flame and dense smoke sprang up twenty meters beyond the wire.

McKay blew off the last rounds of his half-moon clip as blazing figures ran out of the smoke to dash themselves heedlessly against the fence. Screaming with inhuman shrillness, they thrashed at the wire until a burst from the M-2 killed them. McKay rose to his feet holding the Maremont, exchanging the empty box for a fresh one from the Rhodesian pouch on his chest. He worked his gas mask from the case at his belt, pulled it on over his face. He put a hand on Mobile One's rear deck and vaulted up to grab handholds aft of the turret.

"Let's go, Casey. We're gonna clear those shitbirds out."

"Roger, Billy. What about you?"

"I'm with you, kid. Now, move!"

He barely managed to hang on as the big car shot out backward from between the administration building and the linear accelerator, curved back tearing out huge chunks of turf with its tires, and lunged forward toward the sundered gate. It bumped over a tangle of bodies, some of which still moved feebly, and then swirling whiteness enfolded them. The Willie Peter smoke could rot the bones out of you if you got too much of it into you—that was why McKay had pulled on his mask. He was getting an impressionistic glimpse of what downtown Hell must have looked like on a busy night—eye-hurting glares shining through the smoke on all sides, burning people everywhere. Then they were through, skidding on the grass of the park.

The mob was fleeing for the safety of the darkened buildings looming all around. Casey put Mobile One's nose toward the largest lot and charged. The turret swung left and right, spewing death. McKay blasted with the M-60 held one-handed like an outsized submachine gun. From the corner of one eye he caught a man raising a pistol in both hands and bowled him over. The car caught the running pack of rioters and rolled right over them, leaving most of them crushed to dark smears on the sod. McKay sprayed the survivors with a long burst.

"Hang on, Billy!" McKay was almost flung from his perch as Casey hauled the wheel left so that they could rake the backs of the fleeing throng. Rogers flung short spasms of fire after them, sowing clumps of white smoke. The Maremont's bolt clattered on an empty chamber.

"Rein 'er in, Case," McKay said. "They're gone for now." The car skidded to a stop. McKay slumped against the turret, surveying the destruction. There were bodies everywhere, and dozens of wounded mewling like lost kittens. A half-dozen phosphorus clouds squatted like noxious beasts around the park, dissipating slowly in the drifting, chill rain. McKay felt drained, sickened. It had been a massacre.

Fuckers asked for it, he told himself. *What got into them, makin' 'em charge into our guns like that?*

"Billy." It was Sloan, his voice low and urgent. "You'd better come inside."

"Roger." He popped the after hatch and lowered himself to the darkened interior of the car, stripping away his gas mask as he did.

In the passenger space between the driver's and radioman's seats and the turret root, James Okeda lay on the bare steel of the deck with blood running from his mouth and nostrils. "Jesus *shit*," McKay said.

"He's hit in the neck and chest," Sloan said. "I think his pulmonary artery got nicked." He looked up, his handsome face gray in the red glow. "He's going fast."

McKay knelt beside the wounded scientist. Okeda opened his eyes. "S-Sorry to disappoint you gentlemen," he said, and coughed. The blood had the metallic brightness of lung blood.

"We'll get you back into the facility, Doc," said McKay, wondering with a sick sensation if his rampage against the rioters had cost the doctor the vital few minutes in which medical attention might have saved his life. "They'll get you patched up."

Okeda shook his head. "No—no need to humor me." His voice was fading even as he spoke, choking to get the words out through the blood bubbling up from within him. "Something—must tell—"

His thin body convulsed with a coughing fit that sprayed the front of McKay's battle dress with blood. He cradled the dying man's head on his knee. A hand caught McKay's collar, held it with surprising strength. "Ma-mahal—" Okeda gurgled. "Mahal—" He gagged on blood and died.

McKay's eyes met Sloan's across the body. It seemed tiny, scarcely bigger than a child's. "The Taj Mahal?" Sloan asked. "What could he have wanted to tell us about it?"

McKay gazed down. Carefully he eased the body back to the unfeeling steel floor. The gentle little scientist had died as well as any warrior. "We'll never know."

They took the body back to the facility, where Mason stood by, her face taut and drained of blood as they carried it inside and laid it on a desk in the admin building. She stared at McKay and Sloan as if they were creatures out of a nightmare. And so they must have seemed, splashed with blood, reeking from cordite and phosphorus smoke and burned human meat. When they folded Okeda's hands across his chest, she turned and walked silently from the room.

"Tell her we're stayin' till White's boys show up," McKay told a white-faced technician standing nearby, and stalked out into the night.

Over the protests of the other Guardians, McKay walked out past the ruined gates on a mission of his own. His machine gun held ready, he searched among the charred and shattered bodies strewn across the park like abandoned toys. Mobile One crouched outside the gap in the wire, an ominous, primitive form glinting darkly in the rain.

McConnachie, the rioters' spokesman, lay thirty meters from the fence. A phosphorus round had caught him in its searing embrace. His eyes were open in a face like a charcoal mask. "Water," he said feebly through cracked black lips.

McKay ignored the plea. "Why'd you do this?"

The other shook his head, a minute movement from right to left. "Didn't," he croaked. "Tried to . . . stop them."

"You shittin' me?"

"No. Wasn't . . . wasn't for you. Knew it was . . . suicide."

McKay hunkered down beside him, unsnapped his canteen from his belt, uncapped it one-handed and held it to McConnachie's mouth, still keeping his right hand on the pistol grip of the Maremont. The youth tried to raise his head and couldn't. McKay let a dribble trickle down his throat.

"My people were outraged at the way you went into the technocrats' compound, defying their righteous fury." With his mouth moistened, he spoke more clearly. Even what must have been excruciating agony didn't stop him from speaking in his exaggerated, preachy style, McKay noted. "Some of the hotheaded ones saw their opportunity to strike down one of the scientists. The rest took the act as . . . as a signal."

He closed his eyes. "You failed," he continued. "And you will fail. The survivors of this flock are waiting in the safety of the buildings all around us, more determined than ever to wreak the Lord's vengeance on the idolators. And the Prophet Josiah Coffin is spreading his New Dispensation all across the land. Your time is . . . coming."

"Never happen. White's troops are on their way now."

A thin rattle escaped from McConnachie's throat. McKay thought he was dying, but with a shock realized the man was laughing. "That's what will never happen. You'll see . . ." He opened his eyes. They were a startling blue, rimmed in red and black.

"You did this to me, technocrat," he said deliberately. "Finish the job."

"Least I can do." McKay gave him another swallow of water, replaced the canteen, and stood. He aimed the M-60 at where the bridge of the fanatic's nose had been.

"I go to take my place in heaven. I forgive you, and implore you with my final breath to repent—"

A single loud crack cut him off, rang briefly around the deserted building fronts, dwindled to nothing.

"See you in hell," McKay said, and turned and walked back to the car.

Two hours later three armored vans pulled into the streets and began to discharge uniformed K.C. auxiliary cops in visored riot helmets and bulky flak jackets. The relief for the Oppenheimer facility had arrived.

The man who called himself Trajan sat sipping coffee on a corner of his desk, gazing at his collection of framed portraits of himself with various personalities—Nixon, Reagan, Lowell, Dick Helms, Bill Buckley—and thinking about murdering his mistress.

He didn't especially regret mixing business with pleasure by having an affair with his personal secretary. A beautiful and complacent secretary was one of the perquisites of being a powerful man. What he shouldn't have done was permit her to know of both facets of his personality—the public one and the deep-cover one.

All along he'd known he was taking a chance, but he always assumed Elyse, with her melting blue eyes and radiant blond hair, her firm, supple body and skilled mouth, was too enthralled with him to jeopardize his secret. Power was a potent aphrodisiac, to which the girl was far from immune. And besides, an element of risk enhanced the liaison, as fine wine enhanced fine food.

But now that he was de facto head of the Company, she had begun to grow shrill, demanding. She was insisting on almost feudal privileges—not that he had any objection to those, but if he was too busy to enjoy the perks of suzerainty, what with the struggle to seize power over America and execute Maximov's obsessive quest for the Blueprint for Renewal at the same time, he was damned if he'd waste his time making sure the clerical staff toadied some trivial piece of fluff. He tried to explain to her—not in those terms, of course—but she wouldn't listen to reason. The underground quarters they were compelled to share, of necessity quite cramped even though they had the pick of what was available, exacerbated the tension unbearably.

He contemplated a photo by a *Time* photographer of Dick Nixon standing in that stiff marionette's manner of his with an arm raised on Trajan's shoulder, face frozen in an expression of jowly bonhomie. *If the bitch insists on being treated like a queen,* he thought, *then can she complain when I choose to play Henry VIII?* He smiled. Very well then, best to play the role to the hilt. An accusation of treachery would do the trick. Producing evidence would be no challenge. And a suitably messy execution in one of the gyms in front of the assembled staff could be *most* instructive.

The deskcom chimed. He frowned and said, "Accept," preparing to tongue-lash the person from Porlock who'd dared interrupt his delicious reverie.

"Watts, Domestic Ops desk." Germanicus' assistant didn't bother with code names. He wasn't bothering overmuch with the deference appropriate to Trajan's position either. Perhaps an execution for two was in order.

His next words drove all thoughts of royal prerogative from Trajan's mind. "Our assets in Denver can't get to Perkins."

Trajan almost spilled coffee on his ascot. "Why on earth not?"

"This new holy panjandrum from the Bible Belt, Coffin. He landed at Stapleton last night in one of Forrie Smith's Learprop planes. The Federal Center went over to him this morning; whole place is jammed up jelly tight."

A grimace of irritation passed over Trajan's face. The deputy of Domestic Ops had a habit of making allusions to obscure blues tunes which Trajan could never get. "You mean to say that the entire personnel of the Center converted en masse?"

"Nope. Just the ones who counted. Though if the brass has seen the light, I don't doubt the rank and file'll be on their knees shouting glory hallelujah in short order."

Moistening suddenly dry lips with his tongue, Trajan tried to assimilate Watts's tidings. *Our only link to Maximov's damned Blueprint, and the fanatics have him,* he thought. *If only—*

"You should listen in on some of Coffin's broadcasts on KFSU," Watts said. "He's getting progressively wackier with every passing day. The latest bee in his bonnet is raving about the 'ringwraiths' threatening the faithful, for Christ's sake. He must think he's in *Lord of the Rings.*"

But Trajan wasn't listening. An inspiration was taking form in his mind, a stroke of self-admitted genius that would wrap all his problems up in a single tidy red bow.

"Thank you, Frank," he said distractedly. "Trajan out. Call Elyse." Obediently the communicator cut the connection and began calling for the attention of Trajan's secretary in her office next door. *Plenty of time to deal with her later,* he thought. *Now I'm going to reward myself for brilliance above and beyond the call of duty.*

And the thought of what's in store for the lovely Elyse will just be added spice.

They were running on blackout lights somewhere on a back road near Emporia, Kansas, when McKay felt a touch on his shoulder and came instantly awake. Casey was bending over him, his boyish face grim in the red light. "It's the particle-accelerator people," he said. "We got a message coming in from them."

McKay got up from the air mattress spread on the V-450's deck and moved toward the front of the vehicle. They were rotating in two-hour shifts, two on and two off. At the moment Sloan was driving and Casey had the turret.

Kansas City lay several hours behind them. They'd shoved off a little after midnight, having sent in a brief report to Heartland, just as briefly acknowledged. Crenna was too good a leader of men to offer his team either a reprimand or condolences.

Rogers came up behind, having gone immediately from sound sleep to alertness and readiness for action, just as McKay had. McKay slid into the radioman's seat. Without even looking at him, Sloan punched a button on the console. His face could have been carved out of stone for all the expression it showed.

"—coming in through the gates," a woman's voice was shouting. It wasn't Mason's; too young and high-pitched and shrill with mounting panic. "The Mayor's police have pulled out! The mob is back. They're hammering in the doors! Do you read? We need help desperately!"

The sound of pounding and angry voices and gunfire came clearly over the radio. "McKay, Sloan, this is Oppenheimer. They're inside the admin building. They're—*oh God!*"

A splintering crash, rushing feet, and then a scream reverberated in McKay's skull. A welter of indefinable noises, blunt and ugly, burst from his earphone. There was a final metallic crunch. Then static.

McKay's fists clenched until his sleeves threatened to burst around his knotted forearms. His anger against the rioters—and Mayor Dexter White—was hot and wild as prairie fire. "Those bastards. Those—fucking—*bastards!*"

"Do we go back, Billy?" Casey asked. He looked close to tears.

"No. Didn't you hear? It's too damned late!" Casey recoiled, looking hurt.

With all his willpower, McKay kept himself from driving a fist through a million dollars' worth of electronics gear on the console in front of him. He stared out the forward vision blocks, where the wipers fought a losing battle against the rain lashing down.

"It's too late," he said again.

The sun was a bloody eye opening on the flatness of the eastern horizon. The Kansas Turnpike was free enough of

stalled cars to let them roll full out. Not that many people had
driven away from the saturation bombing of the Wichita area
to the west. There was still enough residual radiation register-
ing on their meters that they were running buttoned up.

It was a particular pain in the ass for McKay not to be able
to pop the turret hatch. The Cadillac Gage–made cupola was
designated a one-man machine gun turret, but the one man it
was designed to accommodate was considerably smaller than
Billy McKay. With the receivers for the Browning .50-cal and
the bulky M-19, and the feed devices and ammo storage for
both weapons all crammed in the cupola with him, McKay got
pretty claustrophobic. And that day of all days, he felt the
need to poke his head and shoulders out and purify his lungs
with fresh, cool, rain-cleansed air. He rubbed his face and
looked the sun blearily in the eye.

"Billy." It was Rogers, holding down the wheel and communications on this shift. Stung by the catastrophic collapse
of their mission in K.C., the Guardians felt especially driven
to get to their next objective—Matz, the production expert in
Texas—ASAP. Since they were looking to make miles instead
of trouble, there was no need to have the whole crew on watch
at once. Better to catch sleep as they could and drive on
around the clock.

"Yeah," McKay grunted.

"It's Crenna. Wants to talk to you."

Oh, shit. McKay felt the bottom of his stomach dropping
like an elevator with a cut cable. "Put him on."

"McKay? Crenna here. We have an abort on your Houston
objective. I say again, Houston is canceled. We just had con-
firmation our contact there's a deader."

"Fuck *me.*"

"Negative on that, McKay. You're not my type. Crenna
out."

McKay slammed the heel of his hand against the M-19. It
hurt him more than it did the grenade launcher but still made
him feel a little better. "Break out the maps, Tom," he said
hoarsely. "We're goin' to Colorado."

CHAPTER
NINE ─────────────────────

"McKay." The voice of Sam Sloan, who was driving them across southwestern Kansas, woke him from a fitful sleep. "Lights up ahead on the right."

He stretched, got up, and went forward. His head and limbs felt heavy. The disappointment and tragedy that had met them in Kansas City weighted him like lead. *Or maybe I'm gettin' old,* he thought dismally.

He let himself into the radioman's seat and peered through the forward block. The sky had cleared that afternoon, the unseasonable chill the rain had brought replaced by stifling, humid heat. A profusion of stars glowed coldly above a landscape that was like a taut black blanket. Coming up on the north side of the highway was the yellow glow of lamplight through windows.

Not a contemplative man, McKay had nonetheless always found something poignant about the lights of a lonely house glowing beside a road—and, being an inner-city boy, something strange and almost wonderful as well. Under these circumstances, though, the sight was simply strange.

Skirting the craters Soviet nuclear bombardment had scattered around Wichita had proven trickier than anticipated.

They'd passed through a number of zones that were still amazingly hot for several weeks after the bombing, hot enough in places that you wouldn't want to go outside without a protective suit. By the time the rad count began to drop off, it was well into dusk.

Now it was fully dark, and Mobile One was trucking down U.S. 54, past a succession of small towns, dark and apparently deserted, hoping to catch 154 and cut northwest to meet 50 at or near Dodge City and head for the Colorado border. It wasn't a major highway, but neither was it a back-trail county road that didn't turn up on anybody's map. And therein lay the mystery of the unassuming, oddly inviting warm spill of light against the flank of the night.

Even before the One-Day War, it had become risky for an isolated household to advertise its presence on even so comparatively minor a byway as this. Gangs of bikers and road gypsies regarded such dwellings as easy prey. Now, after the holocaust, the marauders of the open road had been joined by starving hordes of refugees, many of whom weren't too proud to help themselves to whatever more fortunate householders might have on hand.

"Could it be some kind of trap, Billy?" Casey asked from the turret. McKay rubbed his jaw and tried to focus. *A trap?* he thought muzzily. The very innocuousness of the lonely light set his instinctive alarm bells jangling.

"Slow us down, Sloan," he said. "See if the infrared TV scanners show us anything."

"Good idea." The armored car braked to a crawl. Sloan worked the driver's-side cónsóle. A screen on the board glowed to life, showing a high-resolution picture of the road ahead, provided by means of an infrared camera in the hull. The headlights cast IR beams, invisible to the unaided eye, to light up the terrain. IR pictures didn't give as much information as visible-wavelength light. Driving by infrared—even with an easy-to-watch screen replacing the old goggles that gave you a headache inside half an hour—was strictly an emergency proposition. But the infrared cameras were pretty handy for scoping out an area without anyone knowing you were watching them.

They saw a small ranch-style house about a klick away, with

a barn to one side and a tractor in the yard. No pits or obstructions were visible in the road, nor any suspicious piles of trash that might have camouflaged a trap. The whole scene was a picture of innocence.

"Stop us here," Rogers suggested. "I'll snoop ahead and find out what's going on."

McKay frowned. Maybe they were making a big deal out of nothing at all. But, dammit, they hadn't seen lights at night unless they were part of some major encampment, or campfires for raggedy-ass refugees who didn't have anything anyone would want and hardly cared anymore if their fires attracted predators of the two-legged variety.

I want to know what the fuck gives, McKay thought.

"Go for it, Tom. Casey, get your M-40 and spill out to cover him." He used the old Marine designation for a sniper's rifle derived from the Remington 700, even though Casey's custom weapon, with its pistol grip, form-fitting stock, bull barrel, and *Star Wars* electronic scope, bore as little resemblance to the classic Marine sniping rifle as it did to the stock Remington model sold off the rack. Casey's scope could combine IR or starlight night-vision capability with variable magnification and automatic range finding. It'd prove real handy for covering Rogers' ass from a distance. "I'll take over the turret."

He crammed himself into the confines of the twin turret as Casey and Tom melted into the night. He brought up the view from the infrared pickups on the little flat-screen monitor and settled in to await events with his thumbs resting on the firing switches of the two big guns.

As always McKay had to admire Tom Rogers' mastery of a craft in which both were acknowledged experts. Even watching over the fancy see-in-the-dark TV, and knowing pretty well where to look, McKay scarcely glimpsed the ex-Green Beret as he stole forward, taking advantage of every scrap of cover in that apparently dead-flat landscape. Through the hull McKay heard the reassuring chirruping of a cricket.

Tom called in when he was within a hundred meters of the house. He did a complete circuit, then settled in to watch. After ten minutes nothing untoward had happened, and he said, "I'm going in."

McKay's reflex was to tell him the hell with that. But Rogers had done a lot of work with indigenous forces, recruiting for guerrilla resistance to Communist governments in the Far and Near East and to fundamentalist Muslims in the Med theater. He knew how to handle this line of country better than McKay, whose experience in covert ops ran mainly to the skulking, sabotage, and slitting throats school.

Rogers walked up to the front door. A dog ran out, barking. Rogers' earlier reconnaissance had been so skilled the animal hadn't noticed him till now. The sound came clearly over the hull audio pickups. Rogers stepped boldly up on the porch and knocked. The door apparently opened—it didn't show up too well on infrared, since the light from inside didn't register much and the house's interior wasn't much warmer than the muggy night air.

Every nerve and muscle stretched to piano-wire tautness, McKay listened to one side of a brief conversation. Rogers said, "Evenin', ma'am," to whoever had come to the door, and then he identified himself. A moment later he disappeared within.

"I sure hope he knows what he's doing," Sloan muttered.

"Bet your ass he does," McKay growled, thinking, *Sure hope he knows what he's doin'.*

A moment later a voice said in his ear, "Come on in, Billy. It's all clear—and we got an invitation to supper."

"Mostly we trust to the protection of the good Lord," plump Mrs. Thomas said, fussing over the wood-burning stove. "He saw us through the war. We reckon he didn't bring us this far for nothin'."

"Imagine you're right, ma'am," said Tom Rogers, forking up a mound of mashed potatoes in gravy.

The whole scene still seemed unreal to Billy McKay. Here they sat, elbows on the table, stuffing themselves on fried chicken, green beans, potatoes and gravy, and steaming-hot cornbread by the light of kerosene lanterns, chatting pleasantly away with the rail-thin farmer and his corn-fed wife as if none of them had a worry in the world. Casey Wilson was out sitting on top of Mobile One's turret, next to the chicken coop, with his rifle across his lap and a million stars overhead, waiting his turn to come inside and chow down. *Unreal.*

"Have many refugees come by?" McKay asked. He tore into a chicken leg.

Skinny, sunburned Frank Thomas shook his narrow head. "Ain't been much traffic nohow 'long Fifty-four for a spell. And th' only big cities nearby, don't seem many people got out of." With Wichita eradicated, and Tulsa as well, caught in poorly aimed overkill, and Oklahoma City on the far side of a lethal fallout zone, McKay could see the man's point.

"But you're right by the highway," he persisted. "Didn't you ever have problems, even back before the war, with cycle gangs and like that?"

"Oh, no," Mrs. Thomas said serenely. "Frank has a shotgun."

Frank Thomas scowled into his coffee cup. "People hereabouts don't take kindly to bein' terrorized. Reckon this ain't the best part of the country for them road gypsies."

"But ain't you worried, now that things've got all shot to—uh, heck?" McKay still couldn't let it go. "I mean, we're real grateful and all for your hospitality, but you think it's real wise openin' your door to us just like that in the middle of the night?"

Thomas looked at him, then at Sam Sloan. "McKay's a city boy," Sam Sloan said. Infuriatingly, the farmer nodded, as if that explained things. "He's not used to good old-fashioned country hospitality."

"We got plenty for ourselves and more, thank the Lord," Mrs. Thomas said. "Been storin' kerosene 'cause the e-lectricity been gettin' so expensive and all. And, believe it or not, Frank's been usin' a brace of old jughead mules to plow with an' such. Done it off and on for a couple years now, what with the tractor breakin' down all the time and not havin' money to buy one of them new fancy ones."

"Mules?" McKay shook his head.

"Lot of people hereabouts gone back to usin' 'em," Frank Thomas said.

"You a believin' man, Mr. McKay?" Mrs. Thomas asked. McKay hesitated, then shrugged. He didn't know how these folks would take his answer, but he figured he owed them the truth. "Afraid not, ma'am." He'd been raised a Catholic, and been terrorized by nuns until he started attending a public middle school; the experience had left him with little taste for religion.

She looked to the other two Guardians. Rogers nodded, chewing on cornbread. Sloan, who was an atheist or the next thing to it, equivocated, simply shrugging. "Well, that's your own affair. Mr. Thomas and I are Baptist—have been. But lately we been listenin' to the Reverend Coffin on the radio."

It was as if the proverbial twig had snapped in the woods. None of the Guardians reacted in a visible manner, but at the mention of the name each sat a little straighter, listened a little closer. "He don't hold with any one line, you understand," Frank Thomas said, picking up the thread of his wife's conversation. "Fact is, he says there's lots of ways to come to the Lord—and only one Way, you know what I mean. That might sound a touch permissive, but there's somethin' about that man." The farmer shook his head. "Claims he got a new dispensation from God. Reckon he may be right."

"Reverend Coffin calls on them that has to share with them that don't," Mrs. Thomas said. "If them refugees start comin', we'll do what we can for 'em."

The Guardians exchanged baffled looks. The calm goodwill and tolerance of these people could not have been more at odds with the murderous stridence of the rioters in Kansas City. Yet both claimed to follow the vision of the same prophet. McKay recalled what he'd read of the history of the world's major religions. *Sure ain't the first time that's happened.*

Mrs. Thomas bustled over to the table, holding a piping-hot pie in a padded imitation-gingham mitten. "I was makin' up some of my famous peach pie for Mr. Thomas. Always win ribbons for it at the fair." She blushed at her own immodesty. "Glad you boys showed up. We can't eat but a piece or two at a sitting, and with no way to keep it, it'd just go to waste."

"Mighty happy to be of service to men who're servin' their country like you boys," Frank Thomas said. "Believers or not, you're doin' the Lord's work, mark my words."

"In the Lord's name, strike!" the cadaverous man with the shaven pate intoned. The shaggy black-haired youth in the black leather vest stared at him with wild eyes. Then he raised the wrecking bar high with both hands and brought it slamming down on the right arm of the girl spread-eagled on the heavy table.

The nude body jackknifed. The girl screamed. A barely human wail rose to intolerable volume in the confines of the abandoned machine shop before falling away. The slender white form glistened with sweat in the light of torches set in the walls.

The burly former truck driver felt sweat covering his own face, although it was chilly for late June, even up here by the hipbones of the Rockies. He stared at the circle of faces surrounding the captive, disembodied masks lit by a hellish glare, and wondered desperately, *What am I doin' here?*

His skinny, tattooed arms trembling, the young biker handed the wrecking bar to his pal, an equally starved-looking blond youth. The two wore torn and thoroughly befouled T-shirts and greasy jeans. The black-haired one had a leather vest, once black, now faded to scuffed gray. Aside from the captive, they were the only ones in the shop not dressed entirely in black.

A patrol of the Children of the New Dispensation had caught four youths trying to loot one of the food stockpiles they'd set up in Lakewood, at the foot of Green Mountain only a couple of klicks from the new stronghold of the faith. One had been killed. Two more had been captured and deemed worthy of initiation as Brothers of Mercy.

The fourth was the brown-haired girl lashed to the cold, steel-topped table.

Sometimes the ex-trucker almost wondered if he was being fed some kind of funny drug, like meth-5, harmony, or even zombi. Some of them were getting drugs, he knew. The looming, silent kid who stood across the torture table from him licking thick lips had assumed the burden of zombi addiction along with the knife slashes he'd cut into his forehead and his slablike cheeks. The acid-and-spoiled-fruit smell of the drug hung around the giant like a fog. Not even faith in the New Dispensation could save a zombi from dying in convulsions if he was denied his drug. The trucker had seen an article about that shit once, in *People* magazine, where some sociologist called the zombi craze the ultimate rejection of modern society and its values, but it hadn't interested him much.

It had all been okay at the beginning. It had been different then. Reverend Coffin—the Prophet, they called him now—had come to that squalid DP camp in Oklahoma like a fresh wind to blow away the stink of death and despair. He had the power of the Lord upon him—even the redheaded truck driver with the broken arm could see that, and he hadn't seen the inside of a church since he got married. The Prophet had promised them life eternal, and promised them that through faith they'd build a new and better world in the here and now. And the trucker knew it was true, and he pledged himself to Coffin body and soul.

The trucker had felt it a real honor when the Prophet had taken him to one side on that delirious march to Okie City. Though hardly any of them had eaten at all in twenty-four hours, and although they had been living on watery soup and a few crumbs of bread for days before that, they were bursting with a wild, optimistic energy. The advent of the Prophet and his New Dispensation had dissolved all their doubts—not only those springing up from the devastation of the war, but from the grinding disillusionment of the years preceding. All things had been revealed to the marchers; all things were possible.

"I perceive a strength in you," Coffin had said, fixing him with those hypnotic obsidian eyes. "My children's hearts are true, but many lack the strength of spirit to do what must be done at all times and in all ways. You are different. You shall be a Brother of Mercy, and attend me always, and do the Lord's work with all your might."

The truck driver objected that his left shoulder was broken and might take weeks to heal. "But your right arm is strong," Coffin said, and the matter was settled.

So the red-haired man had become a member of Coffin's elite. At that time they numbered twenty-three. At first it seemed the Brothers of Mercy were merely bodyguards. The roads as they neared Oklahoma City were choked with refugees, many of whom were reduced to an almost animalistic state by panic, want, the breakdown of the established order that had guaranteed their behavior as men. On more than one occasion the handful of Brothers had been all that stood be-

tween the Prophet and death at the hands of a mob of unbelievers.

But gradually, subtly, the role of the Brothers had changed.
Even as they streamed into Oklahoma City, the Brothers,
whose ranks had swelled to over a hundred as the faithful
rolled south through DP camps, were sent out to secure food
for the flocks—by whatever means necessary. Coffin had
decreed that those who took him to their hearts should partake
of plenty, while the selfish who hoarded their worldly goods
must be compelled to share their bounty with the faithful. It
was the Brothers who did the compelling, with axe handles,
baseball bats, a few firearms. The ex-trucker took a certain
savage satisfaction in the work they did before the march on
Forrie Smith's Citadel. The thought of fat cats sitting smug on
top of their stockpiles of precious food while he sweltered in
the hopelessness of that camp south of Enid filled him with a
bursting fury that found its outlet in blood.

By that time, they had absorbed a few clumps of road
gypsies and bikers. Many of the faithful, the trucker included,
were disturbed by the presence of such punks. Coffin himself
chided them. "The outcasts, the rejected—these are the
Lord's special children," he announced. "Are not all the
faithful outcasts? Did not the leaders of the land attempt to
sway the people from the true pure faith of Christianity, pol-
luting their children with their evolution and sex education
and banning prayer in schools?

"Let he who is without sin cast the first stone at these new
brethren! In their own way they rejected the values of the sinful society the Lord Himself has cast down in ruin! Now they
are come to the New Dispensation, which is a house big
enough for all who would shelter within." And so it was that
when they marched on N. B. F. Smith University, Mohawked
road gypsies and black leather bikers stood shoulder to
shoulder with the solid workingmen who had formed the
original nucleus of the Brothers of Mercy.

Since then the role of the brethren had expanded. They were
the shock troops of the New Dispensation, protectors of the
Prophet, executors of the redistribution of wealth held by the
faithless, punishers of backsliders. They waited upon the
Prophet day and night; it was they who first heard his revela-

tions from his bearded lips. The brighter and more persuasive among them were sent forth across the land as missionaries, using Forrest Smith's vast stock of transportation to carry the Word as far afield as the Rockies, Canada, and the godless lands east of the Mississippi.

The former trucker had been privileged to travel to Denver in Forrest Smith's luxury Learprop aircraft with the Prophet himself, to spread the word to the Colorado branch of Smith University while a mass of the faithful straggled west in buses and trucks, running on fuel "requisitioned" from unbelievers. Denver was like an upper annex of hell, hit hard by the War and the other Horsemen of Disease, Famine, and Disorder. There had been fighting. Had certain key administrators of the huge Federal complex in the southwestern part of the city not been swayed by Coffin's gospel, perhaps not even Smith's mini-Citadel in the suburb of Arvada would have been enough of a beachhead for the New Dispensation.

But the Lord had provided, as Josiah Coffin assured his followers He always would.

And then had come the military packet jet from the East, arriving in a midnight rainstorm on the darkened runway of Stapleton Field. The trucker had seen pictures of the elegantly dressed man who knelt before the Prophet on that wet tarmac while a phalanx of the Brothers of Mercy stood by, impassive as statues in the downpour, but he couldn't remember who the newcomer was. The Prophet seemed to know. Perhaps God had forewarned him of the easterner's coming.

Since then there had been changes. The easterner had become Coffin's foremost advisor, closer even to the holy ear than Forrie Smith, who remained behind in the nerve center in Oklahoma. Now that Coffin had flown back east to bring the New Dispensation to Kansas City and other places hungering for the Spirit, the easterner was second in command to the administrator who had thrown open the gates of the Denver Federal Center to the faithful, and had assumed command of the Brothers of Mercy there. And under his guidance certain changes were taking place.

The gaunt, skull-faced man who called himself Brother Mace stared at the skinny blond biker with sunken jet eyes. The stink of blood and sweat and urine and feces and just plain fear clogged the air of the derelict machine shop. Outside on the vast grounds of the Federal Center, the army of the faithful rested and gathered its strength for a new day. If any heard the screams coming from the shop, which was one of several built aboveground for convenience and ease of ventilation, they didn't inquire too closely. Many and strange were the ways of the Lord—and dismal indeed the future of those impertinent enough to question them.

"The implement of righteousness has passed into your hands," Brother Mace intoned. "Strike the Jezebel. I charge you, strike!"

His face greenish-gray in the torchlight, the blond youth raised the heavy bar. The girl opened her brown eyes and stared straight at him. "Jimmy," she croaked, "please don't—"

"*Linda!*" he screamed. He threw the wrecking bar aside and bolted for a door covered by a hanging blanket.

"Lobo," Brother Mace said calmly. The huge zombi leaped with a feline grace that belied the bulk of his muscle and fat. An arm thick as a tree trunk fastened around the blond kid's neck. Lobo stuck his knee into the small of the biker's back. Muscles heaved under Lobo's black T-shirt. The boy's eyes started from his head as he clawed ineffectually against the vast arm. A keening like the sound of a trapped rabbit escaped his lips.

There was a splitting crack. The blond youth's struggles ceased. Lobo let him fall, his loose lips hanging in a slack grin.

The biker's companion turned from the table and vomited. At a gesture from Brother Mace, Lobo recovered the wrecking bar, handed it to the redheaded truck driver. "Use that strong right arm," Mace hissed. In the torchlight his face gleamed like bone. "Strike!"

The ex-trucker gazed down at the girl. She stared at him in mute, hopeless appeal. She was a beautiful girl, even though she had soiled herself and had a bright fang of bone jutting through the ruin of her right biceps. She reminded him uncomfortably of the girls he'd known before he'd married Margaret. She'd been pretty good-looking too, in a bovine sort of way, but that was before they tied the knot and she started to sort of balloon from the waist down. He'd hardly thought of her since the missiles came. But there'd been no lithe young lovelies for him since their marriage, and the spectacle of the biker girl naked and helpless before him awoke strange surging tensions.

"Why do you hesitate?" Mace demanded. "Do you feel pity for those who contravene the word of God?"

He licked his lips. He had felt pity, yes. Now he felt—something different.

He raised the bar with his one good hand. Mace's thin lips twisted in a grimace of approval. Unbearable tension knotted in the trucker's belly.

"Nooo!" the girl screamed. The bar swung down and shattered her left thigh with a sound like an axe striking wood. The shock traveled up his arm and blasted into his belly like a million volts. The torch-lit room spun, the tension poured out of the red-haired man in a flood of sensation, and as he dropped to his knees he understood the meaning of ecstasy.

CHAPTER
TEN ─────────────────────

"It looks," Sam Sloan remarked, "like hell with the fire out."

Billy McKay nodded at a score of flares dancing in the darkened city spread out below them, silhouetting ruined buildings like the rotted, broken stumps of poisoned fangs. "*All* the fires ain't out yet."

They were parked hull-down behind the crest of a bluff to the east of Denver, just before the Great Plains turned into the suburb of Aurora. Mobile One's hatches were open, and McKay and Sloan sat smoking on the top deck in front of the turret. The sky was clear overhead, a three-quarter moon washing out most of the stars. It was a hot, dry night. Surrounding radiation was high, but no problem for short exposure; a warhead had burst on the ground in the vicinity of Cherry Creek Dam to the south and west of where they were, and there'd been some particulation and washout from airbursts acting on rainclouds and smog. Fortunately the winds had spread the fallout around, blowing most of it in a wide roostertail extending east-southeast away from town.

The Cherry Creek crater was a good fifteen to twenty klicks away, but they could just make it out in the moonlight—a yawning blackness a thousand feet across and two hundred feet deep, a gleam of vitrified slag along the far rim. McKay thought he saw tiny flickers of light moving around within the crater, but they were faint, almost invisible. He decided he was either crazy or they were some sort of radiation-spawned will-o'-the-wisp. He tried to remember if they'd been briefed on such phenomena during their training. On the whole there was still a shitload about what nukes did, what kinds of effects they left behind, that nobody knew.

Oh well, he thought. *No biggie.*

From the information Crenna had supplied back at Heartland, the war hadn't been kind to Denver. Four airbursts and the one grounder—probably intended for the NORAD headquarters near Colorado Springs a hundred klicks to the south—had slammed the metropolitan area. Why Denver had taken such a pounding wasn't clear. Perhaps the Soviets had wanted to make sure of canceling Lowry AFB and the Rocky Mountain Arsenal to the south and north of Stapleton, which was on the east side of town, as well as pounding a key distribution center. The blast-mirror effect of the mountains west of town hadn't helped matters any. Moreover, it had been raining over Denver the day of the One-Day War, and the warheads had gone off below the clouds—which meant that the thermal flashes had been intensified, even though they had also caused fewer fires.

In the suburb of Aurora below them, a fresh cloud of orange fire boiled up against the night. A few moments later came a spastic *pop-pop-pop*ping of small-arms fire. Sam winced. "Some people just don't know when to quit," he said.

McKay took a long pull on his cigar. "Shit," he replied. Sloan glanced at him sharply, then realized it was the big ex-Marine's laconic way of agreeing. Billy McKay had the habit of falling into pensive moods, and Sloan didn't much care for it. His fits of contemplation made him damn near as cryptic and few-spoken as Tom Rogers, the original Stone Face himself.

Rogers himself emerged just then from the red-lit interior of Mobile One to pass out an extra dose of antiradiation medicine. It consisted of amino acids such as L-dopa and L-cysteine and various other potent antioxidizing agents, to reduce free-radical damage to tissue caused by ionizing radiation—i.e., alpha and beta particles—and by the much more pernicious and penetrative gamma rays produced by the decay of unstable isotopes in fallout.

Casey gulped the horse-sized capsule, chased it down with a swallow of water from his canteen. "Didn't Dr. Okeda have a hand in developing this stuff?" he asked.

Startled, Sloan frowned. He'd never thought about that before. "Yes, he did."

"Shit," McKay said again.

A shift in the wind slammed a sudden assault against their nostrils, a stench like a physical blow. "Jesus *Christ*!" Casey cursed. "What's *that*?"

McKay rubbed his jaw. "Smell of about a million deaders," he said. "After a couple weeks in the sun. Just be glad we weren't here about ten days ago when they were really ripe. By now they must've pretty much dried out."

Tom Rogers stood beside the vehicle, nodding his square close-cropped head and frowning. "I better give you guys a broad-spectrum antibiotic and a mega-C injection," he said, and disappeared back into the car.

Usually the Great Stone Face, Sloan amended mentally. Rogers was the team's medical officer, and when he was wearing his medic hat, he turned into a total Jewish mother.

"I hate those vitamin C shots," Casey remarked. "Like, they make your arm ache for days."

Sloan shrugged. "Better than what'd happen if your immune system weren't on overdrive. Any kind of bug that can bite a human is thriving down there: cholera, typhus, plague, anything."

Rogers came out again, and the Guardians received their hypospray injections in stoic silence. McKay ground his cigar stub out on Mobile One's hull and stuffed it back in his breast pocket, a reflex from his Force Recon days. "Wonder if any stockpiles of Coors survived. Could use a beer." When nobody answered, he shook his head. "I'm goin' to bed. We got a big day ahead of us tomorrow. And I got a feelin' it ain't gonna be fun."

•   •   •

The night sounds closed in around Sam Sloan as he sat alone on watch on the front upper deck of Mobile One. He hunched his knees up under his chin and adjusted his Galil SAR more comfortably in his lap.

Somewhere nearby a cricket tuned up. It was a reassuring sound, the same as the sound made by the midsummer crickets in Sloan's native Missouri hills. The sound filled him with a certain nostalgia. But he also knew it was misleading.

Billy McKay was a city boy born and bred, Casey Wilson a rich California kid who'd done a fair share of backpacking, Tom Rogers an Army brat whose father had taken him hunting from time to time when his family was stationed in an area where it was possible. Of the four, Sam Sloan was the only real country boy. Even though Rogers and McKay had vast experience as infantrymen, mostly of the unconventional stripe, only he had an inborn ease in woods and wilderness.

But this wasn't his country. He was used to the green of Mizzoura (as he pronounced it), which was so rich with forests and farmland it almost hurt the eyes. The land from which the front range of the Rockies sprang as suddenly as a wall was nothing more than a desert to his eyes, desolate and severe.

As dusk approached they had been driving west on little-used state road 36, paralleling U.S. 70, which was choked with derelict cars. They had stacked up in a hopeless jam between Denver and the insignificant farming community of Limon a hundred fifty klicks by road to the south and east of the capital. Limon itself had had the awful luck to have a one-megaton airburst dropped on it. Had this been the best of all possible worlds—or even a closer approximation—they would have kept on trucking along U.S. 50 from Kansas to the unlovely steel town of Pueblo, a smaller replica of Billy McKay's native Pittsburgh, and there turned north on I-25 for a run past Colorado Springs along the beautiful eastern face of the Rockies to Denver. Instead, they had cut north just before the Colorado line. "You don't want to see Colorado Springs," Crenna had informed them in briefings. "Or rather, what's *left* of Colorado Springs."

Just south of Colorado Springs was Cheyenne Mountain, which housed the headquarters of the North American Air

Defense Command. The facility was buried under thousands
of tons of rock and reinforced concrete, resting on over thirteen thousand-ton springs intended to cushion the jolts of
ground-busting megatonners. Supposedly Cheyenne Mountain was bombproof. The Soviets had tried to prove otherwise—and succeeded, at an estimated cost of over fifty
megatons.

The cars junked along the side of the little state road were
already well covered with rust. "They don't usually rust that
way in this part of the world, man," Casey had remarked.
"It's all this rain from the bombs going off. Made the coun-
tryside nice and green, though."

Gazing out the side vision block at the brown landscape,
ever so lightly dusted with a feeble olive green, Sloan had
turned to see if Casey was kidding. He wasn't. To farmboy
Sloan, Colorado looked like hell with the fire out before they
even reached Denver.

After a good look at Denver, though, even with the soften-
ing mantle of night spread across the devastated city, Sloan
realized that compared to it the deserts of North Africa were
no more than purgatory. Denver was about the Eighth Circle
of the Inferno.

From somewhere came a lonesome, trilling cry. Sloan
guessed it was some kind of frog in one of the creeks a klick or
so away. This and the other night sounds were almost familiar
to him, yet still alien.

The sounds of the desert—actually the tag end of the Great
Plains—were not the nocturnal sounds Sam Sloan was used
to, but they were close enough that he knew instantly when a
new sound intruded.

He was gazing at the stars of the Big Dipper when he heard
it. A slight rustle, off in the rabbit brush to his right.

He tensed. His right thumb clicked off the safety catch of
the Galil—reworked by a gunsmith to eliminate the dreaded
"Kalashnikov clack" inherited from the Soviet weapon on
which the rifle was modeled. His left hand slid to the trigger,
then dropped to his side, to the reassuring hardness of a
cluster of small objects like plastic fruits hung on wire vines.

Just a coyote, he tried to tell himself. But he knew better.

He let his gaze slip down to the jagged skyline of the Rockies, remembering the night training exercises at the Guardian camp in Arizona. *In the dark, let your peripheral vision work for you. You can pick up movement from the corner of your eye where you couldn't see a thing by looking straight on at it.*

There. A furtive steal from bush to bush. His left hand tensed. He was aware of other movement in the night all around—black figures hunched but still upright. *Men.*

His left thumb made ready to start throwing back the protective covers of the four clackers—electronic detonators wired to four Claymore mines arranged in a swastika around the V-450. At the press of a switch, he could fill the night with flame and flying steel marbles. But he couldn't fire them until he was sure that the flitting dark shapes were hostile. For one thing he'd look like a damn fool if he blew up a party of helpless refugees—or, worse, blew forty thousand holes in figments of his keyed-up imagination.

But a worse fear nagged at him, clawing at the back of his brain like a rat: *What if they're out there, malignant human presences driven by hunger or greed for our weapons or Christ knows what madness spawned in the flames of nuclear hell? What if they rush us—and I touch off the mines and they don't stop?*

All through the long and arduous Guardian training program, they'd told him incessantly that however much instruction he got, however many exercises he ran and aced, as he always did, he couldn't *know* in the core of him, down deep in his bones, what it felt like to be alone in the dark in hostile territory with the growing conviction that *they* were about to start coming over the wire. He'd always nodded, acknowledged the truth of what they had said—hell, his lack of experience on the ground was the main reason he'd consented to being commanded by a damned gyrene he outranked from hell to breakfast.

But now he knew. The knowledge penetrated him like the chill wet North Pacific wind on watch on the decks of the destroyer *Joseph William Reichert* off the Aleutians. It suffused his soul like the sweet-and-sour gangrene tang of putrefying flesh that rose from Denver and choked his palate every time the wind backed. It shook his soul like a ferret with a rat. The night held shapes, and they were hostile.

He snapped up the trigger shields. His right hand clutched the Galil's pistol grip like a drowning man clinging to a floating plank. *Wake the others!* a voice yammered in his mind. *You can't handle this, Sam. You'll choke and they'll swarm in and cut everybody's throat—hit the panic button now! Call the men who know what they're doing in a case like this.*

His jaw squared with sudden resolution. *The hell with that!* he thought. *I'm one of the best. I can handle it.*

He leaned back against the turret as if he hadn't a care in the world. If the sound of his teeth chattering didn't wake his buddies, he figured everything was shipshape.

An hour later McKay relieved him. "Thought I saw some people skulking around the car," he reported. "They never got closer than fifteen, twenty meters. Seemed to hang around for half an hour or so. Don't know how many there were." He forced a grin. "Heck, I don't even know I wasn't dreamin'."

McKay frowned, shook his head. "You weren't." He settled down with the big machine gun across his lap. "I got a bad feelin' about this place. Stone bad."

Sloan had just settled down on his air mattress on the inner deck aft of the turret root when a noise yanked him back from the brink of sleep. It seemed to rumble up through the tires and suspension and thick hull of the car, a grinding, grumbling, shuddering basso growl. He sat upright.

In the front of the car Casey Wilson hollered, "Earthquake!" and disappeared out the side hatch. Sloan gulped and dove after him.

The night sounds had stilled. The roar rolled over them like surf. Sloan stood staring down at the black-out city dotted with fires and realized the earth wasn't moving beneath his feet.

He became aware of McKay sitting up on the car, leaning imperturbably against the turret. Tom Rogers materialized, holding his own Galil ready. "What's the drill?" the ex-Army man asked.

"Big building going down, I figure," McKay said. "Blasts musta weakened the foundation."

"Awful big one, to make that much racket," Rogers commented.

Slowly the sound died away. "They've been putting up a whole lot of skyscrapers in Denver the last ten years, really awesome ones," Casey Wilson said sheepishly. "Shit. Like, I'm sorry, Sam. It's just, well, all my life a sound and a feeling like that meant one thing to me."

"Forget it," McKay said. "Neither one of you've hung out in bombed-out cities enough to know what they sound like. Go on to back to bed."

Sam and Casey turned back to the armored car. "One thing," McKay said. They looked at him. "Next time you bail out of the car in a hurry—try to remember to take a long arm with you, okay?"

Empty-handed, the two stared at one another.

For the Guardians, it was fortunate that the Denver Federal Center was located in the suburb of Lakewood in the western part of town. It meant that they could avoid trying to battle their way through the ruined heart of the sprawling city—a major struggle even before the war, since central Denver was a confusing diagonal lattice in which all the streets were one way the wrong way, plopped down in the middle of the rationally north-south-oriented grid of the rest of the city. Instead, as a clouded dawn spilled an ugly curdled-milk light across the Plains, they hit out south overland, fording several creeks swollen by the rainstorms that lashed at the mountains.

They swung south of the crater left by the Cherry Creek warhead and crossed the runway of the Arapahoe County Airport, whose buildings had mostly been flattened. The quonset-style hangars remained pretty much intact, but the airplanes parked in and around them looked like toys a petulant child had stomped on in a proper tantrum, their frames buckled and bent by blast wave and overpressure.

Beyond lay an overpass where I-25, running south out of town, crossed County Line Road. The force of the Cherry Creek explosion had dropped it, as well as the cars that had crammed onto it in the panic that followed the word that the balloon was going up. They hammered their way by main force of Mobile One's huge V-8 engine through rusting, burned-out wrecks and bulled due west through desolate, deserted suburbs.

To their right, Denver lay under a pall of smoke. It was not a city much given to huge residential apartment blocks, even though a number had gone up during the up-and-down boom and bust years of the seventies and eighties. Denver still consisted largely of houses, and was consequently spread out. The population wasn't gathered neatly into centralized beehives so that an optimum number could be knocked down by a bomb. On the other hand, except for downtown proper, there weren't that many high-rise structures, which would have been useful for breaking up wind flow and reducing the possibility of a firestorm, according to prewar nuclear pundits. By and large, though, Denverites had built (and fireproofed) well. There was no firestorm.

On the other hand, most of the city was pretty well rubbled by the successive shocks. As far south as Littleton and Southglenn, which the Guardians skirted on the south along the County Line Road, at least half the homes were down, and all showed heavy structural damage. Yet, as always the destruction was freakish, erratic. Even in the hard-hit downtown area, some of the giant skyscrapers still loomed over debris-choked thoroughfares. Empty hulks, many burned hollow, their foundations weakened and structural members dangerously crystallized by thermal pulse and blast, stayed upright only by the tolerance of winds or earth tremors, but stood nonetheless.

Once again Mobile One ran buttoned up. Radioactive decay had taken the sting out of most of the fallout that had settled on the Denver metropolitan area, and even the hot spot of ejected material around the crater had cooled considerably. On the other hand, driving through the dust and ash could conceivably stir up pockets of dust that were still pretty radioactive. Inhaling it didn't pose that much of a problem; the hairs in a human nose are efficient filters. But getting even a few gamma-ray emitters into the car with them wouldn't be helpful, and even fallout that emitted alpha particles, which wouldn't penetrate intact skin, or beta particles, which could only cause superficial damage to skin, could be bad medicine in the close confines of the armored vehicle. If they got into an open wound, or even a fold of skin, the relatively innocuous alpha and beta emitters could cause bad burns. And if a lot of "hot" dust was floating around inside the car, the chance of inhaling fallout, or very dangerous plutonium residue from the warhead, increased greatly.

From time to time they glimpsed ragged figures picking their way through the rubble, foraging for canned goods or God knew what. Mostly these people ducked into hiding at the car's approach. Life in the rubble was a dog-eat-dog proposition. The automatic assumption was that armed strangers would try to steal anything you'd gleaned from the wreckage. Twice the car passed groups of refugees—bearded men, gaunt-faced women, silent, dirty children. They were filthy and clad in rags, carried pathetic bundles as they straggled leadenly along the road. One group was bound west, the other east. There seemed to be no reason for one direction over the other.

Overall they saw few people. Living ones, at least. The air was redolent with the stench of unburied bodies—another good reason to keep the hatches dogged—and hardly a street lacked one or several corpses decomposing in the sun. Not that all the corpses dated from the One-Day War. Many were fresh enough for signs of depilation, flash burns, or just plain violence to show. Others were emaciated, some even to the point of resembling concentration-camp victims in old news-reels. It was still somewhat early for many deaths from starvation alone, but lack of food lowered resistance to the diseases that stalk in the wake of any catastrophe. Diarrhea, caused either by diseases such as cholera or typhus or by extreme exposure to radiation, could whittle a strong man down to a scarecrow in no time.

The state road bridge across the swollen Platte was intact. They bulled through the usual wrecks, then struck out through affluent suburbs of woods and riding stables. The blast waves had been fairly attenuated by the time they got here, so the surface streets weren't badly rubbled. Rain-wet greenery had

retarded fire formation, but thermal flashes had killed most of
the trees. Oddly, the grass seemed unaffected; the rolling hills
were carpeted in a lush green, like a velvet cloth spread out to
offset an after-the-holocaust diorama of stripped trees and
battered houses.

They worked north into the more densely populated town of
Lakewood. Wadsworth Boulevard, the major thoroughfare
leading north toward their destination, was full of frozen traffic. They were getting into the heavy-damage radius of the
warhead that had burst above the University of Denver again.
Many of the cars' gas tanks had been touched off by the flash;
other cars' paint had blistered like burned skin. The blast had
been potent here too. A brown UPS delivery truck had been
tossed thirty yards onto the roof of a chalet-style restaurant.

A few torturous blocks north, McKay did a double take out
a side port. "Jesus fucking Christ!" he yelled. "What's
that?"

What it looked like was a crow the size of a man lying in a
bristle of feathers in the parking lot of a small shopping
center. Nearby lay a handful of small bodies, charred and
badly decomposed.

The Guardians had not exactly been allowing their curiosity
to get the better of them in their wanderings since the war;
they couldn't afford the luxury. Even Sam Sloan and Casey
Wilson, who had fought detached and relatively sterile styles
of warfare, were beginning to grow used to the sight of mass
death and destruction. Sheer attrition wore down your com-
passion—or you went insane. But now McKay ordered Casey
to roll over and see just what the hell this was all about. It was
too damned weird to pass by.

Unwilling to pop the hatches unless it was vital, Casey rolled
over a cindered Mazda and pulled up next to the motionless
apparition. "Oh, God," Sloan choked, clamping a hand over
his mouth.

Suddenly, it was painfully apparent what had happened.
The "crow" had been a man dressed in a bird suit, probably
acting out some silly script for the children. The flash of the
UD blast had caught him in the open and he'd burned to death
in the flaming suit. The smaller lumps were the bodies of the

children who had been watching him in delight when the false
sun rose in the east.

Slowly Casey turned the wheel and drove away. Mobile
One's air conditioner whined loudly in the queasy silence.

Having started life in 1941 as an ordnance plant operated by
the Remington Arms Company, the Denver Federal Center
was an oblong sprawl more than a mile on a side. After the
Second World War, it had taken on its present identity. In recent years it had been massively rebuilt so that, like an iceberg,
most of it lay beneath the surface. Its offices housed, during
working hours, enough employees to populate a not so small
town, and most of them had gotten caught in traffic on the
way to work on the last morning of their lives. Its warehouses
were the repositories for the old records of most of the mammoth machinery of the U.S. Government. The rolling green
hills, crisscrossed with irrigation ditches and dotted with
clumps of trees, surrounding its surface structures looked
more like a wildlife preserve than a bureaucratic nerve center.
For years, injured animals brought in by the Forest Service
had been released on the protected grounds after treatment.
Antelope, mountain sheep, and deer strolled unconcerned
within sight of the vastest federal facility outside Washington,
D.C.

The Guardians' first sight of the complex, as they drove
west along Alameda, was of a small herd of white-tailed deer
cropping the grass just inside the high fence in the shadow of a
stone guard tower. During the unrest of the late eighties, the
DFC's security had been beefed up repeatedly until it now
bore an uncomfortable resemblance to a penitentiary. The
next thing they saw, through green glass so heavily armored it
had survived the direct impact of the blast front, was that the
ten-meter-tall tower was occupied.

"How do we play this, Billy?" Casey asked. He was steer-
ing around a tanker truck that had caught fire and blown open
like a baked potato in a microwave.

Hunched over behind him, McKay glanced at Sloan. "They
don't answer on any frequency I've tried." He shook his head.
"I don't like that much."

McKay's blue eyes narrowed. The DFC's communication

center was buried deep under concrete and earth, and provided with the best state-of-the-art protection against both EMP and lesser-known TREE—transient radiation effects on electronics—caused by radiation emanating directly from the fireball.

Direct radiation wasn't a big factor in causing human casualties, even though it had been responsible for perhaps ten percent of fatalities at Hiroshima and Nagasaki. As weapons got larger, the other fatal effects of a nuclear explosion expanded their radii more quickly than direct radiation, so that almost anyone receiving a lethal dose of direct radiation from a megaton-range weapon would already by struck dead by shock and heat. But electronic equipment was much more sensitive to the free neutrons and high-frequency radiation emitted by a blast.

However, the Federal Center's communications should have survived even the shitstorm they had been subjected to. That meant the current occupants of the facility weren't talking, either because they didn't know how to operate the equipment, or for reasons of their own. Either way, their behavior was rife with implications for the Guardians' mission, none of them very attractive.

"FIDO," McKay said quietly. "Fuck It and Drive On."

Sloan glanced at him sharply. "You sure of that, McKay?"

"Fuck no. But how else are we gonna get Perkins out of there—provided he's in there to start with?"

"Maybe we could put an ad in the personals in *Westword*," Casey said, and laughed.

"Just don't anybody ask him to explain that one," McKay commanded. "Let's go."

The heavy gates that opened onto Kipling, across from Lakewood Park a couple hundred meters north of Alameda, were open. A stream of people flowed in and out between sullen guard towers. A panel van with a huge flashblister obliterating whatever words had been painted on its side was just going through while the pedestrians stepped to either side. The people on foot were of both sexes, and while none of them looked ready for lunch at Top of the Rockies, they didn't have the dirty, shabby appearance or hollow cheeks and eyes of the refugees the Guardians had been seeing. They watched the iron behemoth approach with no visible sign of alarm.

A bulldozer had pushed Alameda clear of derelict vehicles. Mobile One halted on the street in front of the gate, where it wouldn't block traffic. "Want me to patch you into the PA?" Sloan asked McKay.

McKay thought about it for a moment. It was mighty comforting to have the car's armored hide between him and possible danger in an unknown situation such as this. On the other hand, given the resources of the Fed Center, bulling in wasn't really an option, however much it might appeal to the belligerent part of McKay's nature. Christ knew what kind of weapons were stockpiled in there for use by the security troops. Better to try diplomacy.

And McKay was never really comfortable cooped up on top of a load of gasoline anyway.

"Nope," he said. He popped the overhead hatch and boosted himself into the watery sunlight.

The day was humid. Fortunately, there was a light breeze from the west, blowing most of the odors of decay away from this side of town. Still, the air had the familiar taste of death. He boosted himself up to stand erect on the deck. "Hello," he called, cupping his hands over his mouth. "Who's in charge here?"

The van rumbled on up the blacktop toward the slab-sided buildings. People were stopping to watch. In a moment a door opened in the side of one of the towers and a young man stepped out. He had longish blond hair swept back from a long, clean-cut face showing a backpacker's tan. He wore a white polo shirt, jeans, and waffle stompers. His belly was flat, hips narrow, his arms and chest muscular, and he moved with the easy grace of an Alpine skier. As far as McKay could tell, he was unarmed.

"Howdy, brothers," the young man called in a friendly way. "I'm the Lesser Prophet Martin Haskell, of the Church of the New Dispensation. How may I serve you?"

McKay's throat went dry at the mention of the church, but he carried on without a hitch: "My name's McKay. We're on a mission from the President." Haskell looked impressed. "We'd like to talk to the man in charge here."

A grin broke over Haskell's features. "The man in charge here is our Lord and Savior, Jesus Christ, who has bestowed His blessings on us through the First Prophet, Josiah Coffin," he said. "But if you wish to speak with the shepherd of our modest flock, please excuse me a moment while I call him."

He disappeared back into the guardhouse. McKay pitched his voice low so that only his throat mike would pick up his words: "It all depends now on whether these're New Dispensation types like McConnachie's bunch, or like the Thomases."

"Billy," Sloan said in his ear, "there're men up there in those towers. They can't hit us with a rocket from there, can they?"

"Oh, shit yes," McKay said cheerfully. "Probably have Armbrusts just like us. Don't have any back blast, so you can fire 'em in an enclosed space."

Haskell emerged from the looming tower. "It's all arranged," he said brightly. "If you'll let me guide you, Elder Brother Nolan Perkins will see you at once."

CHAPTER
ELEVEN ─────────────────

"Holy shit," Casey yelped. Somehow McKay managed to keep his face impassive. *The man we've come to get's thrown in with these Holy Rollers*, he thought. *Fuck us.*

"Want a ride?" McKay asked. "Just hop aboard."

"Thanks. The Lord doesn't mind His servants making things easy on themselves—long as there aren't lives or souls at stake." He accepted McKay's hand up and let the Guardians arrange him so his long legs weren't blocking Casey's view slit. McKay shut the hatch and rode in front of the turret, making sure to keep clear of the big autoweapons' field of fire.

They rolled out. McKay didn't let himself glance up at the green glass and firing ports of the grim towers looming over the gate. Casey drove slowly up the road toward the blocky aboveground buildings of the complex, past a line of people who waved and smiled. Haskell nodded and waved back like the President in a motorcade.

"Looks like your people are gettin' enough to eat," McKay remarked.

"The Lord provides. We found a wealth of bounty when we

came to this place, stores of food and medicine, and we glean what we can from the ruins. We have plenty of water too. The treatment centers are out, but the water still flows down from the reservoirs in the mountains." A shadow crossed his face. "If only we could help the poor people out in the rubble. We're doing what we can to succor the sick and hungry, but there're so many." He shook his head and brightened again. "Well, we're getting our act together here, and by pulling together and with the help of God we'll soon be able to extend a helping hand to all who need it."

McKay turned away to hide his frown. He'd never been comfortable around ultrareligious types, especially Protestants, and his experiences in K.C. had done nothing to increase his ease around them. Like McConnachie, Prophet Haskell was young and spoke in a preachy sort of way, but otherwise there was no similarity between the radiation-scarred fanatic and this earnest young man with the easygoing sense of humor. The fact was, he was in danger of starting to like Haskell.

They followed the van into a paved central lot. It turned off toward the yawning entrance to a subterranean parking garage. "If you'll be kind enough to have your driver pull in over there," Haskell said, nodding toward the north side of the lot, "I'll take you to our leader."

McKay passed the instructions to Casey in a whisper. He paused a moment, then said, "Sam, you come with me. Tom and Casey stick with the car. Be ready to haul us out if we holler. Or boogie if you have to."

The other Guardians acknowledged without comment. For all their diversity of character, and the frictions that sometimes occurred between them, they trusted one another implicitly to operate as a team—and to do what had to be done to insure success of the mission, whatever the cost. Though Tom Rogers was an experienced liaison man, McKay's instincts told him to take Sloan with him. Sloan was a natural diplomat— a different matter entirely—and McKay had a hunch diplomacy was what was called for here. Besides, he liked having Rogers on tap for a bust-out, if that proved necessary.

Though he had to admit it didn't look like it would be. The

core area of the Fed Center bustled with organized activity of an almost offensively peaceful sort. People were issuing in and out of the buildings, laughing and talking as casually as if the world were still the way it had always been, as if they weren't all within spitting distance of one of the largest mass graves in history. Trucks and vans riding low on their suspensions, under weight of supplies no doubt, disappeared into the subterranean shipping and receiving bays and emerged again to roll back out between the guard points. Off to one side of the central parking lot was a square of green lawn, where a class of about thirty young people sat on the grass watching an older man in jeans and a white shirt write on an easel black-board. It was hard to imagine danger threatening amid such calm and cheerful surroundings, where the dark iron mass of Mobile One seemed a painful intrusion.

But imagining danger threatening was Billy McKay's profession. So Tom and Casey stayed with the car—just in case.

Casey pirouetted the car neatly as a ballerina and brought it to a halt before a low building, whose windowless gray walls were sloped to resist blast waves. Sloan clambered out and was introduced to Haskell. They shook hands.

"Late Federal Paranoid-Style Architecture," Sloan remarked, taking in the building. "It's even uglier than Bauhaus."

"Yeah," McKay said. "But it served its purpose."

"True." Sloan glanced between low bunkerlike buildings, frowned, pointed. "What's going on out there?"

Martin Haskell's gaze followed Sloan's finger west to where about twenty people were running and crawling over the green hills. Several figures stood over them, apparently calling orders and instructions. The instructors were all clad in black.

The Lesser Prophet hesitated. His tongue quickly moistened his lips, and for just an instant his eyes filled with pain. The expression was gone so quickly that McKay wondered if he'd imagined it. "It is our mission to help mankind as best we can. But there are people who'd like to share our bounty by force—and more than a few who don't like the way we think. I'm sure you know what I mean."

"Yeah," McKay said, eyeing the maneuvers. They weren't

too snappy—any skirmish line that advanced that haphazardly
on maneuvers in the Corps would be patrolling the kitchens
for a month. But the men in black seemed to have their
charges pretty well in line, all things considered.

"Much as we regret it, we must take steps to defend ourselves. The New Dispensation is a light that mustn't be allowed to go out of the world. Some of us are forced to learn
what we can of the profession of arms to preserve it."

"Who're your DIs?" McKay asked. Haskell looked puz-
zled. "Just professional interest. I used to be a drill instructor
at Parris Island. In the Marines," he added.

"Those are Brothers of Mercy," Haskell said. "They're the
First Prophet's private guards." He smiled—it looked a touch
strained. "If you'll come along, please, gentlemen, I'm sure
Elder Brother Perkins is eager to make your acquaintance."

They followed him into the building. The windowless room
would have been pitch black inside without artificial lighting.
Kerosene lanterns hung along the walls. They contrasted with
the achingly normal federal-office plainness of dropped
acoustic-tile ceiling, pasteboard walls, and thin carpet, the oily
smell of kerosene out of place against the everyday odors of
disinfectant and stale cigarette smoke.

Young men and women moved with quiet purposefulness
along the hallways. McKay glanced at Sloan. Given the fact
that the Church of the New Dispensation had just moved in
and set up shop here, the level of organization was almost
uncanny. *'Bout what you'd expect*, McKay thought, *if the
man runnin' the show's one of the ones supposed to be straw-
bossing the reconstruction of America.*

Sloan's thoughts seemed to parallel his own. "Maybe our
boy's just playing along with these folks for reasons of his
own," Sam said hopefully as Haskell led off down the hall.
He was subvocalizing; his words were inaudible to anyone but
McKay.

"Dream on," McKay muttered back.

A couple of turns down the lantern-lit corridors brought
them to a doorway through which Haskell entered. It gave
into a reception area, with a receptionist's desk and a scatter
of chairs and a couple of low tables with magazines on them.

The guttering light of a single lantern gave the banal surroundings an air of cavernlike mystery, and cast slightly demonic highlights onto the features of the two men who stood before the opposite door.

Both wore black from head to foot. One was a burly redheaded dude almost as big as McKay, who despite the unusual color scheme of his cowboy shirt and jeans looked like an Okie trucker out of any roadside diner in America. His left arm was bandaged and cradled in a black sling. The other made McKay stare despite himself, a wolf-lean man barely taller than he was, with a pointed beard and a spinal crest of black hair rising from a narrow shaven skull, a gold ring hanging from his right earlobe. He wore black leather and studded wristbands; the tattooed arms folded across his chest were bare and sinewy, with thick veins worming down the bulge of his biceps. His cold gray eyes met McKay's without flinching. "If that ain't a road gypsy," McKay subvocalized, "I'm a novitiate nun."

"I think you can kick the habit," Sloan said.

"Mr. McKay, Mr. Sloan," Haskell said, holding the door for them, "our Elder Brother Nolan Perkins and Brother Summerill."

The two Guardians stepped into a room lit by several Aladdin kerosene mantle lamps that cast almost as much light as the dormant fluorescents would have. A man in shirt-sleeves was just standing up behind a metal desk and extending his hand. "Gentlemen," he said, "I bid you welcome in the name of the Lord."

Resisting the urge to glance at Sloan, McKay took the man's hand. His grasp was dry but perfunctory. He was a small-framed sort, with gray hair thinning back around a high forehead, eyes indistinct behind thick glasses. He was medium height but seemed smaller—on the whole, just the way McKay had pictured him.

He glanced past Perkins at the man who stood behind him, in front of a corkboard wall covered with schedules and lists. Like the road gypsy out in the hall, this man was taller and narrower than McKay. There the resemblance ended. The man behind Perkins was not lean but skinny and stoop-shouldered.

Despite the muggy closeness in the office, he wore a natty navy blazer and a white turtleneck exquisitely tailored to minimize an incipient kettle belly. Light brown hair swept back from a lordly profile dominated by an aquiline nose down which the man regarded McKay with a certain haughtiness. He did not offer his hand, and McKay didn't feel like pressing the point.

Sloan looked up from shaking hands with Perkins and his eyes widened. "Summerill—is that W. Soames Summerill?"

Finely shaped brows rose. "You're familiar with the name?" The words held a slight dry edge of sardonic disbelief.

Sloan stepped forward eagerly. "Of course. I've read all your books. In fact, I just finished *Sightseeing in Babylon: The New Conservative's Guide to Post-Moral America* before, ah, things blew up." He stuck out his hand, which Summerill, obviously bemused, accepted with his own well-manicured fingers.

"McKay, allow me to introduce America's foremost conservative gadfly, Soames Summerill. You might have seen him on TV; he's always on the late-night talk shows. Political commentator, attorney, editor, philosopher, author of a number of best-selling suspense novels—a regular Renaissance man. They call him the Bill Buckley of the nineties. I don't hold much with his politics, I have to admit, but he's one hell of a writer. 'Scuse me, Brother Perkins," he added hastily at the systems analyst's wince.

McKay walked past the desk and grudgingly took Summerill's hand. "Always a pleasure to meet one of our boys in uniform," Summerill murmured. He seemed to be scrutinizing McKay minutely from beneath languidly lowered lids.

"Yeah," McKay grunted. He pivoted smartly to face the Elder Brother. "Dr. Perkins," he said brisky, "we're here regarding the Blueprint."

Summerill's eyebrows rose higher. Perkins' eyes blinked rapidly behind the Coke bottle lenses of his glasses. "Oh," he said. "Oh my." He sat down behind the desk and began carefully to rearrange the papers stacked there with enormous precision.

McKay held forth a thick envelope closed with the Presidential seal. "Our bona fides are here, if you wish to inspect them," he stated formally.

But Perkins shook his outsized baby bird's head. "No, no, Mr. McKay, it isn't that simple. Not that simple at all."

He looked up at McKay. His eyes were huge behind the glasses. "You see, I won't be able to accompany you. You must consider me as having resigned from Project Blueprint."

CHAPTER
TWELVE ——————————

McKay and Sloan stared at Perkins in dawning horror. He'd just blurted a top-secret name in the presence of Summerill and Martin Haskell, who hovered reverently in the doorway. And if the two Brothers of Mercy on sentry duty outside were like any sentries McKay had ever encountered, they had been stretching their ears wide for anything juicy they might overhear from the inner sanctum. He felt the familiar snafu dread seeping out from the pit of his belly.

Sam recovered his composure first. He turned to Summerill. "Excuse me, sir. Would you please permit us to speak with, ah, Elder Brother Perkins in private?"

Perkins' head bobbed. "Yes, Soames. Leave us for a moment, please."

Summerill frowned. "Elder Brother, do you believe this to be wise? These men—do we really know what they want? They are, after all, armed."

"I know who they are," Perkins said wearily. "They mean me no harm."

Don't be too fuckin' sure of that, McKay thought. He was mad enough to screw the barrel of his combat-modified .45 in Perkins' shell-like ear and haul him the hell out of here.

135

"Very well," Summerill said. "I shall be outside in case you need me, Elder Brother. Good afternoon, *gentlemen*." His nose elevated with aristocratic disdain, he stalked from the room.

Haskell stood there with his handsome brow furrowed in confusion. "It's all right, Martin," Perkins said. "Leave us."

The Lesser Prophet nodded obediently. He flashed a quick grin to the two Guardians and backed out, shutting the door behind him.

Outside in the gloom of the antechamber, W. Soames Summerill lowered himself into the swivel chair behind the receptionist's desk. Since the secretary who normally occupied that station during working hours was one of the huge majority of Federal Center employees who'd been incinerated in the thermonuclear pseudo-sunshine of the One-Day War, Summerill might have been forgiven a twinge of sentiment at the framed pictures of a small boy and girl set next to the telephone, seeming to look expectantly toward their mother's chair. But he didn't notice them at all.

Instead, he nodded back perfunctorily to the brief bows the two Brothers of Mercy gave him, acknowledging that he had received the deference due him as their commander. Then, leaning back in the chair, he began to smile.

"Doctor Perkins," Sloan said urgently as the door closed, "do you realize what you're saying?"

Perkins smiled sadly. "Yes, Mr. Sloan. All too well."

"Listen, Doctor," McKay said bluntly. "You volunteered for Project Blueprint. Now the time has come, and you're sayin' you won't."

"That is correct."

McKay brandished the sealed envelope. "But you got your orders here, direct from President MacGregor."

Perkins' eyebrows rose. "So President Lowell didn't make it. Well. I fear Mr. MacGregor is rather a shallow young man, though he's always seemed to appreciate the role of the federal government in American life more than his predecessor." He squared a sheaf of papers on the blotter before him. "Not that that matters anymore."

McKay was dumbfounded. Was this little geek refusing a

direct order? In the Corps McKay had had obedience, instant and absolute, drilled into him, and even though he'd come to stretch that standard himself more than once on the field of battle, it was still deeply ingrained in his nature. The little bastard had *volunteered*, for God's sake! McKay felt precisely the sensation he would have if as a small boy he'd tagged a playmate who had turned around and flatly refused to be "it."

"Now, Doctor," Sam Sloan interposed smoothly, "you assumed a grave responsibility when you volunteered to take part in the Project. You willingly joined a band of experts charged with reconstructing America. Surely you can't turn your back on that?"

Perkins peered at his desktop a moment. Then he looked up and smiled shyly, as if imploring approval. "I've found a better way, don't you see? America—before—was rife with materialism. People had lost their reason for living. Life became an endless, mindless seeking after money, after momentary pleasure. It was all so empty.

"You'd have me go back to help rebuild all that. I can't. Josiah Coffin opened my eyes. He revealed to me the Lord's purpose in bringing down the whole rotten edifice of modern society. The evils of materialism are to be expunged, and from the ashes of the war, from all the suffering and pain are to emerge a better people, strong and resolute in the love of Christ."

He raised his head, and his face shone in the kerosene light. "I am doing what I swore I would do, gentlemen. I am helping rebuild America. A better America than the designers of the Blueprint for Renewal could ever have conceived."

Outside, the afternoon had clouded over totally, accurately mirroring the moods of the two Guardians who emerged from the low bunkered building with a troubled-looking Lesser Prophet Haskell trotting at their sides.

Perkins had remained resolute in the face of all McKay's bellowing and Sloan's gentle reason. At the end he had agreed to consider it overnight and speak to them again in the morning. But he assured them his answer would remain unchanged.

Casey and Rogers had popped their hatches. Rogers had

raised his seat so that his head and shoulders were out of the turret as he smoked and enjoyed the freshness of the unseasonably chilly breeze blowing down out of the mountains. Casey had boosted himself to sit on the edge of the hatch with his feet dangling, talking to a half-dozen young women who'd clustered around the car. He looked up and grinned and nodded a greeting as his comrades strode toward the vehicle.

Irritation flashed through McKay. He'd never exactly lacked for feminine companionship himself, but both Casey and Sam Sloan had something, some easy knack of attracting and dealing with women that he himself lacked. Sam Sloan could combine down-home gallantry with manners buffed to a Continental gloss at the Naval Academy, while Casey had a happy, boyish charm few women could resist. "Wilson!" he snapped. "Clear the decks of them broads. We're clearin' out."

Casey's head jerked back. It tilted to one side and he blinked exactly like a puppy who'd been slapped for no apparent reason. McKay knew he was being a prick. He *wanted* to be a prick just now.

He stalked to the near side of the V-450 and hauled open the door. "Oh, Casey," one of the young women called, "you don't have to go now? Our t'ai ch'i lesson's just about to start!"

"Sorry." McKay could almost feel the ex-fighter jock's grin as he climbed into the car. "Like, duty calls."

McKay slammed the door.

Sloan let himself down the hatch above the electronic systems operator's seat. "Did you see the blackboard they were breaking down as we came out?" he asked. McKay grunted. "It had the weirdest stuff on it. Astrological symbols, what looked like some sort of Aztec or Mayan pictographs, and what I'd swear was elvish runes from *Lord of the Rings*."

"Bunch of fuckin' lunatics," McKay said, seating himself in a fold-down and crossing his arms over his chest.

"They seem like nice people," Casey said, slithering down into his own chair.

"Shit," McKay said firmly.

Dusk still lay like molten amber across the vast ruin that was

Denver, but here in the campground hidden in the trees off the road to Idaho Springs, it was already as good as dark. "There's just one thing we can do in this situation," Billy McKay announced to his teammates over plates of freeze-dried rations that had been reconstituted with water from an icy brook nearby and heated in the V-450's microwave.

"What's that, Billy?" Casey Wilson asked, spooning up a forkful of rice. He, Sloan, and McKay were sitting at a concrete table for their dinners while Rogers ate at his post in the turret. They had followed a circuitous route out of Lakewood, just in case any of the Children of the New Dispensation might get ideas about following them, and headed up for the mountains to laager down for the night. With the Claymores out and the vehicle's audio sensors cranked up full—and with their own voices filtered out by computer—they felt able to let down and relax, if only for a few moments.

"Bust Perkins the hell outa there."

Sam and Casey stared at McKay in stunned silence. "Kidnap him?" Sam blurted. "Is that what you want us to do?"

Chewing, McKay nodded.

"My God, have you gone crazy?" Sloan burst out.

"Nope. But Perkins has. You talked to him. He's like a Moonie or something. He's nuts. He won't even tell us what he *knows* about the friggin' Blueprint!"

"Jesus, Billy," Casey said. "We can't go around kidnapping people."

McKay slammed his plate down. "What the fuck is the *matter* with you people? We're Guardians. We got a mission. We're supposed to bring back this Perkins so they can start piecing the goddamned Blueprint back together."

"But he isn't willing to go with us, man," Casey said.

"It's his *duty*." He looked from one to the other. Their features were indistinct in the near-total darkness. "Listen, you know how urgent this Blueprint deal is. We got to get America back on the track before these damn Europeans come swarming in here to loot the continent for our own good."

He waved a hand at the city decomposing like some dead leviathan in the darkness beyond a fold of mountain. "There's people out there starvin', people out there dyin' of diseases that ain't even been heard about for a hundred years, people

out there killin' each other for what little there is left. A few
months from now it's gonna be winter, and even if that whole
Nuclear Winter thing turned out to be a load of shit, the climate boys back at Heartland say it's still liable to be the worst
in two hundred years. You think what this Perkins asshole
wants is more important than all that?''

He was shouting, all thoughts of security forgotten. Sloan
and Wilson sat their ground, seemingly undaunted by his
vehemence.

"We're officers, gentlemen, and Guardians, McKay,"
Sloan said. "Not kidnappers."

McKay glared at him. "*Fuck* being officers and gentlemen.
This is war. The fate of the fuckin' *country*'s at stake."

"It's no good, Billy," Casey Wilson said gently. "We can't
make Perkins be a scientist for the Project if he doesn't want
to."

"Tom! Talk some sense into these bozos. You cut your
teeth in covert ops. You know the real world ain't some
fuckin' game, with a lot of pretty rules and everybody sayin'
'Excuse me please,' and 'Thank you kindly, ma'am.' "

Rogers hesitated. "We got our duty," he said at length,
slowly. "But I don't know if I hold with comin' between a
man and what he figures he owes God."

McKay leaped up from the bench and stomped down to
stand beside the stream. "I don't believe this. I don't fucking
believe this. The fate of America's in our hands, and we sit
here blowin' the breeze about some crazy-ass Jesus freak who
don't want to do his goddamned duty!"

"Billy," Rogers said, his usually quiet voice pitched to the
edge of inaudibility, "if we ain't fightin' so a man can be free
to keep his own faith with God—what're we fightin' *for*?"

The argument raged on until the idiot face of the moon
hung high above the pines on the crestline to the east. McKay
was adamant that the only thing to do was haul Perkins out
whether he wanted to come or not. The fact that Perkins was
surrounded by the stone walls and steel doors of a federal
facility especially rebuilt to provide maximum security against
the unrest of the late eighties—to say nothing of a thousand or
two religious fanatics—didn't impress him. The Guardians

were the best. They were trained to go through walls and doors —and fanatics—if that was what it took to complete a mission.

Casey and Sam Sloan were just as insistent that even if it *could* be done, it *shouldn't*. They *were* the best, and part of what they were there to protect with their lives was the freedom of Americans to act in accordance with their conscience. Tom Rogers, for his part, was used to playing by the same roughhouse rules McKay had learned with Force Recon and later with Studies and Observations Group, Southwest Asia Command, the euphemistically named snatch, sabotage, and slaughter corps charged with waging a savage three-cornered covert war with Communists and fundamentalist Muslims in the Mediterranean theater.

But Rogers alone among the Guardians was an intensely religious man who felt that in serving America he was serving Christ. Coffin's message, such as they'd heard of it, spoke to him in a number of ways. He wasn't swayed from his commitment to the Guardians or to recovering the Blueprint for Renewal, but Rogers respected the fact that Perkins had hearkened to that message.

"We don't even know how Christian they are, Tom." A part of McKay was shocked at himself. The tone in his voice was almost like pleading—something he hadn't done in more years than he could count. "They were teaching people a bunch of weird shit about Aztecs and Hobbits back there at the Center. And we told you what kind of a monster they had guarding Perkins' door for him—a fuckin' *road gypsy*. *They* ain't got any more religion than a cockroach."

"The Thomases told us Coffin's gospel embraced all men," Rogers answered calmly. "If Coffin's got even road gypsies listenin' to his preaching—well, that says to me he just may have somethin' here."

"Christ."

McKay was stuck in a crack. He could order the Guardians to kidnap Perkins, and they'd do it just like that. And there was a time when McKay would have ordered them to do it, and enforced the order with his sledgehammer fists if he'd had to.

But somewhere along the line McKay the hardass, McKay

the Parris Island DI who'd come within a hair of being
cashiered for busting the jaw of a fellow drill instructor who'd
told him he was being too hard on the boots, McKay the combination of Clint Eastwood, Sly Stallone, and a junkyard dog,
had changed.

McKay bossed the Guardians. But they were no normal
grunt outfit. Each man was a specialist, as skilled as a brain
surgeon in his own line. Each was already a hero before coming to the Guardians. McKay knew damn well that every man
of the Guardians had more than proved himself as being as
good a troop as McKay—and Billy McKay was the maximum
Marine. No tougher, truer Marine had ever slogged in puttees
through Belleau Wood or pried Nips out of the stinking lava
of Iwo at the point of a bayonet.

He could order his men to kidnap Perkins—but he couldn't.
They were all pros. If they were that dead set against doing
something, then hard as it was for him, McKay had to acknowledge there must be a reason. At the same time, he
couldn't let go of the compelling force of his own arguments.
That left one course of action. One that Billy McKay hated
worse than Communism.

He had always been independent—"bloody-minded" or
"insubordinate," as his commanders were more apt to phrase
it. What he'd liked about Force Recon and SOG was the
latitude he had. You got the briefing and you got the objective
and then you went out and pulled it off without having to
radio back for permission every time you wanted to wipe your
ass after a crap. He liked a style of warfare where the brass
would shut up and *let* you soldier, soldier.

And now he said, "Sloan, get me Heartland."

Stunned silence settled in around the camp as Sloan rose
and went into the car. The Guardians knew full well how
tough-minded and contrary their CO was. But this wasn't just
a tactical or operational question; this was *policy*. Even
McKay had to admit there was legitimate question as to where
their real duty lay.

It was a question that had to be answered at the highest
level.

Casey had to shinny up a ponderosa pine to string an antenna before they could punch a signal through to Heart-

land. McKay went into the car alone, spoke first to a comm tech, then to the officer of the watch. Then the gravel voice of Crenna crackled over the air.

A few moments later McKay stepped out. He stopped and filled his massive chest with mountain air, pine tangy and chill.

"We're to go back to the DFC tomorrow and try to talk Perkins into comin' with us," he said in a curiously subdued voice. From the open door behind him came a muted hum of machinery. "Barring that, we're to proceed to our next objective. Under no circumstances are we to attempt to coerce Dr. Perkins. Our electroprinter's cutting a hard copy of our written orders."

"From Crenna?" asked Sloan, surprised.

"No," McKay said. "From President MacGregor."

Though the morning was bright and the sky clear, there was little traffic on the tarmac strip that led from South Kipling to the central area of the Federal Center. An unsmiling man in black waved the V-450 through the gate and stepped back into the right-hand guard tower as the huge car trundled up the road.

No classes were under way on the quad, and no skirmish lines wended their uneven ways across the hills. A few people were abroad, glancing curiously at the squat armored vehicle and hurrying on. Perhaps there was some sort of chapel service in progress, McKay thought.

It had been an uncomfortable ride down from the mountains. Nobody had had much to say since the word came down from Heartland the night before. Perhaps the other Guardians felt bad about compelling McKay to go upstairs for direction—crying to their superiors like a second looie lost on patrol. Or maybe they, like McKay, were tasting in advance the lead-and-ash bitterness of yet another failure. After Perkins they had one lead: the economist Marguerite Connoly, holed up somewhere called The Freehold in the San Luis Valley of southern Colorado.

With our luck, McKay thought sourly, *a fucking meteorite will hit the place just as we drive up.*

The Lesser Prophet Martin Haskell stood in the open doorway of the building in which they'd met Perkins yesterday. His fine straw-blond hair was blowing in a brisk warm breeze, and his teeth were very white against the tan of his face. In his chambray shirt and jeans, he looked insufferably young, fit, and healthy, like something from a beer commercial. He gave them a cheery wave as Casey reined the big beast in.

"Good to see you, friends," he called. "The Elder Brother's ready for you. He's waiting in his office."

McKay nodded brusquely. Sloan managed a smile and a "good morning." "Hope you'll be able to join us for lunch later," Haskell said. "Some of our young ladies have been pestering me to find out when Mr. Wilson was going to be back." He grinned. "I'm afraid they're not concentrating on the religious studies as much as they should be."

"Yeah," McKay said. "Look, could we go ahead and get to it?"

For an instant Haskell looked taken aback. Then he smiled. "Sure. I guess I'm wasting time, standing out here chattering. I like to talk; that's how I knew I had a vocation as a preacher."

He led them into the low-slung building. As before, the hallways were lit feebly by kerosene lamps, though there seemed to be fewer people wandering around. For his part, McKay was hoping the low light would cover for a slight change in his profile.

The day before, he'd worn his sidearm in a Kevlar holster with a full flap, the way he usually did in the field. Today it had been replaced by a custom cowhide combat rig made by Milt Sparks of Idaho City, Idaho. McKay wore it when he couldn't tote around his Maremont and thought there might be trouble.

Not that he felt that way today. He was just pissed off at the world in general and at T. Nolan Perkins in particular. Or that's what he'd told himself when he'd buckled the holster on that morning.

Haskell ushered them into Perkins' waiting room. The same two plug-uglies stood in front of the Elder Brother's door, and McKay fleetingly wondered if they stayed there all the time. This time, though, there was a pretty young woman in the room with them, in jeans and a Red Rider T-shirt, with

straight blond hair hanging to her waist. "This is Sally,"
Haskell said. "She's got coffee and doughnuts, if you'd like
some refreshment while you're waiting for Elder Brother
Perkins."

McKay refused anything to eat or drink. Sloan accepted a
cup of black coffee from a metal urn as Haskell excused
himself and went into Perkins' office, saying he'd be back in a
few moments.

When the door shut McKay fixed the left-hand guard with
his gaze. "You, Mohawker," he said. The gray wolf's eyes
narrowed, but the road gypsy didn't speak. "What do you get
out of this? What're you doin' here?"

For a moment the man in black leather returned McKay's
gaze with flat, cold hostility. "They accept me here," he
growled at last. "They told me God'll take me like I am."

McKay snorted. "Didn't think you gyps cared shit about
God."

A long-standing motto of the road gypsy breed was, "If we
can't get along, let's get it on"—although in practice the gypsies showed little inclination toward the former. To talk to one
the way McKay had was an open invitation to mayhem. Mc-
Kay had busted enough Mohawked heads to know that
well.

But the man returned McKay's derisive laugh. "Didn't
know he cared shit about *us*, man. Not till Coffin came
around."

The door opened. W. Soames Summerill stood there in a
gray crew-neck sweater, smiling as if it hurt his face. "Gentlemen, come in if you will. The Elder Brother will see you
now."

McKay looked at Sloan. The ex-Navy man gulped his coffee, and they went in together.

McKay just had time to pivot on one heel as an axe handle
thudded into his left shoulder.

CHAPTER
THIRTEEN ─────────

Back during his misspent youth, during the phase of samurai fever every red-blooded young American male seems to undergo, Billy McKay had seen Akira Kurosawa's classic flick *The Seven Samurai*. In it, various would-be warriors for hire had been tested by being asked to pass through a door inside which lurked a peasant with a block of kindling upraised to clonk them on the head. The experienced samurai—or more correctly, *ronin*, since they were all unemployed—all sensed his presence and evaded the danger. The hayseed peasant lout, played by Japanese superstar Toshiro Mifune, had walked in flat-footed and gotten skulled.

Nothing could better have pointed up the difference between Billy McKay and Sam Sloan. Even as he stepped into Perkins' *sanctum sanctorum*, McKay was in motion, knowing without knowing how that the shithammer was coming down. Sam took his axe handle squarely at the crown of his skull and went down moaning.

McKay's left arm went instantly numb at the impact. Nevertheless, he managed to swing it with the momentum of his spinning body, clublike, knocking the axe handle on against the door frame. At the same instant his Colt roared in his right hand. A black-clad body thudded back into the wall, a beefy face going blank at the awful impact of a 230-grain slug in the belly.

With a vicious whistle, a hardwood haft slammed down on the radius bone of McKay's right arm a few centimeters behind the thumb. The big pistol dropped from nerveless fingers. McKay turned quickly, forming his left hand into a spear to take his second antagonist in the throat.

Arms fell around him from behind, pinning his arms to his sides. He strained to break free, but his unseen attacker was massively powerful. With his left arm all but useless, McKay lacked the strength to get free. A strange stomach-churning stink, acrid yet sweet, filled his nostrils.

He had a wild impression of Nolan Perkins sitting ashen-faced behind his desk, Soames Summerill standing by with a smirk on his thin features, Lesser Prophet Haskell lying crumpled by a filing cabinet with blood matting his blond hair, and the bearded face of another road gypsy, grinning in gap-toothed triumph as he raised his axe handle above his Mohawked head.

The handle whined down. It slammed into McKay's skull with a sickening thud. An electric arc exploded behind his eyes. His knees folded beneath him. The huge arms wrapped around him let him drop into the soft embrace of the carpet.

His gut seethed with nausea. He was aware of Summerill looming over him, a million miles tall. And then a voice was saying urgently in his ear, "Billy, this is Tom. Pull out of there fast! We're takin' fire from the buildings—"

"Clear out! That's an order, Tom. We're—"

The Mohawker struck again. Thunder roared in McKay's ears, drowning out Tom Rogers' voice. McKay's eyes turned in, the stars came out, and that was fucking that.

McKay was drowning.

He struggled, seeking the surface, seeking air and light, but his arms were trapped. His lungs and head were bursting. Faint light hung above him. He strove for it with all his might, thrusting . . .

His eyes opened. "A bucket of water in the face," a voice said. It was soft and supercilious and smooth as oiled velvet.

"Clichéd, but it serves. Something I've often tried—mostly in vain—to point out to the critics of my novels. Conceits generally don't become clichés unless they contain more than a grain of truth."

His mind and eyes focused on the slim figure standing before him. Or rather leaning, with one buttock propped on a table of sturdy planks. "Summerill," he said through gritted teeth. The word was a curse. It made his head ring like a bell struck with a twelve-pound sledge.

"The great man himself," said a familiar voice. McKay's head was certain to topple off his neck like an overripe melon from a vine at the least motion, but he made it turn ponderously so that he could see the speaker from the corner of his eyes. It was Sam Sloan, strapped to a chair with his arms behind him. Sweat glinted on his ruggedly handsome face in the yellow light of lanterns, and his dense, dark hair was matted to his flat-muscled chest. A trickle of blood ran from the corner of his mouth. "You'll find his wit is a lot like fine wine."

McKay sensed that Summerill was drawing himself up to receive a compliment. "It doesn't travel well," Sloan finished.

Air gushed from Summerill's lungs in a sharp exhalation. "Lobo. Show our friend what we think of his feeble japes."

A huge shape moved into McKay's field of vision. With it came a reek as if a bottle of hydrochloric acid and a jar of rotting fruit had been opened side by side. Something clicked in his soggy brain. *Zombi!* A fist the size of a Volkswagen differential cracked Sloan across the face. Its owner turned a pale, expressionless, deeply scarred face on McKay, then lumbered away. The impression of unnaturally deep-sunk eyes lingered in McKay's mind.

"Now that we have our relative positions established beyond a shadow of a doubt, gentlemen," Summerill murmured, "perhaps we can talk as reasonable men."

By this time McKay had muzzily worked out that he was in the same state as Sloan, bare-chested and propped in a chair, both hands tied behind him. "Go fuck yourself," McKay said.

Summerill smiled. "You're rather more forceful than your friend. Also more limited." The zombi stench welled up in

McKay's nose, and his head was rocked back by an open-handed slap.

McKay blinked back the blood that leaked abruptly into his left eye from a split brow. He was assimilating more of his surroundings now. They were in some sort of shop or workroom, with a concrete floor, heavy tables, various tools hung about the shadowed walls. From the almost subliminal hum vibrating in the air he gathered that they were underground, and that the Federal Center retained some power other than that provided by muscle and kerosene.

There were at least three men in the room: Summerill, Lobo, and a tall, thin man whose long black robe set off a face the color of uncooked dough. The last stood behind Summerill and to one side, near a drain set into a depression in the floor. His nose was a blade, his domed skull smooth and bare. His eyes were as far recessed as Lobo's, though whether he was a zombi or not was hard to tell. From the dark glitter well back in his eye cavities, McKay guessed not.

"Allow me to introduce my associates, Brothers of Mercy Mace and Lobo." The tall, thin skull face nodded deliberately. The pallid, reeking flesh mountain didn't so much as blink. "If you cooperate, you need not make their acquaintance any more . . . *intimately*."

"You've been coming on so strong with this Ming the Merciless act, you've forgotten to tell us just what it is you want," Sam Sloan said. None of the smartass lilt had left his voice. McKay felt a stab of admiration. Sloan was real hard-core, even if he was a goddamn black-shoe Navy son of a bitch.

He expected Lobo to hit Sloan again, but Summerill smiled. "You have a point, my friend. Lobo, Mace—leave us."

Mace frowned. "Praetor—"

Summerill held up his hand. "Do you doubt me? Go." Mace folded his arms inside voluminous sleeves, turned, and stalked out of McKay's field of vision. Lobo followed, silent as a stump.

The elegantly clad man looked at Sloan. "You seem bemused at the title I've awarded myself. I think it's both refined and fitting. Do you not agree?"

"I'm reminded of the Praetorian Guard," Sloan said.

"And an old saying: *Quis custodiet ipsos custodes*?"

Summerill laughed delightedly. " 'Who shall guard the guardians?' Why, I do, for the nonce. But I see you've perceived the truth behind my title. You have the makings of an educated man, Mr. Sloan. For I know all about the both of you, you see."

He stood up, paced a few steps. "Let me tell you a story. Many years back a very wealthy man named Yevgeny Maximov became concerned about the state of the world. He was convinced civilization was collapsing, that the West had begun the long slide into anarchy. He gathered together a consortium of like-minded men and women, people of power, wealth, and influence. He began to lay the foundation for a new world order that would arise, phoenixlike, from the ashes of the old."

"Maximov," Sloan repeated, furrowing his forehead. "Maximov—the Internationalist Council!"

Summerill inclined his head. "Just so."

"Didn't they just set themselves up as rulers of that FSE deal in Europe?" McKay asked.

"Very perceptive. But you're getting ahead of the story. By various means, financial and otherwise, the council began to put out feelers and secure contacts and friends in every corner of the globe. In government, the news media, commerce, the military, intelligence operations—"

"In a word, traitors," said Sloan.

A flicker of irritation crossed Summerill's face. "Please don't persist in interrupting me. Lobo hasn't hurt you half as much as he could—and would very much like to."

He took a handkerchief from inside his sweater and mopped his brow. "Beastly hot in here. We're only able to run the climate control a few hours a day, to keep the air circulating. We have to conserve power.

"Where was I? Ah, yes. Among his many contacts, Mr. Maximov numbered members of a quite influential faction within the Central Intelligence Agency. A faction alarmed at both the erosion of America's position in the world and that of the Agency within America—whose members understood the two phenomena to be closely interrelated."

"Pennsylvania," McKay said suddenly. "The ambush at that Company airfield. It was your boys we shot the shit out of!"

It was as if a mask had been whipped from Summerill's face. The urbane ease disappeared and was replaced by hatred, feral and unrestrained. "Yes. It was our men you butchered. Our plan you disrupted. We could have had the reorganization of a new America well under way by now if you hadn't interfered! But you thwarted us, and what remains of the nation will pay the price for years!"

Summerill smiled, half ruefully. "Excuse me. I tend to feel these matters very strongly. Patriotism, unfashionable as it is, is very much a part of me."

"So you sell your country out to some foreign moneybags who's made himself emperor of Europe," McKay sneered.

"Are you so simpleminded? The anarchic, fragmented state of the world cannot be allowed to continue. Look what it's brought us—decades of unrelenting strife, culminating in the greatest single catastrophe in the history of the human race. The world must be brought together under a single strong, guiding hand. That hand is Yevgeny Maximov's."

"I've been wondering what you were doing out here in the boondocks mingling with the herd," Sloan said. "Never thought fundamental Christianity was much in your line. A little too unwashed for you."

Summerill smiled. "I think you've already guessed what I'm doing here. Coffin appeals to the gullible, the superstitious, a broader spectrum of the American public than any charlatan in recent history. Thousands, even millions, who feel they have been cast adrift on a sea of calamity will turn to him for solidity, for something to cling to against the tossing waves. Properly cultivated, he will do the hard work of pulling a shattered nation back together."

"You mean you don't buy this holy rap," McKay said.

"I?" Summerill laughed again, incredulously. "Cuisinart mysticism, a hodgepodge of tent-revival preaching and every crank cult to roll down the pike in the twentieth century! Everything Coffin's heard in his life has been churned into the brew, from *Star Trek* to Scientology, from the Aztec gods to Zen. It's part of his appeal—his genius, I daresay. He literally offers something to everybody.

"But *believe* in him? The man is mad! Utterly, deliciously mad! As a religious quest, he seeks out remaining zones of high radiation and makes pilgrimages to them. He claims the Lord protects him from being harmed, and God knows he must have some immunity, for he shows little sign of radiation poisoning. And he has recently revealed to the inner circle that God is demanding human sacrifices to atone for sins so numerous and foul that even this holocaust could not expunge them. He is a confirmed lunatic, and every day his grasp on reality grows more tenuous.

"No, Commander Sloan, I am not a believer in the First Prophet Coffin. That I leave to Elder Brother Perkins, who I regret to say is a fully sincere convert—in fact, the man who threw the Center open to Coffin. I am, however, a believer in the power of his New Dispensation. And when he has consolidated the nation under his holy banner, he will be gently eased into a purely nominal role as figurehead—or permitted to become protomartyr of a new theocratic state. He is an innocent, our Reverend Coffin. He was only too glad to turn the tool he had crudely begun to forge, the special guards he calls his Brothers of Mercy, over to me to be finely honed into an instrument of what he feels to be the Lord's policy."

"What about all these people out there." McKay jerked his head around. "The ones like Haskell, and those girls with their t'ai ch'i classes. What do they think of your bone breakers?"

"As little as possible, Lieutenant McKay. They know that the New Dispensation is threatened from without by hordes of hostile nonbelievers and from within by heretics and backsliders. They are content to leave the less savory aspects of redemption to those appointed inquisitors. But don't be deceived, my friend. Each and every one of the faithful, young and old alike, stand instantly ready to do whatever their prophet commands of them, at the cost of their own lives—or of what they've been taught was their humanity."

"This is all mighty nice," Sloan drawled, hitting the Mizzoura hard, "but if you'll just let us up out of these chairs, we'll be moseyin' along."

"Your facetiousness doesn't fool me. You and I are working toward the same end: the rebuilding of America. And we're looking for the same tool to do it with."

"The Blueprint for Renewal," McKay said dully.

"But of course."

McKay spat.

"That goes for me too," Sloan said, "in spades."

Summerill smiled thinly. "Don't be too hasty, gentlemen. Consider the penalty for refusal. You are totally within our power."

"*McKay to Mobile One, acknowledge*," McKay subvocalized, shutting his eyes and lowering his head as if in despair to camouflage the act. "*McKay to Mobile One. Are you there, Tom? Casey? Answer me, for God's sake. You have to get the hell away from here.*"

"Perhaps it's occurred to you to try to raise your compatriots. You'll find that endeavor fruitless. First of all, we took the liberty of removing your cunning little communications device. The debacle at our airfield in Pennsylvania indicated you possessed some such contrivances, so I was on the lookout for them. And second"—he steepled his fingers before his narrow chest—"I regret to inform you that your comrades were killed when their vehicle was destroyed by antitank rockets. A painful necessity, I assure you."

McKay squeezed his eyes tightly shut. *Casey, Tom. Oh, shit, did I fuck up. Sorry I let you down like this.*

Sloan was cursing Summerill in a toneless voice: "Murderous, scum-sucking, pig-fucking son of a whore and a billy goat—"

"Now, now." Summerill shook his head. "Your friends died in the line of duty. But there's no need for you to join them. All you need do is cooperate with us. It's really for the good of the country. The fate of America lies in our hands. Help us keep it safe."

"You go straight to hell," Sloan told him.

Summerill sighed. "I feared you'd take that line. So I arranged an object lesson in the hope of shocking you out of your adolescent stubbornness. You inquired a little while ago, Lieutenant McKay, about your friend the Lesser Prophet Haskell. Perhaps you should interview him yourself on the subject of the New Dispensation—and the Brothers of Mercy."

He clapped his hands. McKay and Sloan heard a door open behind them, heard the creak of wheels on ungreased axles. A moment later Mace and Lobo reappeared. The huge unspeaking zombi was wheeling in a nightmare on a steel gurney.

It was a pink man, hairless, his nude body a bundle of fibrous masses overlaid with a tracery of very fine pink and blue lines. It looked like one of those Visible Man anatomy models they used to sell in hobby shops. For a weird disjointed moment, McKay thought they'd brought in some kind of painted mannequin as an incomprehensible prank.

Then the thing turned its dripping head and *looked* at them. The eyes were huge and blue and utterly mindless.

"The Lesser Prophet Haskell took it upon himself to differ with a policy decision made by the Shepherds of the Faithful," Summerill intoned. "He tried to warn you of the, ah, reception we'd planned for you in the Elder Brother's office." He gestured airily. "Quite a good piece of work, don't you think? In his wisdom—might I say, revelation?—the Prophet Josiah Coffin collected men into his Brothers of Mercy who displayed far more aptitude for detail work than did, say, the Iranian oafs we tried to train for SAVAK."

Sloan had his head turned aside and was vomiting onto the bare cement. McKay felt his lips curling back from his teeth. The man had been expertly peeled of every square centimeter of skin—and somehow, horribly, remained alive.

"And now," Summerill said, "you see more clearly the options we offer."

With a convulsive heave of his shoulders, McKay broke the bonds that held his wrists together. He lunged at Summerill with a savage snarl, arms outstretched to hurt, to break. He could do it—he was trained, he'd done it before. He'd make that smirking bastard envy poor Haskell.

He pitched forward, his face slamming the concrete. His feet were lashed to the front legs of the metal chair, and in the stupor of having been beaten unconscious, he hadn't noticed. Blood gushed from his broken nose, streamed into his eyes, blinded him.

Summerill's laughter, high and shrill, pealed out above the throbbing of blood in McKay's temples. He was dragging himself toward the sound when Lobo brought his booted foot down on the back of his neck.

"Yes, Excellency," Summerill said into the microphone. "We learned one very valuable piece of information from them—the name of another participant in Project Renewal."

"That is all?" Attenuated by distance, the deep bass voice of Yevgeny Maximov still eloquently conveyed disbelief and displeasure. Summerill felt a stab of annoyance. *What does this monomaniac want?*

"Not precisely," he said. "They actually knew the names of four Blueprint personnel, one of whom is Perkins. The other two are dead. As of now we know as much as those confounded meddlers in Heartland—which in itself is a valuable datum. It took an application of the latest synthetic truth drugs to get the information from them. They proved remarkably resistant to physical persuasion. Even the application of electric current to the genitals did not break either man." Summerill didn't try to mask his admiration. "The electric treatment makes tough men weep like frightened children."

"Torture? Crude. I am surprised you employed it."

Sweat beaded on Summerill's fine upper lip. "But, Excellency, the truth drugs are highly experimental. I thought it necessary to exhaust other avenues before resorting to them. And I thought you yourself used—that is—"

A rich chuckle rolled out of the speaker. "It is a pleasure to know that I can reduce one such as yourself to inarticulateness. Yes, I do employ torture when I deem it appropriate. Little makes a deeper or more lasting impression on the susceptible. But I believe such men as these are not among that class of humanity."

A pause. Just when Summerill felt the echo-dampening walls of the communications center closing in on him, Maximov said, "It is of no consequence." Summerill sighed with relief. "In the meantime, what have you learned from this fool Perkins?"

"He knows nothing, Excellency. We have confirmed this."

Summerill spoke just a touch too quickly and prayed that the uncertainties of communication around the globe would make Maximov overlook the lapse. He was lying through his perfect teeth.

The fact was that Perkins refused to discuss the Blueprint for Renewal with Summerill as adamantly as he had with the men from Heartland. Had Maximov gotten any inkling of that, he would have insisted that Perkins be taken apart immediately, by drugs or torture, as Summerill "deemed it appropriate." And that would endanger Summerill's setup here. Even if he could arrange for the Elder Brother—handpicked by the First Prophet!—to have an accident of some suitably innocuous sort, the fact remained that Perkins was an organizational genius—an Einstein, a Toscanini of bureaucracy. His talent alone could keep the Church of the New Dispensation alive and growing here in the West.

If I can prevent Maximov from spoiling things, he thought, *I'll give him America on a silver platter—Blueprint for Renewal or no Blueprint.*

And if the tentative feeler he had sent out toward that radical group in Quebec developed into what he hardly even dared hope it might, the time might come when he could stand up and defy that bearded madman across the water.

He waited. Maximov was almost supernaturally sensitive to a man's moods, and especially to anything that smacked of dishonesty—or treachery. Would he call Summerill out?

But the thick Ukrainian voice said, "Very well. If we are groping in the dark, our colleagues in Iowa do no more. Should your interrogation have left anything of your subjects, try to recruit them. I always have need of men of fortitude and courage. Otherwise dispose of them.

"Press on quickly to this newly discovered member of the Project. I've clamped martial law on Europe and am making moves to expand into Russia and even the Near East. But production is at a standstill, and without production even my police cannot keep order indefinitely. I must have the Blueprint, and have it soon!

"Very much depends upon it—for both of us, Trajan, my very good friend."

• • •

Caught in the clutches of a nightmare of pain and blood and horror, McKay writhed in his sleep. Then a foot in the ribs booted him awake and he realized that while it might have been a nightmare that held him, it was unfortunately no dream.

He was prodded to his feet at gunpoint. The torture he'd undergone had been capped with a night curled up on the cold cement floor of an empty broom closet, so that now he could barely stand upright, let alone move. Just the same, the grim, black-clad guards gave him no chance to try to escape, even by making them kill him. While a half-dozen rifles and shotguns covered him, a chain was fastened to the manacles clamped about his wrists and he was yanked off balance into the corridor.

"Mornin', McKay," a familiar voice drawled. "Hope you slept better than it looks like you did."

A few meters down the corridor, Sam Sloan stood, manacled and under guard. He looked like death warmed over—and allowed to congeal again. "Not worth . . . shit before my morning coffee," McKay mumbled.

They were hustled to an underground garage. A few lanterns pushed the blackness feebly back, giving the echoing emptiness an eerie, cavernlike appearance. A black van, gleaming flanks reflecting the orange lamplight in ripples, awaited them with its rear doors open. McKay was prodded inside and the manacles about his wrists chained to a bar welded firmly to the uprights of the frame on the right-hand side. Then Sloan was dragged in and secured to a similar bar on the left.

A half-dozen Brothers of Mercy clambered into the back of the van, and the doors were shut. Another pair got into the front seats. The driver started the engine, turned on the headlights, and after a quick glance back at the captives, set the vehicle rolling up the switchbacked incline of the ramp.

In the light washing back into the van, McKay could see the guards were armed with new-issue M-16A2 rifles, with heavier barrels than the old A1s, three-shot burst regulators, and symmetrical foregrips like those on the little CAR-15 but larger.

That wasn't too unusual; even the regular-force cops back in
K.C. carried the M-16A2. But what disturbed McKay even in
the depths of his misery was that two of the other black-clad
guards carried H&K Close Assault Weapons Systems, fancy
bullpup 12-gauge shotguns that could fire either ultra-potent
000 buck charges or exotic ammo like depleted-uranium
armor-piercing slugs that could waste a BMP, on semi or full
rock 'n' roll. The newly developed weapons were on provi-
sional deployment with the Army, awaiting final approval and
requisition. The fact the Brothers of Mercy had them meant
Coffin's people had knocked over at least one important ar-
mory—and not just a National Guard post with a yard full of
rusted-out tanks and rump-sprung jeeps.

Shit, he thought. *No one's gonna stop 'em now. They're on
the loose, armed to the teeth, and stone crazy.*

If only . . . He glanced across the rocking cab at Sloan. The
lanky Guardian lay slumped against the side of the box, head
down, blood-matted hair hanging in his eyes.

Get real, McKay, a voice said in his head. *You've fucked
up. You lost Tom and Casey, lost Perkins, lost Connoly, lost
the whole fuckin' Blueprint.* He knew he'd blabbed his guts
loose on some kind of dope—could remember the agony ebb-
ing away, being replaced by a weird wet-warm amniotic glow
of euphoria. Summerill had been his friend, his father, his . . .
love. It wasn't that he felt guilty over talking under the influence of the drug, whatever it was. He knew he couldn't
have helped himself, no matter how hard-core he was.

But the way Summerill had peeled open his mind, his *soul,*
and rummaged around with his slimy fingers . . . McKay
reckoned he maybe had some idea now of what it was like to
get raped.

But overriding everything else was the misery of knowing
that the Guardians were gone, that the vital mission entrusted
to them—to him—was a failure beyond redemption. Coffin
and his psychopaths would win, with Soames Summerill pulling the strings like some satanic puppet master. And across
the ocean, Yevgeny Maximov would pick up a couple million
square miles of real estate and a few million more slaves.

The van broke out into blinding daylight. The driver paused

for a moment to call in a check over a CB radio mounted under the dash. Then he gunned the engine and rolled out toward the gate.

McKay laid his head against the vibrating skin of the van and closed his eyes.

Vaguely, he became aware of voices. The Brothers riding shotgun in the back of the van were discussing some kind of big push coming up. A kind of mass crusade, with Coffin himself returning from Oklahoma to lead it. From the snatches of speech that penetrated the fog of exhaustion in McKay's head, he gathered they were about to knock over some kind of earthly paradise, a green and pleasant valley brimming over with stockpiles of food and tender young women, well-fed and clean. Apparently, nonbelieving women were considered loot in the armies of the New Dispensation, the exclusive privilege of Coffin's black guard.

A moan escaped his crushed lips. He stirred himself, realizing he'd been riding in a half-waking dream. He raised his head, blinked crust from his eyes.

"Welcome back to the land of the living," said Brother Mace from the front passenger seat, "for however long you may enjoy it."

For some reason, a picture he'd seen in *National Geographic* a long time ago popped into his head—shit, must've been when he was with the peacekeepers in Lebanon. There were these monks, it seemed, who lived somewhere in Constantinople or Asia Minor. When members of the order died, they dried them down to bare bones and kept them in alcoves.

If you took a long, dead stick and stirred it around in those dry bones, you'd about have the sound of Brother Mace's voice.

"What Brother Mace is saying, in his own quaint and circumspect way," Sam Sloan said, "is that we're to be sacrificed for the greater glory of the church, or to keep the sun burning, or some equally worthy cause."

He sounded almost normal. *Good old Sam*, McKay thought. *Even in the jaws of death, he's still a smartass.*

"Why—" The word sounded like a twig breaking, and felt about the same way down deep in his throat. He tried to bring

up some saliva. Brother Mace rapped a word, and a skinny
Brother with black sideburns and a faded black leather jacket
held a canteen to the Guardian's lips. McKay felt an urge to
refuse, but realized that would be pretty pointless, and drank.

"Why couldn't you just do us back at the Fed Center?" he
rasped. "Afraid your poor little lambs couldn't take it?"

The skull face smiled, the gleaming bone-white head shook.
"Human sacrifice is a doctrine for which the flocks have not
yet been prepared, it's true," he said. "But that's not the
reason for this little excursion." The smile widened, showing
teeth, and it was almost a shock to McKay when he realized
they *weren't* pointed. In the daylight Mace looked like
something from one of the *Star Wars* flicks, or maybe a *Judge
Dredd* comic book. "You are to be honored by being sacrificed at a most holy site."

"Where's . . . that?" McKay croaked.

"We're almost there," Mace said, and turned around.

Since the rear windows were painted over in black, McKay's
view was restricted to trying to see out the front windows of
the van. He got the impression that they had yellow prairie on
one side, dappled by the shadows of drifting clouds, and the
blue loom of mountains on the other—which put them,
roughly, between Wyoming and New Mexico.

Think, Marine. McKay frowned with the effort of concentration. It literally made his head hurt. They had plains to the
left, mountains on the right. That meant they were going . . .
south, south along the Rampart Range. South from Denver
to . . .

An idea began to form in McKay's brain. An idea he didn't
like one single bit.

For a time they swung away from the mountains, east it
must have been, rattling along unimproved roads or jouncing
overland. When the sun was high overhead and the inside of
the black van was beginning to get pretty warm, they cut back
west. McKay had the impression they were climbing. A final
laboring of the engine up a particularly steep ascent and then
the van turned and halted. McKay and Sloan were unshackled
from the frame and prodded out the back door.

The view that met them looked as if someone had made a
mountain out of sand or mud—or mashed potatoes, if you

saw *Close Encounters of the Third Kind*—and then taken a few golf balls and dropped them on top of it. See the pretty pattern they make, circles interlocked with circles. Then a baseball—a hardball—had been dropped on the mashed potatoes off to one side from a good height.

The two Guardians stood blinking into sunlight barely diffused by a wash of cirrus clouds high overhead. They stood on the edge of the biggest of a scatter of craters. But instead of being baseball sized, the crater stretched a good half mile from rim to rim. McKay felt his hair rise at the nape of his neck.

"Cheyenne Mountain," he breathed.

The muzzle of a CAWS poked him in the kidneys. "This is it," a Mohawker growled. "You're goin' down—down into the crater!"

CHAPTER
FOURTEEN ————————

Shadows chased each other across the huge expanse of the crater. It was really quite pretty, spread out there beneath their feet. They were chained to posts set into the wall of the crater perhaps thirty meters down, roughly at the juncture between the fallback of debris thrown up by the surface burst and the "rupture zone" of soil and hard rock where both had been compacted and disrupted by the shock. That left most of the crater's two-hundred-meter depth in a breathtaking panorama below them.

Somehow McKay couldn't appreciate the view.

"Wonder how hot it is hereabouts," Sam Sloan said casually. He didn't mean the temperature.

"Dunno." McKay tried to pull his mind together to sort the problem out, but his concentration had a tendency to fly off in all directions like startled quail. Concentrations of radiation sufficient to produce a rad count of upwards of three thousand after one hour were considered to qualify as hot spots, and only in the area immediately surrounding ground zero of a surface burst did such concentrations occur. And the potency of fallout dwindles rapidly; after the weeks since the war, a three-thousand-rad per hour hot spot might have settled back

163

to not much worse than background.

But McKay couldn't remember ever seeing data for inside a crater proper, where the most heavily irradiated crud would tend to settle. And Cheyenne Mountain had been hit *hard*. McKay didn't know how much of a mountain the NORAD facility had been tucked under, but now it was a sort of flattened mound. What happened to debris when it was cycled through a mushroom cloud time and again, permitting ever more incandescent plutonium and other such pleasant stuff to condense on it?

Finally, the big crater had been made by a weapon of upward of twenty megatons—probably a twenty-five-megaton grand slam, the maximum in anybody's arsenal. What kind of residual radiation would a beast like that leave in its crater?

And what difference does it make? We're gonna die.

"I almost hate to say this," Sam Sloan remarked cheerfully, "but I hope it's hot as hell in here. I'm not too keen on dying of thirst." He sighed. "Too bad. It's kind of a pretty old world, even after all we've done to it. Look at those mountains up there—Pike's Peak, the rest of them. Be a shame to leave it."

But McKay was drifting, drifting—

He came awake suddenly, aware that he was cold. He opened his eyes. The sun had fallen out of sight behind the great wall of mountains off to their right. Purple gloom filled the crater. He realized that he was still bare-chested.

"Sloan," he called. No answer. Speaking louder: "Sloan! *Sam!*"

"Huh? Oh. Guess I must've dozed off. Getting on toward evening, isn't it?"

McKay frowned. "I feel a kind of tingling in my legs and gut. You think that's radiation?"

"Who knows? The blood-count boys say you can't feel it, but back in Arizona I read accounts from Hiroshima and some of those tests the Army ran. Men who'd been exposed to hard radiation said differently. Might be imagination, and it might not."

McKay craned his neck around. Above, the rim of the crater bulked like a dark rampart against the mauve sky. "I ain't trackin' too well," he said slowly, "so you'll have to remind me. Our whole honor guard came down with us when they tethered us down here, didn't they?"

"Right so far. Brother Mace gave a stirring little sermon about how we were making a little installment on the blood-debt humanity incurred at Calvary a couple thousand years ago. They chained us to these poles, and then they all went trooping back up the slope. Heard an engine leaving the area a little later, so I reckon they headed back to Denver with the comforting sense of a job well-done."

"They ain't stickin' around for the show? Is there anybody up there?"

"Affirmative," said Sloan. "At least a pair of black leather boys. They peer over the rim at us from time to time. They seem to have a half-dozen or so guards living in tents just beyond the continuous-ejecta zone. I gather they take turns keeping tabs on us."

"Jesus. These people are fuckin' *crazy*."

"Roger that—as you always say."

McKay thought furiously. His brain was clearer than it had been in—in—had it just been a day? Whatever. He was back on track again. It wasn't going to be a hell of a lot less lethal on the outskirts of the band of rock and dust spewed out of the crater than it was down here in the belly of the goddamned thing. Did the Brothers of Mercy know that? The conviction that they probably did would have horrified him, if he had thought he would be around long enough to deal with them. Then he thought of the people in the San Luis Valley, and the shitstorm of sadistic fanatics about to descend on them, and *that* horrified him.

"Sam." His voice was as cracked as the hard earth of the rupture zone above them. "If the radiation's slipped back to, say, a hundred rads an hour, then we'll suck up a lethal doze in about twelve hours at max. You check?"

"So far." A dose of upward of two hundred rads could kill, but wasn't likely to. Over a thousand was pretty sure to do the job. Of course, if they were getting a hundred rads an hour, it wouldn't just stop when it hit lethal level. It'd keep on sleeting through their tissues like some invisible acid rain.

"If it's really hot—over a thousand an hour—we'll be dead by morning."

"Check."

"So fuck it. I don't feel like waiting." He twisted in his bonds and bellowed up at the crater's lip. "Hey! You black-shirted bozos—why don't you come down here and suck my cock?"

"Jesus, Billy," Sam said. "What're you trying to do, get us killed?"

"Yeah."

For a moment Sloan stayed silent. Then: "You're right. It's been a pleasure serving under you."

McKay moistened his lips. "Pleasure to serve *with* you." For some reason he had a hard time forcing the words out of his parched throat.

The Brothers of Mercy definitely observed their own strange discipline. It took a volley of the most imaginative and obscene abuse old Marine McKay could muster—directed at them, their mothers, and the First Prophet Coffin—to eke a response out of the sentries on the crater rim. Then he and Sloan finally heard an angry shout, saw pale dust swirling up around booted feet as a Brother skidded down the slope toward them.

"As a Navy man it pains me to admit to being outdone in anything by a Marine," Sloan said admiringly, "but you had some things to say this ol' farmboy never heard nor dreamed of."

The Brother who arrived in response to McKay's oratory was a man of medium height with short, bowed legs, a big belly, thick chest and shoulders. He had a wide, fat-cheeked face framed by dark sideburns, a mashed-looking nose, hair combed back from the forehead, and angry slits for eyes. He looked like another trucker out of Waco. He wore no protective gear at all, unless a black leather vest counted. "Smart-ass," he puffed. "What makes you think you can say those things about the Prophet?"

"You can tell him all about it the next time you're kissin' his ass," McKay replied.

The man slugged him in the face. The world spun. *I'm gettin' too old for this,* McKay thought.

"I know how to take care of cheap scumbags like you," the

Brother said. With a click, a switchblade opened in his right hand. The light of the three-quarter moon rising in the east danced evilly on the blade.

"Hey! Hey, Mac!" A voice floated down from the rim. "Don't kill 'em! Brother Mace will peel our hides off if we don't let the Lord take them in His own time. We—"

The voice of the other sentry cut off abruptly. "I know what I'm doin'," Mac called back. He regarded McKay with contempt. "I know what you're tryin' to do. You're tryin' to get out of feelin' your punishment. It ain't gonna work, shithead."

"Gotten any since you last saw your mama, shit-kicker?"

The plump face tensed. "I ain't gonna kill you, never fear," he said, "but I can cut out your tongue so you don't act so fuckin' smart with me." He grabbed McKay's jaw and raised the knife—

—and his head exploded in a cloud of blackness like a squid's sudden ink.

A strange whimper escaped the Brother's slack mouth. From the bridge of the nose up, his face and forehead were gone. His body dropped and thrashed briefly in the radioactive dust. McKay blinked, felt dizziness bubble up over him. He fought it as long as he could, but it swirled him away into oblivion.

"Billy. Billy! Can you hear me?" He opened his eyes. A face hovered like an insect above him. He opened his mouth to speak, then turned sideways and jackknifed as nausea hit him. Sour vomit gushed from him.

"Sam," the strange creature said, "give me a hand. You strong enough to help me get him to his feet?"

"Yeah. He got beaten unconscious. I'm pretty sure he's got a concussion."

Hands pulled at McKay. He got his legs under him, shrugged the hands off. " 'Mokay," he slurred. "C'n walk by myself. Who . . . who're *you*?"

"It's Tom. Tom Rogers."

The dirt came up and slapped McKay in the face.

●   ●   ●

An insect stung him in the arm. He moaned, and then the stimulant shot through his system like wildfire. He sat up and looked wildly around.

What he had thought was an insect was really a stocky man in a protective suit. He and Sloan stood over McKay. A few meters away, the half-decapitated body of the Brother of Mercy cooled in the moonlight.

"I took out the other sentry up top," said the ghost of Tom Rogers. "Casey got the one who was down here and then headed back for the car. You ready to move, Billy? There're still six or seven of those bastards in the tents."

"Drive on," McKay croaked. They moved as rapidly as they could toward the rim of the crater. As they neared the top, they heard a soft blatting sound—and there was Mobile One, squat and ugly as ever, gleaming dully in the moonlight. It was the most beautiful sight Billy McKay had ever seen.

Rogers—it really was him, it had to be—yanked open the side door, helped McKay and Sloan into an interior lit by dim red night-vision lights. Casey Wilson held down the driver's seat, practically vibrating behind the big wheel. His young face was taut and white.

Tearing off his mask and hood, Rogers tugged McKay toward an air mattress on the deck aft of the turret roof. McKay resisted. "Dust—fallout contamination—" he croaked.

"No time." Rogers got him down, strapped him in, then strapped Sloan on a mattress beside him. Then he swarmed up into the turret. A moment later they heard him sing out, "Ready for it."

"Fire the bastards up!" In all the months he'd known Casey, McKay thought with fragile lucidity, he'd never heard such hatred in the kid's voice.

The grenade launcher and heavy machine gun sang in brief harmony. Then Casey spun the wheel and Mobile One roared into the night.

Voices sounded in a void.

"—accumulated dosage somewhere upward of three hundred rem. The protective drugs he'd been given in advance, plus the shots you gave him after rescue, minimized the effects insofar as possible. The chelating agents you administered are flushing his system nicely. Apparently some radioactive dust got into his boots; he's exhibiting minor signs of beta-ray burns, but they're no worse than what you got going into the crater. For the rest, he seems to have the constitution of a bull. He'll suffer some ill effects from his exposure, but I think he'll pull through."

It was a feminine voice, crisply professional. McKay thought about rolling over and opening his eyes for a look at its owner, but decided it was too much trouble.

He turned his attention back to the voice. "Three cracked ribs, multiple contusions, loosened teeth, and assorted trauma. The genital burns are superficial, thank God. I'd ask what kind of monster would do this to a man, except I suppose it's the same kind who'd deliberately expose human beings to high doses of hard radiation." She paused. "I fear for the future of this valley."

"We'll do what we can, ma'am." It was Tom Rogers.

"What worries me," the doctor went on, "is the repeated trauma to the head. Mr. Sloan informs me that whereas he was struck once and stunned, McKay was hit repeatedly and actually knocked unconscious. That's most serious, most serious indeed."

"I know."

McKay stirred. He wanted to tell them he'd be all right, that Marines had thick skulls, but somewhere along the way he got lost and slipped away again.

Voices.

Casey Wilson: "Doc Vasquez says Billy ought to be coming around soon. Like, I don't think you'll be too keen on his politics, Angie, but he's the finest man I ever met. You'll like him."

What's this shit about politics? McKay thought. He decided he'd dreamed it.

A voice—and a face.

"You're a lucky bastard, McKay," Sam Sloan said. "You slept like a baby and never had to go through the vomiting stage."

McKay tried to pry open an eye. To his surprise, he succeeded. Sam Sloan sat by his bed in a sunlit room. "You look like the moths been at you."

Sloan grinned ruefully. "Seems I'm more susceptible to radiation sickness than you are. I'm losing some hair, my white blood count's dropped through the floor, and I'm going to have some beauty marks for a while." McKay realized that Sloan's face was splotched with small patches of purple called petechiae—subcutaneous hemorrhages caused by exposure to radiation. "You managed to avoid all that. On the other hand, we were afraid you'd slip into a coma for a while."

McKay tried to sort out his time sense. "How long I been out?"

"Ten days."

He snapped upright. *"Ten days?"*

"That's what I said. Ease on back there, partner, or Vasquez'll give us both an enema for letting you get worked up. If I hadn't already learned better, to my sorrow, I'd be amazed a woman that good-looking could be that mean."

McKay fell back. He'd intended to ease himself down, but it hadn't worked out that way. He was weak as a baby.

"What the hell happened?" he asked.

"Well, in the beginning God created the heaven and the earth—or the Big Bang created everything, if you like that version better."

"Everybody's a goddamn comedian. I mean, what happened to us, Sloan? Why aren't Tom and Casey dead?" He thought a moment. "And why aren't *we?*"

"The answer to the one implies the answer to the other. We're not dead because Casey and Tom aren't. That bastard Summerill lied to us—but he didn't know it, in that one case."

As McKay and Sloan strolled unconcernedly into the ambush in Perkins' office, Brothers of Mercy had opened up with light antitank weapons from the concealment of the buildings around Mobile One. Fortunately, they weren't very good shots. Rogers returned fire and then reluctantly ordered Casey to obey McKay's final order.

Casey had taken off over the grounds of the Fed Center with fifty bad guys shooting at him. He'd hit the fence south of the gate, and the ten-ton V-450 had never slowed. A couple of truckloads of blackshirts had followed. Rogers had flamed one, and then an antitank weapon had skimmed the front deck and they pulled back across Alameda. The Brothers of Mercy pursued on foot and in vehicles. Rogers greased a number of them, how many he was uncertain. Then a rocket had blown loose a pump at a gas station near where Mobile One was trading shots with her pursuers, and an underground gas tank that had survived the bombing went up in orange and black glory.

"The Brotherhood reported a kill. Casey got it on Mobile One's radio. He and Tom holed the car up in the service garage of that Sears across the intersection from the Center, and sat up all night hatching schemes to haul us and Perkins out. Come dawn they intercepted transmissions from the van taking us to the Springs, and just followed a few klicks behind.

"Casey parked the car in an arroyo," Sloan continued, "just beyond the ejecta zone, and they snuck in just about the time you started serenading the sentries. Rogers cut the throat of the one on the rim, Casey popped the other one in the head with that wonder gun of his, and the rest is history."

McKay was too dazed even to wince at Sloan's misuse of the word *gun* when he meant *rifle*. "Where are we now?"

"A community called The Freehold, in the foothills of the scenic San Juan Mountains. And they are scenic too. I'd love to have a chance to do some running in them."

McKay closed his eyes. Trust Sloan to daydream of running up a fucking mountain when he was losing his hair and breaking out with spots from radiation sickness.

A tentative rap came from the door. "There's your lunch," Sloan said. "Get something in you, and I'll be back in a while. There are some people who want very badly to talk to you."

The skinny kid in the plaid Pendleton shirt who brought his tray would never replace a pretty nurse in whites. But McKay managed to put down a surprising quantity of the fruit juice, milk, and (of course) chicken soup he brought on a tray. Feeling at least ten percent human again, he took stock of his surroundings.

He was in a room with whitewashed walls and a ceiling held up by massive wood beams. The chair to the side of the bed looked as if it had been put together from old railroad ties, and the bedside table was a cable spool, but both had been finished and shellacked expertly. On one wall was a print of a primitive drawing of some dude in a funny hat riding a white horse over a bunch of dead guys with beards. On the other was a framed copy of the Declaration of Independence, with the words "Void Where Prohibited by Law" stamped over it. He couldn't make head or tail of either, so he transferred his attention out the window.

He saw a hillside covered with short, khaki-colored grass. Black cattle with white faces grazed on the slope, and farther up a pine forest commenced, marching up into a serious-looking snowcapped mountain range. It was very rural and peaceful, quite pretty if you got off on hills and cows and mountains and trees.

McKay took another sip of fruit juice and closed his eyes.

Two hours later he was awake again and wishing he weren't. His room was full of people, and a fever dream of a girl, with glossy black hair that hung clear to her waist, had just fixed him with eyes the blue of the Rocky Mountain sky and said, "Mr. McKay, the Church of the New Dispensation has invaded the San Luis Valley. Unless something is done to stop them they'll be here in a matter of days.

"They say they've come for my mother—and for you."

CHAPTER
FIFTEEN ——————————

"Now, Angela," said the woman who occupied the folding chair which had been·set under the print of the guy on horseback, "don't you think you're overstating the case somewhat?" The oldest of the three women crowded into McKay's bedroom with the four Guardians, she was in her middle years, not exactly attractive, but with a sturdiness shading toward pleasing plumpness. She had round cheeks pink with high-country good health, gray-shot black hair pulled back into a bun, and light blue eyes that danced behind big rimless round glasses. In her red plaid flannel shirt, blue jeans, and well-broken-in hiking boots, she looked like a cheerful lady geologist, or maybe some kind of Forest Service biologist. Something outdoorsy, at any rate.

Despite appearances, she was Dr. Marguerite Connoly of Yale University, one of America's most influential economists and the sole known participant in the Blueprint for Renewal who still happened to be alive and available.

Now she turned a pleasant, half-apologetic smile on McKay. "My daughter has always had an inclination toward the melodramatic. It shows in her politics." McKay vaguely remembered hearing somebody—Casey?—mention politics when he was out. It seemed important somehow, but McKay reckoned he'd get it sorted out later. It was all he could do to take in the important stuff right now. "What has happened is that a number of members of the Church of the New Dispensation have moved into the valley, both in the north through Poncha Pass and in the south through La Veta Pass, east of Alamosa. So far they haven't tried to do anybody any harm."

Sitting across from her, beneath the framed Declaration of Independence with its curious addition, Angelina Connoly shook her head in exasperation. McKay liked the way her hair, unbound and as glossy-black as coal, whipped about her shoulders. In fact, he liked just about everything about her—her slender, athletic body, her fine-featured oval face, eyes like the sky reflected in a mountain stream. Her breasts were a little small, but he was a big enough man to make allowances. *I might just get to like it here*, he thought, *wherever here is*.

"Those fools from the Northern Rio Grande Federation had the passes closed off to prevent *anybody* coming in," Angelina said heatedly. "What do you think happened to their people on guard?"

"Mayor Westlake told us they'd heard from them and they hadn't been harmed." Dr. Connoly's smile had gone sad and tolerant. "In spite of the horror stories we've heard from these gentlemen"—she gestured to the Guardians—"I sincerely doubt we have anything to fear. I don't think we can hold the whole church responsible for the deeds of a few misguided zealots."

McKay caught Tom Rogers' eye and nodded. Tom nodded back almost imperceptibly. He and McKay shared a professional's grim knowledge of the way the world really worked.

"I don't like to sound stupid," McKay said, "but could you maybe fill me in for a bit on where I am?"

"You're in the Freehold," said the third woman in the room. Dr. Ruby Vasquez had hair the color of burnished copper done up on her head, big black eyes, a snub nose, and skin the color of coffee with lots of cream. Her cowboy shirt and jeans did nothing to disguise the fact she had one hell of a figure, even though she couldn't have been more than five feet tall. "You're in bed. And there you'll stay until you've recovered from the ill treatment you received at the hands of our misguided friends." From the tone of her voice, it was apparent she thought as much of Dr. Connoly's assessment of the Church of the New Dispensation as McKay did.

"Thanks, Doc." It was a little jarring to call a woman "Doc," especially such a tiny bombshell. He wanted to pat her on the ass and bundle her into bed, but he had the distinct impression she'd take his arm off at the shoulder if he tried. "But, uh, could you give me a little better idea of just what the Freehold is? Our briefing didn't exactly cover it. Is it some kinda commune?"

The other three Guardians sat on the other side of McKay's bed from the women. McKay had raised a brow when they all trooped in; was leaving Mobile One unguarded a hot idea? Just as quickly he'd dismissed the thought. Tom Rogers was in command when McKay was out of action, and McKay trusted his judgment the way he trusted his own.

Now Angie looked past McKay and caught Casey Wilson's eye. Casey grinned and hunched one shoulder up slightly. McKay felt a weird pounding at the base of his throat at the look that passed between them. He wasn't exactly a stranger to having a good-looking woman look at him with lust in her eyes, or even to having her speak with love. But to have a woman as fabulous looking as Angie Connoly looking at you like that—and be able to look back at her the way Casey was—that was something Billy McKay had never experienced. He felt a sudden hollowness inside him.

"Freehold's a proprietary community," Angie said. "We have a hundred fifty households—families, pairs, some singles—here at the foot of the San Juan range. Since you weren't in any shape to notice when you drove in, that puts us on the west side of the San Luis Valley. Rio Grande comes out of the Garitas just a little way north of here."

"Don't beat about the bush, Angie," Dr. Connoly said. "Mr. McKay, you've fallen into a den of anarchists. Not the mad-eyed bomb-throwing type, I'll give them that. Heaven knows they mean well. But they're dewy-eyed idealists, the lot of them. Romantics."

McKay was thunderstruck. *Anarchists?* Jesus. They'd just gotten loose from a bunch of crazies. All they needed was more.

Angie's exquisite face looked pained. "Some of us would accept Mother's label—myself among them. But we're not leftists, not socialists masquerading as anarchists like most of the ones you may have heard of. By 'anarchists' we mean 'anarchocapitalists' or 'anarchoagorists'—believers in total freedom, including a free market. And not all of us go that way; we have a lot of minimal-government types. You could call us libertarians, though no more than half of us were ever party members."

McKay looked at his team. Sloan seemed mildly amused. As always, Tom Rogers would have looked perfectly at home carved into the side of Mount Rushmore. But Casey worried him. Was it just horniness and infatuation behind the yellow shooting glasses, or was he actually *buying* this crazy woman's rap?

"You can fill me in later on the details," he said. "What've you heard from Coffin's loonytunes?"

"They want to be allowed to send missionaries into the valley," Dr. Connoly explained. "We had some of their people out here yesterday to speak to us. I find their tenets simplistic, but the potential of this religion is tremendously exciting. It could be the key to rebuilding America!"

Oh shit, oh dear. Not another one. McKay found himself wishing Dr. Connoly would settle down and be an anarchist like her daughter. Anything to do with the New Dispensation was too fucking much for him right now.

"Don't worry, Billy," Casey said. "These people, like, know how to keep their mouths shut."

Ruby Vasquez had taken a slim black cigar from a pack in her hip pocket. "Sometimes," she said, lighting a match with her thumbnail and applying it to the cigar.

"They didn't tell Coffin's people anything about us," Casey said. "They just let them say their thing, and said goodbye."

"We're fairly sure they want us to give them food," Angie Connoly explained. "The valley has rich farmland. We've got enough surplus to take us into next year's growing season

—even though the Federation's been pressuring us to share the wealth with them."

"The Northern Rio Grande Federation has been attempting to form a central authority for the valley," Marguerite Connoly said. "My daughter's drawing-room radicals won't cooperate, even though I've tried incessantly since the war to convince them that only a strong government will see the people of this valley through."

"We've been preparing for the Third World War since we started settling here ten years ago," Angie said. "The political bosses who've assembled this Federation kept their heads in the sand until it was too late. Now they want us to bail them out."

"Can I ask a personal question, Dr. Connoly?" McKay asked.

"Why, certainly."

"Just what are you doing here anyway?"

"Taking a well-earned sabbatical to try to make my only child see the error of her ways." She smiled. "And also to relax and do some hiking in these gorgeous mountains."

"Oh." McKay hesitated. His head still felt a little fuzzy. He knew enough to realize just how lucky it was it still worked at all. In spite of endless movies and TV shows, it was tough to knock somebody out by hitting them on the head—and impossible to do so without causing some kind of permanent damage. It was McKay's good fortune that whatever harm the Brothers of Mercy's axe handles had done to him could apparently be handled by the damage-control system inside his brain.

Now he fixed Dr. Connoly with his eyes. She recoiled slightly, though she had the grace to cover it. He was gaunt cheeked and hollow eyed, and his gaze was piercing, uncanny. "We've come for the blueprints," he said.

She nodded. "I know that. Guardian Rogers already told me. I'm eager to do my part for this country."

Relief flooded him. "Great. Dr. Vasquez didn't think to tie me down to this bed, so I'm ready to boogie any time. How soon can you be ready to go?"

She smiled. "Just as soon as we've got this ridiculous contretemps with the Church of the New Dispensation settled."

•   •   •

Outside, the sun had slid down the sky toward the western peaks. A rich amber light filled the room. It reminded McKay of beer, and suddenly he was very thirsty.

"Well?" he demanded of the other three Guardians. The Freehold contingent had left them alone at his request. "What the fuck do we do now?"

"If it were the Perkins situation," Sam Sloan said, sitting back in the railroad-tie chair and crossing his long legs, "I'd say to go ahead and drag him out by the scruff of the neck. You were right about that situation all along. But this one's different."

"Matter of fact," McKay said slowly, "I *wasn't* right about that. We can't make somebody take part in anything as big and complex as the Blueprint if they don't want to. But you're right. This is a different situation. Recommendations?"

Sloan licked his lips. "We could bundle up Dr. Connoly and try to bust through the church's cordons," he said. "We're fast, we've got the firepower of a frigate. We could maybe pull it off."

"But you don't like it." It wasn't a question, and Sloan knew he didn't have to respond. "Casey?"

"I can't get behind just leaving these people here for the crazies to get, Billy."

"That your considered opinion," McKay rasped, "or just your balls talkin'?" Casey looked devastated, and McKay instantly felt like a fresh dog turd. "Sorry. That wasn't fair. Tom, what do you think?"

Rogers stared out the window at the cool evening darkness of the pines. After a moment McKay decided he hadn't heard, though it was definitely not like the ex-Green Beanie to daydream. He started to repeat the question.

"We got a mission," Rogers interrupted, not looking around.

McKay sighed. "You're right, Tom. We just better move on."

"But we should remember what the mission really *is*." It was as if McKay hadn't spoken. He blinked. Rogers sounded almost emphatic. "We're supposed to be helpin' rebuild civilization, ain't we? We might not agree with what these folks

here stand for, but they are buildin' somethin'." He rubbed
his jaw where the hairline of an old scar shone white against
his tan. "Reckon we'll be doin' our job if we do what we can
to keep this false prophet Coffin from tearin' it all down."

Coming from the taciturn Rogers, that was quite a speech.
Sloan leaned forward and put his head in his hands. His hair,
falling out in mangy clumps, would have looked comical in
another situation. "I want to agree with you, Tom. But if we
get involved trying to right every damn wrong we run across,
we might as well write off the Blueprint."

Casey started to say something, looked at McKay, and
turned away again in silence. McKay grimaced. It was a hell of
a situation when one of his team hesitated to offer his opinion
when it was asked for—and it was McKay's own damn fault
for being such a prick.

"No," McKay said. "I think this is something special.
Maybe I'm being unprofessional, but I'm fucking sick of running from these bastards. I want to break Coffin's little toy
church across my goddamned knee. I don't know if we got a
hope in hell of beating them—the church has a whole lot of
people in this valley, and what looks to be a real good setup
for transport and resupply. But the thought of tucking our tail
between our legs and running off without a fight just grates
my nuts."

He looked hard at Sloan. "I think we owe 'em a little something, Sam."

Sam raised his head. "You're right," he said. "You *are*
being unprofessional, McKay." A grin spread slowly across
his square face. "But you know what? I agree with you. Let's
show those sons of bitches what it means to mess with the
best."

It wasn't that simple, of course. McKay the Marine, the
Force Recon team leader, or SOG specialist would have been
tempted to abide by the time-honored principle of "what the
brass doesn't know won't hurt them."

McKay the Guardian leader was tempted too. But he
couldn't play it that way. Crenna had given him as much
latitude as a subordinate officer had ever had. But a question
like this was rightly settled at the top. Somehow it didn't sit

right with McKay, the thought of trying to pull a fast one
when he did have such splendid freedom of action.

Much as he hated to do it, he had to talk to Heartland.
Again.

"This better be good, McKay," Crenna growled when they
raised him over Mobile One's radio. Vasquez had disappeared
after she had seen Casey and Tom help McKay out through
the living room of what turned out to be Angie Connoly's
semisubterranean home. It gave McKay several kinds of a
twinge to see the way both Casey and Angie pitched in like a
team to mollify the angry Chicana physician, but he was glad
they did. Ruby Vasquez was like a cross between an Army
nurse and a Parris Island DI; McKay admired that in a
woman, but didn't think he could put up with her abuse just
now.

"Hate to bother you, Major, but we got a question of policy
here again." Tom Rogers had radioed in a complete account
of what had happened in Denver after they arrived at Freehold. McKay outlined the new problem tersely. "We'll stand
by if you need to talk to President MacGregor."

"No need to bother the President, McKay," Crenna said.
"Sam Sloan summed it up nicely: you can't afford to get hung
up righting every wrong you stumble across."

McKay's heart sank. *Oh well*, he thought. *Casey ain't
gonna take too well to havin' to leave his foxy lady to the
Brothers of Mercy*. Neither did he, come to think of it. Angie,
Vasquez, all of them may have been anarchowhatsits and mad
as hatters, but they seemed like pretty good people. And even
if they'd been mad-ass Marxists, it still didn't seem right to
abandon them to the mercies of Coffin's fanatics.

"Yes, sir. I'll tell—"

"Let me finish, McKay. Tom Rogers was also correct, in
that your major mission is the reconstruction of American
society. The Blueprint is vital to that, but so is the kind of
work the people of the San Luis Valley are doing.

"Don't forget this Summerill character. It's important that
you spike his plans, both as they concern Coffin and the
Blueprint itself. If you can cancel his number permanently, so
much the better."

A crackling pause. "Sloan was right about another thing.

These inappropriately named Brothers of Mercy knew of your mission and tried to take you out anyway. I think a lesson needs to be taught.

"You're the men to teach it. Make it happen, McKay. Crenna out."

Later McKay had some of the gaps in his memory between his and Sam's rescue from the crater and his return to full consciousness filled in by his cohorts. Mobile One was of course well stocked with medicines, especially the latest drugs for treating radiation sickness. Rogers had tended the two sick and unconscious men while Casey drove south toward Poncha Pass.

The pass itself had been blocked by a contingent of armed ranchers who claimed to be representing the Northern Rio Grande Valley Federation. They were there, they said, to prevent stragglers from the stricken cities of Denver, Colorado Springs, and Pueblo from invading their valley. They thought the Guardians might qualify, and were totally unimpressed by Tom Rogers' insistence that they were on a vital mission from the U.S. Government.

A burst of M-19 grenades into a stand of aspens overlooking the highway, however, had impressed them. They let the Guardians through, and by dawn Casey was driving up the graded dirt road and through the barbed-wire fence that surrounded the sprawling community that called itself the Freehold. The sentries at the gate, however, were a handful of teenaged kids who held assault rifles—illegal since the late Eighties—as if they knew how to use them. They were dubious about allowing the big armored car inside until Casey told them that they had urgent business with Dr. Connoly, and two gravely ill men aboard.

A black girl with a 7.62-mm Galil had ridden up with them as a guide. She directed them to the sprawling semisubterranean home owned by Dr. Connoly's daughter Angelina, who they would learn was about the closest thing to a leader this crazy bunch had. She met them herself, a tall, willowy woman with long glossy black hair, blue eyes, and a pistol at her hip. Casey's hurried explanation that they were on a secret mission from the government failed to make an impression on her.

The information that two of the Guardians were desperately ill from maltreatment by the Church of the New Dispensation did; Angie directed that they should be put up in her own home.

Rogers and the diminutive firebrand Vasquez, summoned from her own home nearby, went into a low-voiced professional huddle over Sloan and McKay. Casey naturally wound up explaining to Angie Connoly just who they were and what they were doing. "I know it was, like, a breach of security," he acknowledged now, "but it didn't seem right to try to hold out."

"I wonder just how hard you *tried*," McKay rasped. "Looked like you and Connoly Junior could barely keep your hands off each other at that confab earlier."

Casey flushed and stammered. "Now, McKay, he's right and you know it," Sam Sloan said, frowning. "These folks've done us some mighty big favors. They're entitled to some explanations. And anyway, Dr. Connoly's probably told her daughter the whole story by now."

McKay wondered about that. Mother and daughter were cordial, but their relationship was clearly strained. Hell, Dr. Connoly probably *enjoyed* playing the national security game.

He waved a big hand dismissively. "Sorry, Case. I'm an asshole when I'm sick. Most of the rest of the time too, but that's in the line of duty."

In any event, Billy and Sam had been under intensive care for several days. During that time, the freeholders had learned of the approach of Coffin's crusaders. Angie and Casey had been thrown together a good deal of that time. At first they'd discussed politics, each curious as to what made the other tick. Not that Casey was especially interested in political discussion for its own sake. None of the Guardians were, although Sloan had picked up a lot of fairly standard liberal notions somewhere. A deeply held patriotism, which each Guardian possessed in plenty, had been considered more important in the selection process than any particular political axe to grind.

But Angie had wondered how Casey could spend his life in uniform, dedicated to restoring a government that on the evidence hadn't done such a hot job of providing for the security and welfare of its citizens. In his turn, Casey was amazed that

Angie could so totally reject the very concept of the nation state and all that it implied—patriotism included—and found himself intrigued with her crazy notion that somehow humans could get by without government, or with little to speak of. Little by little they found there weren't really so many areas of disagreement between them after all; Casey had always pretty much held with live and let live, and Angie could identify with strong commitment to a cause, even one she didn't especially believe in. And the fact that the Guardians weren't engaged in trying to force people to do anything favorably impressed her.

And after the second evening they found they'd talked the moon down into the Sangre de Cristos. Now, Casey was quite a handsome dude, in a boyish, tanned, blond sort of way, and Angie was a very lovely woman as well as a very intelligent one. They got along so well, so *naturally*.

Grinning, Billy McKay scratched a match alight on the rough-hewn table by the bed and lit the cigar which Sloan, over Rogers' unspoken disapproval, had brought him. "All *right*, Case, you don't have to give us the gory details." He puffed noxious blue smoke. "If I had a stone fox like Angie Connoly snugglin' up to me, I might hoist the black flag too. Good thing that motherhumper Summerill didn't think of having one of those cute little cheerleaders for Jesus try to seduce me. Or maybe two."

He laced his fingers behind his bull neck, lay back, and stared up at the beams running across the ceiling. "Now clear out and let me get some sleep. You lucky son of a bitch."

Next day they drove down with Ruby Vasquez to the town of Gilpin, which appeared to be the headquarters for the Northern Rio Grande Federation. "I thought Alamosa was the big town hereabouts," McKay had said through the steam rising from his big terra cotta coffee mug that morning. He leaned back from the butcher-block breakfast table beneath the skylight in Angie Connoly's dining room. He and the other Guardians were just finishing a plentiful meal with the mistress of the house.

Angie polished off the last of her scrambled eggs. "It was. Then the plague hit."

Sam Sloan raised a patchy brow. "Typhoid? Cholera?"

"The real thing. *P. pestis* in pneumonic form. The most infectious disease known to man. One of the most fatal." She sipped from her own coffee cup. "This part of the world we get outbreaks every couple of years. Usually they don't amount to anything much, except for the dozen or so people who catch the bug." She shrugged. "This time the breakout happened right after the war hit. Started downriver in New Mexico, spread up this way. Alamosa's virtually a ghost town now."

McKay tried to remember if any of the locals had shown a tendency to cough the night before. "And, uh, what happened here?"

"Nothing. Dr. Vasquez had a supply of the vaccine on hand. Most of our people had themselves inoculated. A few didn't, but that's their decision."

"How about Gilpin and the other towns up the valley?" Sloan asked.

Angie made a face and set down her cup. "Mostly shot anybody who tried to come up from the south. Same thing they did in the passes to keep out refugees from Denver, Pueblo, and the Springs. Caused a lot of ill feeling around here." She bit her lip. "Those people the Federation set to watch the passes. They're dead now, aren't they?"

McKay looked at Casey. "Uh, I hope so," the younger man said.

"Poor fools. Well." She stood up, stretched. This morning she had on a striped halter top without a bra beneath. McKay tried not to admire the display too visibly. Casey was his buddy, after all. Had he been any other male on earth, he wouldn't think twice about trying to cut in. But never with a buddy—and especially not on this mission. "Time for you to be on your way, I guess. Though I don't think you'll get much out of Mayor Westlake and his cronies, other than a demand that we share our food with them."

Now they rumbled down a country road into the San Luis Valley. The landscape was a bewildering combination of lush green farmland and desperate-looking sagebrush and grama-grass desert, real Zane Grey country. "Too bad you weren't awake when we came through, man," Casey informed McKay from the driver's seat. "There are, like, *sand dunes* all over the place, on the eastern side of the valley. Looks like Death Valley or something."

McKay grunted. The passing terrain didn't show him much, but he still concentrated on mapping and storing it for further reference, in case they had to fight over this ground. He'd rather have concentrated on little Doc Vasquez, who sat on the fold-down across from him, holding on to a leather strap as casually as a subway commuter—an image belied by the Ruger Blackhawk .357 Magnum revolver with a barrel nearly as long as her arm strapped at her hip. She was along to perform the introductions and act as interpreter if needed, since much of the valley's population was Hispanic. Casey spoke Spanish well, and so did Tom Rogers. But McKay didn't. Since there was more to talking to people than just speaking their language, McKay was pleased for more than one reason to have her along.

"Would you mind telling us more about Freehold, ma'am?" Sloan asked Dr. Vasquez. "I'm sure Casey and Tom have heard the story, but McKay and I sort of slept through it." He gave her his most charming smile. McKay gave him a poisonous look.

Vasquez explained that Freehold had started in the middle eighties when a consortium of libertarian-minded investors had started buying up property along the east slope of the San Juan Mountains. They wanted to establish a combination survival retreat and experimental community where like-minded folk could attempt to live in accordance with their principles. It was about the end of the survivalist craze, and before the big real estate spurt of the latter part of the decade, so they were able to get a substantial chunk of property well supplied with water by the San Juan watershed.

"They—Angie, Dumont, and the other founders—would've preferred a location away from such a high-risk target as the Springs. But the prime retreat properties in the Northwest were pretty well gone by then, or the prices jacked up sky high. And there aren't a lot of places in Colorado that're suitable. Water—that's the problem."

"Angie was one of the founders?" Casey asked.

Vasquez grinned and winked at McKay. He didn't mind.
"She doesn't look like an old lady, does she? She isn't, unlike
me." Vasquez was a very fine-looking woman somewhere in
her late thirties, if McKay was any judge, and he was. "She
was one of the first computer networkers; started while she
was at Andover. She was a good way into her first million by
the time she started college."

The community—development was the wrong term—of
Freehold required purchasers of lots to sign a declaration of
principle, amounting primarily to a promise to avoid initiating
force, to respect the rights of other community members, to
accept arbitration of disputes among members of the community. "I thought you believed in total freedom," McKay
said.

"We do."

"But you laid all these requirements on people before letting them come in."

Vasquez grinned. "Foremost among freedoms are freedom
of association and freedom of disposing of your property as
you see fit. Nobody was required to stipulate anything about
morals or lifestyles. Only to leave their neighbors the hell
alone and not go dragging the government in on intramural
hassles. Anybody who didn't like those terms could buy land
anywhere else they wanted—just not from the Freehold Company."

"Ain't that just like a government?"

"No, because you could elect not to play the game at all.
Try telling the former US of A you don't like playing by their
rules."

McKay frowned. He wasn't sure he saw the distinction, but
he decided to let it pass. The Freeholders sure didn't seem like
commies, and that was the one brand of politics he really objected to. Mainly they seemed to stand for just letting people
go to hell their own way. He didn't see too much wrong with
that, though a lot of their ideas struck him as pretty funky.

The Freeholders were a lively, argumentative lot, but for the
most part they abided by the rules they set for themselves. In
the early years, a few caused some unpleasantness and were
bought out. "There's not much any two of us agree on," Vas-

quez said, "but one thing we all hold by is that everyone's right of person and property is absolute—but their ownership stops at the outside of their skin and property line."

Many of the Freeholders had gone into ranching or farming to some extent. Others, such as Angie Connoly, had pursued occupations that enabled them to work out of their homes, largely in information processing of one sort or another. But almost all of them consciously pursued the goal of self-sufficiency. Freeholders tended to practice high-yield organic farming, not from any weird misconceptions about biochemistry, but because such methods tended to be cheaper, better for the land, and were not dependent on the vast and vulnerable petrochemical industry for fertilizer. Freehold vehicles ran on alcohol. Rabbit hutches were as common as pickups—and windmills and solar homes.

Since most of them were consciously committed to living by the principle of laissez-faire, they got along well with most of their non-Freehold neighbors. The surrounding area had a large population of Hispanics, who by and large didn't care for *gringos* that much—and even less for the blacks who moved in, including Pete Dumont. Pete was the solar adobe wizard who'd built most of the Freeholders' homes and was one of the community's founders. But the Hispanics were also hardy and self sufficient and came to appreciate neighbors who minded their own business. North of the Freehold were several other survivalist retreats, including a cluster of what could only be called hippies and some kind of Minuteman ex-colonel's stronghold. Though many of the survivalists disagreed with the politics of Freehold, they treated one another civilly, even helping each other out from time to time.

The townspeople of the bottomlands were a different story. They tended to distrust the retreaters of whatever stripe, and certain elements among them had launched litigation and even some legislation in the State House to drive them out. Among the residents of the Freehold were a couple of the nation's top attorney's, who'd gotten pissed off enough to handle all the survivalists' defense free of charge, which brought hippies, Minutemen, and anarchosomethings closer together. It hadn't hurt matters with the Hispanics either, since some of the

developers who were going after the survivalists had managed
to lump a lot of the *nativos* in with them, hoping to grab a
little extra land.

"Thought you'd be natural allies with the developers,"
Sloan said.

Vasquez scowled. "Not much wrong with development per
se. But the people down in the valley are by and large the kind
who try to use the government to turn their profits for them.
They were squeezing people so they could buy land cheap; crying to the state for help when they made stupid investments
and lost their shirts, the way they did when the condo craze
gave way in the eighties." She gestured out the viewport. They
were getting near Gilpin now, and in the near distance loomed
what looked like a partially bombed-out high rise. Instead of
being knocked down, it had never gone all the way up. It had
been in the process of becoming a condominium, Vasquez explained, until capital had run out. The valley was full of such
mouments to financial misjudgment.

"We've built fine houses and productive ranches in the
hills," she said, "and they've tried everything they could to
screw us out of them."

"But that's ridiculous," Sam Sloan said. "How could they
do that?"

"The Emergency Farmland Reclamation Act, for one. It
was in part an antisurvivalist law anyway. They tried to con-
demn our land out from under us."

Sloan frowned out his vision block. "You're a Chicana,
Doctor," Casey said. "What do *you* think about all these
gringos who've moved in?"

"I lived in this valley all my life," she said, "but I was also
one of the founders of Freehold. My people aren't used to
gringos who pay for what they take and only take what's
freely offered, *querido*. It's kind of a welcome change."

Mayor Westlake was a tall, lean man with a red face, a pink
shirt, and a string tie with a silver and turquoise cow's-head
clasp. He had thinning hair, wore a gray suit, and exuded a
general air of weariness. He exchanged icy courtesies with
Vasquez, then turned on his real estate agent's professional
heartiness when he was introduced to McKay and Sloan.

"Glad to meet you gentlemen," he said, pumping Sam's arm as if he were trying to make water spurt out of his mouth. "Always proud to meet a man serving our country. Always been a strong supporter of our boys overseas. Not like some." The last came with a meaningful glance at Vasquez.

The San Luis County Courthouse, the seat of the Northern Rio Grande Federation, was a quaint, whitewashed two-story structure with a pitched roof looking down on a cottonwood-shaded plaza. The look was very different from the rest of Gilpin, which consisted of a few dumpy, blocky southwestern-style adobe houses and a whole lot of cinder-block boxes intended to look like dumpy, blocky southwestern-style adobe houses. At least McKay thought they were dumpy. He got the impression Casey liked these adobe heaps, but then he was from California.

Inside, though, the courthouse was all modern, with acoustic tile and air conditioning. The latter was running today. Though the power station was closed down to conserve energy and fuel use was rigorously rationed, the generators were still going all-out to keep the wheels of government running cool in the midsummer heat. McKay hoped he wouldn't catch a cold as Westlake waved them to Naugahyde chairs in his office, which featured a lot of sports photos along the walls and a huge map of the San Luis Valley over the desk.

The Mayor was amused when he learned the Guardians had come down to offer aid in defending against the Church of the New Dispensation. "You gentlemen are wasting your time," he said expansively. "We don't expect any trouble from these folks. We got us a militia, been drilling hard ever since, uh, things broke down. We don't have nothing to fear from a bunch of Hairy Krishna types. Fact is, we just today sent them a delegation to ask them to move on. We're tryin' hard to conserve what we got in this valley. We don't take kindly to all these city folk movin' in and trying to put the arm on us."

He leaned forward and placed clasped hands earnestly on the desk in front of him next to a cutesy plastic statue of a funny-shaped guy standing under a tree looking dolefully up at a bird on a limb and saying, "Go ahead—everyone else does." "Matter of fact," the Mayor said, "there is something you could do to help us: talk some sense into these crazy people at Holdout or Freelove or whatever they call their cozy little commune. They're balkin' at accepting the authority of the Federation, even though this Dr. Connoly, who don't have too bad a head on her for a woman, has been tellin' 'em up and down that a strong authority's needed to pull this valley through the crisis.''

He worked his long face into an expression of utmost gravity. ''In fact, I'm very much afraid those people are guilty of the worst crime that can follow in the wake of catastrophe—hoarding.''

By this point, McKay judged, a glass of water thrown on Doc Vasquez would turn to steam long before it hit her skin. Fire flashed from her black eyes. She opened her mouth. McKay kept a straight face, but inside he was grinning in anticipation. As a former drill sergeant, he had a professional's respect for a fine ass-chewing, and he had a feeling he was about to witness a masterwork of that art.

A knock came at the door. Irritation crinkled Westlake's sunburned forehead. ''What is it?''

A worried young man in white shirt and tie poked his head in. Despite the air conditioning, his face gleamed with sweat. ''Your Honor, we just received a message from the Church of the New Dispensation,'' he said, almost stuttering the words in agitation.

Mayor Westlake scowled. ''What'd them punks want?''

''Th-They said we were to begin dispensing our food stocks among them tomorrow morning at six o'clock. Otherwise they—they're going to attack us!''

CHAPTER
SIXTEEN ─────────────────

The Battle of Gilpin was a disaster.

The Rio Grande ran from northwest to southeast in this part of the Valley. Gilpin lay mostly on the southwest bank. Two bridges—one a four-lane highway bridge, the other a more modest two-lane affair—led across the river from the town. The river was swollen by rains up in the mountains so that it filled its hundred-meter wide bed and then some. A used car lot and a few houses on the edge of town were underwater.

Across the torrent the Federation militia's trucks rolled in the gray false dawn. Farmers and townies armed with rifles and shotguns, they were smoking and joking confidently as they climbed off the flatbeds and dispersed into a sort of company line parallel to the river and about two hundred meters beyond it. A couple dozen Colorado Highway Patrolmen in Smoky Bear hats and short-sleeved tan shirts seemed to be acting as cadre. A captain in a billed cap with gold spaghetti on the front of it positioned his car near the north end of the highway bridge and stood by with one excruciatingly polished boot propped in the door, microphone in hand to direct the battle's progress. By six-thirty they were in position. By seven, they had just about decided the Churchies had thought better of facing them. Their deadline had come and gone an hour ago without any sign of the enemy appearing on the slow dull-green swell of the prairie.

Having deposited Dr. Vasquez back in the Freehold, Mobile One took its place anchoring the left flank of the battle line, such as it was. Casey had found an abandoned adobe house near some cottonwoods, two hundred meters from the river and a half klick from town. It was another mud-brick block, but McKay could see a little more reason for the architecture now: the thing had been built to *last*. The walls were crumbling, melting under the onslaught of rain and wind, but mostly they still stood. The roof was gone, but thick beams, bleached whitish-gray by the sun, still spanned the walls.

Mayor Westlake had offered to enlist any Freehold men who were willing to swear an oath of allegiance to the Northern Rio Grande Federation. Predictably, none had stepped forward. The view back at the Freehold was that every able body would soon be needed to defend his or her own home after the Federation lost its battle with Coffin's faithful. That Westlake would lose was doubted by none but Dr. Connoly.

The Guardians had their own reservations about the Federation militia, but they were there to defend civilization, so they trundled back to Gilpin to place themselves nominally under the command of Captain Ortega for the duration of the fight.

How nominal that command was became painfully obvious at once. Ortega, it appeared, wanted the Guardians to lead off, spearheading a glorious attack in advance of the militia. Since the Guardians knew for a fact that Coffin's people had antitank rockets, they turned him down cold. Leading with the chin against rockets like that had led the Israelis to get their asses wiped by the Egyptians during the fight for the Bar-Lev Line in the Yom Kippur War twenty-odd years before, and it hadn't become any better an idea since. Instead, the V-450 would take up a concealed position to the side in order to give covering fire with its heavy weapons. With poor grace, Ortega had conceded the point, since he hadn't any choice.

Billy McKay lay on his belly fifty meters south of Mobile One with his light machine gun beside him, peering through a chamisa bush with binoculars and hoping there weren't any scorpions around. This country reminded him lots of North Africa. North Africa was lousy with scorpions.

At five and a half minutes after seven, he said, "Something's happenin'," into the mike taped to his Adam's apple.

During his youth, going to movies was a lot more acceptable in his circle—and his family—than his secret vice of reading. So he spent a lot of time at the movies: new releases, rereleases, midnight movies, anything. One of his favorite (along with everything Clint Eastwood ever did, except for the *Every Which Way* series) was a flick made clear back in the sixties called *Zulu*, about a radically outnumbered British force defending a desolate outpost in the middle of South Africa against several *impis* of tough Zulu warriors. He'd rooted impartially for both sides; the Limeys were heroic, of course, but the Zulus were amazingly hard-core.

In one memorable scene, a ridge overlooking the station at Rorkesdrift had suddenly been lined with hundreds of Zulus, standing like a grim black wall. McKay eventually learned that the same scene was always being replayed by hostile Indians in old Westerns, but it had been particularly well handled in *Zulu* and the impression it made remained.

Something like that happened now.

Along a long low rise two hundred meters away, more a furrow than a ridge, a line of men materialized. They stood as silently as the Zulus had in the movie, dark against the gray, threatening sky and the jagged mountains beyond. McKay lowered the binocs and stared. He remembered that those distance-blued peaks were named Sangre de Cristo—Blood of Christ. He hoped it wasn't prophetic.

Shouts came from the right, then an electrically amplified bellow. The breeze was blowing from the east, making it harder to hear what was going on to the southeast, but McKay gathered that Ortega, via his car's loudspeaker, was ordering the Children of the New Dispensation to disperse.

Two figures broke past the unspeaking ranks and ran toward the militia, shrieking, wrapped in flames that danced pale orange in the uncertain sunlight. "Jesus," McKay heard Sloan say in his earphone. *Must be Westlake's emissaries,* he thought. The Churchies had soaked them in gas and touched them off.

"Put 'em out of their misery?" asked Rogers, manning the .50-cal and the M-19 as usual.

"No," McKay said, though it wrenched him. "Can't give away our position yet." He heard somebody start to say something, Casey or Sloan, but that person changed his mind as the realities of warfare on the ground sank in a touch deeper. The easterly wind carried the screams clearly to their hiding place.

Siren wailing, lights flashing, a highway-patrol car lunged forward. What the cop thought he was going to accomplish, McKay never knew. The driver headed straight for the mindlessly running, burning figures until a machine gun stuttered from the crestline. From the fast, high-pitched snarl McKay recognized a Minimi. Characteristically, the light 5.56-mm rounds didn't stop the cruiser.

Then the throaty growl of an M-60 sounded. The car veered right, ran through a quarter circle, and stopped. No one got out.

The two charred figures collapsed into the short grass and finally stopped screaming.

With a roar the line on the rise surged forward like the surf.

"Fucking amateurs," McKay said with relief. For a moment there he'd been uneasy; it seemed the machine guns were pretty well sited. But they'd do no goddam good with two hundred of the faithful between them and Gilpin's defenders.

Prone in the low brush, the militia opened fire with everything they had. Much of it did no good, since the charging faithful were well beyond shotgun range. But figures started falling.

McKay raised the glasses. He saw only a handful of black-clad Brothers of Mercy among the attackers. He was surprised. Maybe Coffin was unwilling to risk his elite goons in battle.

If so, it was going to cost him dearly. At first the faithful came on with great spirit, and little discipline—running flat out, hollering like mad, firing from the hip as if that would accomplish anything but burning ammo. The Federation militia may have been a bunch of sad sacks, but there were some old deer hunters among them who actually knew how to shoot,

and the targets were cooperating by running straight for the
muzzles of their rifles. A dozen attackers went down, a score,
then McKay lost count. The charge began to falter.

Just the same, the gap between the faithful and the militiamen narrowed rapidly. "Fire 'em up, Tom."

Mobile One rolled to the side to clear its field of fire. The
.50 started thudding, like the back-space key on a gargantuan
typewriter. Even from better than a hundred fifty feet away,
the muzzle blast of the big machine gun struck McKay like
small fists. Rogers walked the stream of slugs right across the
attacking front. The faithful wilted like reeds in a firestorm.

All at once the attack fell apart. The cries of the Children
changed in pitch, from bellowing battle lust to high-pitched
panic. In an eye blink they were washing back toward the ridge
like a retreating tide.

The militiamen lunged after them like wild dogs after a fleeing calf. Shouting hoarse cries of triumph, they scrambled to
their feet and ran forward. A half-dozen highway-patrol cars
went bounding off over the desert in pursuit of the routed
enemy, crushing the writhing bodies of wounded Children as
they went. The two machine guns yammered from the ridge.
Tom sowed a line of death from the M-19 along its crest, and
the machine gun fire ceased.

"Sloan! Get me Ortega on the double!" McKay barked. He
was covered with sweat, and it wasn't from the muggy heat.

"We have them on the run, McKay!" Ortega's bull voice
boomed in his ear. "Go after them, don't give 'em no chance
to regroup!"

"Call those men back, you silly son of a bitch! It's a trap!"

"What's the matter?" The captain's voice dropped an
octave into oily contempt. "You afraid? What's amatter, you
got that big armor car—"

From a rocky hummock north of the rise the attack had
come from, a puff of white smoke jumped suddenly into the
air. McKay's heart damn near jumped out of his chest.
"*Casey, gun it,*" he screamed. "TOW!"

"Whose toe?" Ortega demanded. "You gone crazy—"

McKay wasn't listening. He had his hands on the Maremont
and was pumping rounds at the mound as fast as they'd crank

through the tube. Something might conceivably have caused a
puff of smoke like the one he'd just seen besides a Tube-
launched, Optically aimed, Wire-guided missile powerful
enough to break open a heavy tank the way a mallet cracks a
Maryland blue crab, but if so nobody'd ever told him about it.

As long as the enemy missileman kept the optical sight
aimed at the target, impulses sent along a hair-fine wire un-
reeling behind the twenty-kilogram projectile would steer it
unerringly toward its destination. Mobile One's single thin
hope was that if the enemy was killed or even distracted before
the missile hit, it would "go ballistic," fly off out of control.
All McKay needed to do was hit somebody he couldn't even
see four hundred meters away.

The automatic grenade launcher fired from the V-450's
turret. A hundred fifty meters away the characteristic starfish-
shaped bursts of white phosphorus grenades and the dirt foun-
tains from high-explosive shells sprang up. *What the fuck?*
McKay thought. The TOW-gunner was three times that distance away.

Then he saw that the distant hummock was hidden behind a
dense curtain of white phosphorus smoke. And if he couldn't
see the hill—

Uncontrolled, the TOW struck a corner of the abandoned
house and blew up in the front room. A fist-sized chunk of
adobe brick struck McKay in the back. "Tom, Casey, Sam,
are you all right?"

"Affirmative, Billy," Casey replied.

McKay looked back at the ridge. The counterattack had
mounted almost to the top. But it seemed to be losing momentum somehow. Militiamen had started reeling aimlessly, falling down. Two light planes were cruising slowly overhead,
spilling white vapor from their bellies.

Without conscious thought, McKay was pulling his gas
mask out of its holder at his belt. "Nerve gas," he shouted.
"Button up and get ready to *go*." He snagged the mask on
over his face, took the Maremont in one hand and the binoculars in the other, and ran like hell for Mobile One.

The Guardians were brave men. In fact, two of them, Sam
Sloan and Casey Wilson, had acquired a certain brief fame for
their exploits in the Mediterranean theater. None of them was

quixotic enough to throw away his life battling for no other reason than to provide a footnote in future histories of someone else's lost battle. The V-450 was protected against chemical weapons; they could hang around and shoot up the faithful until someone put another wire-guided missile in them.

That might hold off the fall of Gilpin for as much as half an hour.

They forded the river northwest of a highway bridge choked with fleeing survivors. None of them paid any attention to the iron monster churning up the river. The Federation's militiamen had thrown away their guns and run like motherfuckers. McKay didn't blame them. Which nerve agent the faithful were spraying them with McKay didn't know for sure, but whichever it was it would kill or incapacitate pretty much on contact with skin. The militia didn't even have gas masks.

Mobile One rolled up out of the brown water like a sea turtle coming ashore to lay eggs, and circled north of the doomed town. They had almost covered the forty klicks to Freehold when Sloan picked up the radio broadcast announcing that Mayor Westlake had surrendered the entire Northern Rio Grande Federation to the Church of the New Dispensation.

CHAPTER
SEVENTEEN ─────────

"Billy." The word, falling soft as an autumn leaf in the darkness, still jarred McKay from uncertain sleep like the blow of a fist.

He sat up. A Colt MkIV .45-caliber automatic was heavy and cold in his right hand. It felt unfamiliar; his own customized sidearm had been confiscated by the Brothers of Mercy. This weapon had belonged to Freehold founding father Peter Dumont—dead in a raid, was it two days ago?

In the spill of starlight through the window of his bedroom in Angie Connoly's house, McKay made out the distinctive cinder-block shape of Tom Rogers standing carefully out of arm's reach. He knew better than any other Guardian how careful you had to be waking up an old SOG-groupie like McKay.

Without apology McKay tucked the pistol away. "What's up?"

"Sentries on the road just escorted in a couple of prisoners who say they want to talk to us. Bikers."

Bikers? McKay's impulse was to have them taken out back and shot. Somehow Coffin's Dispensation extended to cover even the most violent children of the road. Roving bands of bikers and road gypsies had been harassing the Freeholders and the other communities of the western side of the valley since the debacle at Gilpin a week before. The Freeholders, however, could pitch a fit sometimes if you got up to things like greasing prisoners.

He recalled the way Pete Dumont had taken a round in the hip that night on Trinchera Creek, the other side of Gilpin. They'd hit a camp of several hundred faithful, snooping and pooping into the woods above the camp on one side while Casey somehow maneuvered Mobile One onto an outcrop of volcanic rock above it on another. They'd raised holy hell among the bad guys, with Rogers dropping measured bursts of grenades and .50-caliber on them while the Freeholders cut loose with rifles; McKay and Sloan had played accompaniment on the Maremont and the M-203 grenade launcher. But there'd been a contingent of black-shirted Brothers of Mercy around, and they'd hit back hard and fast while their brethren were running around like decapitated chickens. They'd sent Mobile One reeling back with a volley from light antitank weapons, and close-assaulted against the snipers in the trees with assault rifles.

An M-16 round had smashed the ball of Pete Dumont's right hip. The Brothers were right on top of the raiders, so sudden was their counterattack. The inexperienced retreaters had gotten confused, disorganized, started wandering around in the dark shooting in all directions. Dumont had crawled off to the side and drawn the Brothers of Mercy to him with long bursts from his HK-91—a 7.62-mm rifle illegally modified to fire full automatic. The distraction had given the Guardians time enough to round up the other raiders and get them the hell out of there.

These anarchists had some silly ideas. But they died like men.

"What time is it?" he asked.

"About 0213."

McKay stretched, yawned, grabbed his shirt off the hand-carved wooden bedstead. "Let's do it."

A kerosene lantern cast an uncertain sphere of light in the

living room. To one side stood Sam Sloan, like McKay just
buttoning up his shirt, and a little way away were Casey and
Angie, holding hands. When neither was on watch, they spent
the night together. It didn't bother McKay. It might be their
last chance to catch some brief exhausted moments together.
And he was doing the same thing, on the rare occasions when
he and Doc Vasquez had some free time together.

Somewhere on the far side of the San Luis Valley, Tom
Rogers was using his old Green Beret skills to try to drum up
some trouble in Coffin's backfield. The faithful had descended on the valley like a cross between an occupying army
and a plague of locusts. From the refugees streaming into
the San Juan foothills, the Guardians had learned that the
Brothers of Mercy kept the conquered beaten down with fear,
but had generated enough hatred in the locals that a skillful
operator might well get some of them to overcome their fear
and strike back. As highly as he regarded Rogers, McKay
didn't expect much from the attempt. But then he didn't expect much from anything these days, except for the inexorable
advance of Coffin's mad army.

On the far side of the lantern glow stood the two bikers.
One was a tall, lanky black dude in a jump suit, with trim
beard and mustache, and hair that hung in dreadlocks to his
shoulders. The other was a woman in a Mohawk and a torn
leather aviator's jacket. Beside them, carefully positioned so
their comrades were out of their field of fire and they wouldn't
foul each other, stood a pair of teenagers, a boy and a girl,
covering the bikers with rifles. The muzzles were held very
still. The bikers were very still too.

"Can't Coffin get it through his head we won't surrender?"
McKay demanded.

The Mohawked woman sneered. "It ain't that," the man
said.

"Did Summerill send you?" Angie demanded. "We're still
not going to hand over the Guardians to him." She smiled
wanly in the lamplight. "Nor my mother."

The bikers looked at her with interest. "You the Connoly
girl?" the Mohawked woman asked. Angie nodded. "Summerill's got a price on you too."

"Shut it, Snake," the man said. "My name's Callahan. Friends call me Dreadlock. You can too. Don't matter none at this point."

"A Rasta, in with Coffin's gang?" Sloan asked disbelievingly.

Callahan's locks swung in emphatic denial. "Never a Rasta. Just like the natty dreads." He flashed a quick grin. "Never one of Coffin's people. Not willingly."

"You tryin' to tell us you was drafted, asshole?" McKay asked. This whole scene was a waste of time, and he badly felt the need for sleep.

"Yeah." Callahan stared him defiantly in the eye. "The Cruisers—they're my pack—we never looked to hurt nobody. Scavenging in the ruins was what we were into. That's *all*, man. No strong-arm stuff, no stealin' from anybody still had a use for the stuff. You be doin' it too, you live long enough."

That was true enough. "Get to the point," McKay prompted.

"The Brothers of Mercy." The woman called Snake spat the words out on the hardwood floor. "They caught us on the outskirts of Pueblo."

"Bunch of fuckin' road gypsies and some rednecks," Callahan said. "We were in a warehouse fulla canned goods, all kinds of good shit. They hit us like a thunderbolt, man. All over us at once. Seems the good Lord gave 'em every scrap of food left in the world for their very own. They even thanked us for *findin'* it for 'em."

"So what happened?" Sloan asked, not ungently.

Callahan made a helpless gesture with one hand. "Lost three good riders, just like that. They said join or they'd do us. We been around for a while, man. We know how these Mercy people *do* you. So we joined." He shrugged. "What the fuck? I won't lie to you, man. We figured we might as well go along. If it's a dog-eat-dog world, we might as well run with the Dobermans, you know what I mean."

McKay felt the skin drawing taut over his cheekbones. "What the hell do you want? Sympathy?"

Another grin. "Be nice. But no. We fought some, raided some. Survival, man. Now we want out."

"Coffin shorting you on spoils?" Angie asked. Her voice

had turned hoarse over the last week. The fatigue was wearing her, wearing them all down.

"Coffin! Lady, you think you know what crazy is. You don't know crazy unless you laid eyes on *that man*."

"He's got a pact with the devil," Snake said. "Don't look at me like that; you don't *know*. He spends the night at the bottom of those craters by where Colorado Springs used to be sometimes. Hot enough to kill you like that." She snapped her fingers. "He says it's meditation. *And it doesn't hurt him*."

"He's crazy," Callahan insisted. "This afternoon he hauled this steel surgical table from the clinic out onto the plaza at Gilpin and had his killers hold some chick down while he cut her heart out with a knife." Callahan stared at them with a haunted expression. "He held the heart up and *squeezed*, man, and the blood ran in his mouth and down his chin and all over his face. He says that's holy." He looked at the floor and his voice fell low. "If that's holy, man, I hope there's room in hell for me."

Sloan's face was the color of typing paper. Angie had buried her face in Casey's shoulder. McKay was used to atrocity stories. He'd seen some in the making, maybe even caused some himself, depending on your point of view. But Callahan's tale still made his scrotum shrink. Coffin and his crew went beyond cruelty, beyond insanity. They had entered some transcendental realm of horror.

"So what do you want with us?"

"He's on his way here. Be here tomorrow—no, today. They move slow. You been hurtin' him with those raids, but you haven't stopped him. And you won't."

"Tell us something we don't know," McKay snarled. Mayor Westlake had been bombarding them the last several days with radio broadcasts, personal appeals to "surrender and face a righteous justice." He promised them all just treatment. Somehow that didn't reassure anybody.

"Just one thing you can do," Callahan said. Flame jittered in his eyes. "Kill him. Kill him, and this whole crazy church comes tumbling down."

He smiled. It was an expression better suited to a corpse than a living man. "Let me tell you how—"

*   *   *

"Casey," McKay said, his voice softly echoing in the hangar, "this is without question the nuttiest idea I've ever heard."

"Hand me the wrench, will you, Billy?" The young Californian raised his head and turned to Billy. A smudge of grease on his cheek made him look younger than usual. "You say something?"

McKay sighed. "You seriously think you're gonna shoot down Coffin's air force with this fucking toy airplane?"

"Huh? Oh, yeah, no problem. Could you please hand me that wrench, Billy?"

McKay sighed again and handed Casey the wrench. They were working on the toy airplane in the sole hangar of the Freehold's toy airfield. Casey diddled with something. A voice emerged from the cockpit. Casey nodded and diddled it again. *He hardly knows I'm alive,* McKay thought.

But McKay understood. Flying combat was like the Holy Grail to a fighter jock. Since the time Casey had shot down five Syrian MiGs in a single dogfight and been permanently grounded as too valuable to risk, Casey'd known he'd never feel the hot and cold rush of flying a fighter into battle again.

Except he was about to. Sort of.

The craft he'd be piloting into action was a far cry from the trim little high-tech marvel that was the F-16 in which he'd scored his quintuple kill. It was a state-of-the-art Cessna canard job, which meant that to an untrained eye it looked backward: it had the propeller in the back, no tail, and miniature wings like a tailplane sprouting from its pointy snout like Salvador Dali's mustache. It was the eighth wonder of the world, according to both Casey and its owner, a stocky middle-aged novelist from the Freehold. It used less fuel than a conventional plane, ate less runway to take off and land, turned on a dime, but never, ever stalled. As part of his Guardian training, McKay had received a modicum of flight instruction, so he knew enough of aviation to realize that the bass-ackwards white Cessna was quite the compact miracle of modern science.

But it wasn't a fighter. Not even the installation of two obsolete Browning M-1919A4 .30-caliber machine guns in the nose by Casey, the owner, and a beefy ex-cop from Denver who was Freehold's gunsmith and armorer, would change that.

Where the machine guns had come from, McKay didn't know and didn't really care to. He was, after all, an official of the U.S. government, and possession of even one fully automatic weapon was heavy-duty illegal. Even the sale of semi-automatic versions of assault rifles, such as the FN, the Galil, or the M-16, had been outlawed for several years. Private ownership of autoweapons had been banned, period, in the late eighties. The Freeholders not only had assault rifles, they had ones that had been quite skillfully modified to fire on full automatic like the original military versions. That was easy to overlook; they might have bought them before the ban, they may have modified them after the One-Day War. But there was no way anyone could legally possess full-dress machine guns.

McKay wondered privately about the colonel who lived higher up in the mountains and was said to be a Minuteman. He'd never laid eyes on the man himself. Maybe he really *was* a Minuteman.

The bushy head of the armorer stuck out the side door of the small five-place airplane. "Casey? Could you come inside a second and check the trigger assembly?"

"Sure. Hang on to this a minute, will you, Billy?" Casey handed McKay back the wrench and clambered into the plane. McKay scratched between his shoulder blades with the wrench and eyed the craft dubiously.

Something had to be done to neutralize the faithfuls' aircraft. Most of the dwellings within the Freehold were semisubterranean or earth sheltered, mainly for insulation but also as protection. At least half the homes could serve as fallout shelters on a moment's notice. They didn't have them, they *were* them, with stockpiled food and water, thick earth revetments to keep out the gamma radiation, solar- or wind-powered ventilation with multiple redundant filters, the whole nine yards. The same thick walls or bunkering offered protection against bullets, and as a rule, houses were designed with firing ports in mind. Finally, though the Freehold occupied thousands of acres, the houses were mostly sited so that they provided mutual fire support. All in all, the peaceful and un-

assuming community of Freehold was like a colony of pill-
boxes.

And very little of the protection and tactical foresight built
into the community would do the slightest good against the
nerve gas Coffin's crew had looted from the Rocky Mountain
Arsenal. People who could get inside well-sheltered homes and
seal up had a chance—but fallout's a lot easier to filter out
than gas.

The Guardians had several Stinger shoulder-fired surface-
to-air missiles stocked in Mobile One. Unfortunately, light
private propeller-driven aircraft like the ones the Children of
the New Dispensation were using didn't exhaust enough heat
for the missiles' infrared eye to lock on them. The armored
car's .50-caliber might knock an airplane down, but it
couldn't be elevated high enough to be much use as an anti-
aircraft gun. And McKay knew full well he could spray the sky
with his modified M-60 till the next nuclear war with little
chance of hitting even a low, slow-moving plane.

That reminded McKay of yet another problem. Though the
Freehold used alcohol as fuel, distilled largely from their own
crops and waste products, some of the non-Freeholders on the
west side of the valley had stockpiles of diesel. Some of them
had been willing to donate it to the cause; others had sold to
the Freehold. As far as ammo, the Freehold and the other survivalists had between them stocked enough ammo to fight a
war, but not a stick of it was .50 caliber, to say nothing of
linked 40-mm grenade.

The guns of Mobile One were running dry.

Their only chance against the threat from the sky was Casey
in his toy airplane. Their only chance against the threat on the
ground . . . McKay's throat clenched. Hard-boiled as he was,
he could barely bring himself to think about it.

Casey's head popped out the door. "Billy? Could you grab
hold of that machine gun on your right? We can't get it seated
quite right."

For a third time McKay sighed. He took hold of the perfor-
ated barrel. *I hope to Christ this scheme'll work,* he thought.

He knew damned well it wouldn't, but they didn't have any
choice but to try.

• • •

"I don't want you coming with me tomorrow," Casey said for the third time.

Angie Connoly shook her head in the darkness. "We've settled that already."

"No." He lay on his back with his fingers laced behind his head and stared at the roofbeams. "We've settled that I need a bombardier to chuck grenades out of the *Sparrowhawk* to help Billy and the rest of them on the ground after Coffin's air force is out of the way. Not that you're going."

She propped herself on an elbow beside him. They were both bone tired, desperately tired, so much so that they hadn't made love that evening, though each was in bitter need of that reaffirmation against the black prospect of tomorrow. But this matter had to be resolved, and there would be no other chance. She said slowly, "This is my fight. My home, my friends. It's my job to go."

He shook his head. "Somebody else can do it."

"I'm as well suited as anybody to do the job. It's my responsibility. You're doing your duty as you see it. Let me do what I think is mine."

She sensed his frown. "Didn't think you believed in duty."

"Not the way you see it, as some sort of inborn obligation like that of a vassal toward some uncaring feudal lord." She felt him tense, but she didn't have time to spare his feelings. There could only be truth between them now. "I have a duty to myself, to fight for what I believe in. I have a duty to fight for my friends because it is a burden I have knowingly and willingly assumed."

She leaned over him, hands gripping his bare shoulders. "A dozen of our people have died already, for the same reasons I'm going to be risking my life with you tomorrow. Except I have one more—and that's that I love you and want to fight beside you.

"Or don't you think I'm good enough to die with?"

He clutched her arm. "Don't think that! It's just I—I love you too. I don't want to expose you to danger."

"I'm exposed to the danger," she said, marveling that her voice stayed so level. "It's part and parcel of living in this

world. And since I have to face danger, I'd rather face it with
you."

He pulled her down, found her mouth with his, crushed her
to him. She tore the sheet from between them, writhing on top
of him, and pumping at him with her fingers while he moaned
and kneaded her buttocks and back. Their coupling was quick
and violent, and over all too soon.

When he was asleep she raised herself again, looking down
at him in the faint starlight coming in the windows. *How
young he looks,* she thought.

In time she laid her head down and went to sleep as well.

CHAPTER
EIGHTEEN ───────────────

"The assault goes well, First Prophet," W. Soames Summerill, newly promoted to Elder Brother and Prophet Plenipotentiary—whatever that meant—said to the Reverend Josiah Coffin.

Coffin sat in an ancient overstuffed flower-print chair that he'd picked up in his travels and now insisted on hauling around with him everywhere he went. The First Prophet was a great one for forming sentimental attachments to various articles he came in contact with, as though he were aware they'd become holy relics in time and wanted to afford them the proper appreciation. For example, the gaudy tent Coffin had ordered erected as his command post here, a kilometer back from the beleaguered commune, had started life as the bingo tent at some dreary county fair in Oklahoma and subsequently served as a makeshift hospital in a displaced persons camp—or so the legend went. Summerill was skeptical of the tale, but it was certainly typical of Coffin.

"They resist?" he asked. His voice rolled out like thunder. His eyes blazed like black spotlights.

From the spirited popping of gunfire from the west side of the rise, and the streams of armed men flowing by on both sides of the hill on which the tent had been set up, Summerill thought Coffin might just be able to infer that the Freeholders were indeed resisting. Well, the First Prophet would have his little foibles, lunatic that he was. *He's getting paler,* Summerill thought. *I wonder if it's all that radiation he's exposing himself to.* He had to confess that Coffin's tolerance for ionizing radiation was little short of miraculous.

"They do. Their eyes are blind to wisdom; would they not have acknowledged your ministry otherwise?" *The things I'm called on to say. On the other hand, I do say them with my accustomed eloquence and panache.*

The CB set on the cafeteria table a few meters away crackled. Summerill's communications men had run a coaxial cable to an old windmill halfway down the side of the hill, which had once pumped water into a now-dry stock tank at the bottom. It made quite a serviceable antenna. "Elder Brother," reported the voice of platoon leader Harkings, "we're taking heavy casualties from several of those buried houses. And the house we just overran was empty except for two bodies; the unbelievers had some kind of escape tunnel."

Coffin's habitual frown, as of great and protracted concentration rather than anger or annoyance, didn't change. He merely lifted fingers like the legs of a giant albino spider and stroked his matted beard. Summerill frowned enough for both of them. *Who'd have thought a passel of anarchists would prove so tenacious?*

He took up the microphone. "Do not trouble us with inconsequentialities," he said. "Continue to do your duty, and the Lord shall guide your arm."

"God will give us victory! Harkings out."

"No doubt He shall," Summerill murmured, "in His manifestation as Dow Chemical Company."

"What did you say, my brother?" Coffin asked from the depths of his reverie.

"Should you not call down your winged avengers on the infidels? They will chasten them for their persistence."

"Oh. You are right, Brother Summerill. Let the merciful breath of heaven fall upon them."

Summerill caught himself at the brink of gaping. Truly, here was a wonderful talent for twisting truth and reworking

meaning, like a combination of Joseph Goebbels, Oliver
Cromwell, and Cecil B. De Mille. Allowing himself a grin, he
called for his aircraft to move in. Almost as an afterthought,
he called Harkings back. No point in wasting good Brothers of
Mercy. He had great plans for them once this foolish skirmish
was gotten out of the way.

The Brothers of Mercy, in black leather harnesses, formed a
ring around the hilltop pavilion. Several on the west side were
pointing and muttering. "What is it?" Summerill asked.

"Some of our riders are returning," said the red-haired man
who commanded the guard detail. He had a hook for a left
hand; he'd had a broken arm, Summerill recalled, and it had
turned gangrenous. He chided himself mentally for cluttering
his mind with such details. "They've got prisoners, it looks
like."

Kiting among the thermals over the San Juan Mountains,
playing hide and seek with a friendly cloud, Casey Wilson
abruptly grinned. He'd wanted to go head-hunting, aggres-
sively seeking out the enemy craft and destroying them.
McKay wouldn't let him. There was no telling what kind of
anti-aircraft weapons the Children had, so Casey was under
orders to wait for the enemy to come to him. Casey wanted
very much to please McKay, so he bowed to the ex-Marine's
wishes, even though he felt McKay underestimated him.

And now the enemy was coming to him. Three of them, low
and slow and stupid.

Better than anyone Casey understood the limitations of his
little plane. It wouldn't stand the g-forces of the violent
maneuvers that were the fighter pilot's stock in trade, it lacked
power, and for a gun sight he had a circle with a cross in it
painted on his windscreen. He was like a Kentucky Derby-
winning jockey forced to ride a donkey—with three legs.

Moreover, the little plane was overloaded for this sort of
work. Three of the four passenger seats had been pulled out to
lighten the craft, but no fighter pilot, especially a single-seater
jock like Casey, was happy about getting into a scrap carrying
the weight of even one extra person. To say nothing of all the
other crap they carried. Several crates of grenades—frag and
phosphorus grenades for Angie to drop on the bad guys if the

opportunity arose—plus the supplies McKay had insisted they take along in case they were forced down—sleeping bags, rations, even mountaineering gear, with rope, pitons, and grappling hook, for Christ's sake.

On the other hand, this wasn't the Derby. And the boys in Coffin's crates didn't even know it was a race.

And Casey Wilson knew beyond the shadow of a doubt that he was the best there was.

"Belted in?" he asked.

"Yes."

"Hang on." He put the plane into a diving turn. And smiled.

Dreadlock Callahan swaggered up the hill as though he were thinking of buying it. A Ruger Redhawk double-action .44 Magnum revolver rode in a shoulder holster under his left armpit. It had well-worn custom Hogue grips specially modeled for his hand. At his side walked Snake, stepping out in her thigh-high boots, her head held up, and her powerful shoulders thrown back. It made her big, well-shaped breasts stand out and called attention to the fact that she wasn't wearing a bra under her brown leather jacket and her T-shirt, a sight that never failed to attract the Prophet's attention.

In the past, both Callahan and Snake had been leery of attracting too much attention from the First Prophet or his favorites. Mohawk and all, Callahan's second in command was an attractive woman who exuded the harsh sexuality of a tigress. Now they were going for anything that would muddy the waters.

Behind staggered two men with faces so covered in blood and filth as to be barely recognizable, their hands tied together behind their backs with two ends of a long rope. Each had a noose knotted around his neck; for the benefit of the First Prophet, they had been brought to his presence leashed to Callahan's and Snake's bikes, trotting desperately in their dust to avoid being throttled. Now the bikers led them up the hill like lambs to the slaughter.

Prodding them from behind was a pair of Cruisers, one with a pump shotgun, the other holding a shiny submachine gun of a type Summerill alone recognized. Snake wore its mate on a long sling around her neck, complementing the sawed-off shotgun she wore along one thigh, Mad Max style, and the bowie-bladed trench knife with knuckle duster hilt she wore along the other.

The two biker leaders strode past the circle of Brothers of Mercy without deigning to notice them. Yanking on the ropes, they sent the captives spinning into the dust at Coffin's feet. "We caught a bunch of the bas—that is, the unbelievers tryin' to sneak around on our left flank," Callahan said. "These two're what's left."

Summerill's aristocratic nostrils dilated. "These are two of the four men who've been bedeviling you, First Prophet. The very ones who escaped their just punishment in the crater."

Coffin leaned forward, black eyes wide. "The very leaders of the Devil's Militia," he rasped.

"Lieutenant William McKay and Commander Samuel Sloan," Summerill murmured, "Allow me to introduce his Most Holiness, the First Prophet of God on Earth, Josiah Coffin." He smiled. "It's a pleasure to see you gentlemen again."

"Wish we could say the same," Sam Sloan said through puffed lips. It was a lie. Sloan was as glad as he could possibly be to see Soames Summerill's smiling face again, but he didn't dare say so.

Groveling in the dust, the Guardians studied the First Prophet as he rose from his armchair throne. He looked just like Rasputin: tall, gaunt, wide shouldered, and sunken cheeked, with the same recessed, mad, compelling eyes. He radiated pure power. Sloan could see how even sensible people would follow him, how even decent people would turn to monsters at his command. The Browning high-power 9-mm pistol stuck inside his pants dug him in the small of the back, and he hoped the signal to use it wouldn't be long in coming.

Never thought this mother's son'd grow up to be an assassin, he thought wryly. *Not too sure it's conduct becoming an officer and a gentleman.*

But there wasn't any choice, not anymore. If Coffin died, the whole insane edifice of his church would come tumbling down. He might become a martyr, but seeing the man for the first time, feeling the awful impact of his presence, Sloan understood that in this case that didn't matter. Without the cohesive force of Coffin's personality, the eerie alliance of zombi and Jesus freak, of road gypsy and truck driver, of biker and Baptist, would shatter.

He glanced at McKay. McKay's nearer eye was purpled over and swollen half shut. The mud and blood were cosmetic, but McKay's shiner and his split lip were real. There hadn't been time to fake those convincingly. Sam still felt a tad guilty at the pleasure he'd taken in blackening McKay's eye, but he reckoned McKay had paid him in full. The Freeholders had grinned at the exchange, but Guardians took care of their own.

"Mighty nice guns they got," a redheaded man with a hook said. Sloan had seen him before, outside Perkins' office. And that huge bald guy with the zombi look—he was the one who'd pinned McKay's arms when they got bushwhacked.

Snake hefted her submachine gun. "Got 'em off a couple of deaders."

"They are Heckler and Koch MP-5s," Summerill said, "with integral silencers, manufactured in .45 caliber for the use of antiterrorist forces." He gestured airily. "Take them away—and the other weapons as well. Our dear friends and allies are attempting treachery."

A hawk had come among the chickens.

An ancient high-wing Piper labored under the load of the pressurized tanks slung beneath it. Brother of Mercy Willie flew with a cautious eye on the ground beneath. If they bent the damned—er, accursed—airplane, lethal VX nerve gas would inundate the faithful who were falling back from the Freehold to let the planes go in. Also, it would not do one bit of good to Brother Willie or Brother Frank, his bombardier.

Brother Willie was a roly-poly little shit-kicker with a smile for everybody and a private pilot's license. He was extremely conscious of his honor, leading the flight of three aircraft against the bastions of unrighteousness. Their job was to gas the first few ranks of Freehold homes while the other two planes sowed their vaporized death deeper into enemy territory.

Brother Frank had spent his life worrying until he wasn't

much more than skin and bones, Adam's apple and googly eyes and not much chin. He had a Caterpillar tractor hat pushed back on his head and was twisting his hands together to keep them from grabbing the trigger in his lap too soon. Brother Frank had a sense of his own limitations, if not much else.

" 'Nother hill, we'll be ready to hit it," Brother Willie warbled. He was fit to bust. He'd flown the gas attack on the Federation at Gilpin and it had just been peachy. He could hardly wait to get at the Freehold. "Quit playin' with yourself, Brother Frank, and git ready to punch that button."

Frank moistened his lips and fumbled at the safety cover shielding the button that released the gas. He was the one they had in mind when they dreamed up foolproof safeties.

Suddenly he froze like a rabbit caught in a semi's headlight. He blinked his prominent eyes rapidly and said, "What's that sound?"

"Say what? Git ready with that darn button."

"Heard somethin'. Sounded like rippin' cloth."

"Aw, hellfire, Frank," Willie said. "Keep your mind—"

The plane shuddered spastically. Brother Willie said "yurp" as a .30-caliber bullet punched through his left shoulder blade, went through his lung, and knocked bits of rib and gristle and gore all over his instrument panel coming out. His left hand quit obeying instructions, his right just naturally wandered up to find out if it could possibly be true that some of him, parts of his actual *body*, had been somehow knocked awry, and his eyesight started getting blurry and dim.

Then jittery Brother Frank *really* had something to worry about—for the six seconds before the Piper collided with the state of Colorado at two hundred klicks an hour.

Casey zoomed into a short, steep climb to lose speed. He'd circled around and stooped on the right-hand plane of the three strung out in a sort of line over the San Juan foothills. He felt hot triumph welling up his throat from his belly. He'd had to hunt for his target some with that makeshift sight. But during the early years of the Second World War, Soviet fighter-drivers had gotten by, if not well, using exactly the same system, and Casey was sure he was as good as any damn

Russian. He'd just proved it—the eighth kill of his career lay smoking in the grama grass while a lot of armed Children of the New Dispensation stood watching in terminal fascination as nerve gas billowed out at them.

Wild-eyed, Angie Connoly stared at him. She had climbed into the Cessna that morning with the man she had, in spite of everything she and he believed, come to love. Now she flew with a total stranger, a taut-faced, terse man who didn't even speak in the same voice as the Casey Wilson she knew. The fierce exultation on his face when the Piper crashed shocked and appalled her.

She might have been more appalled had she realized Casey was committed to a maneuver he'd never so much as tried before. He'd never flown a canard job, though he knew a lot about them; he hadn't dared take *Sparrowhawk* for a test flight for fear of tipping their hand to the Children of the New Dispensation. But he knew a canard plane was almost impossible to stall. He intended to use that fact to score his next kill.

Since he'd bled off the speed he'd picked up in the dive on his first victim, the other two planes had pulled out ahead of him again. He was back above and behind them, and he wanted to get out of a climb and after them fast. He pulled the nose up toward the vertical. In another plane he would have been going into a hammerhead stall, pulling through the point at which the wings no longer gave lift, and fallen onto his back and done a wingover, a quick and dirty way to reverse direction. Instead, he brought the little plane to a stall, at which point the airfoils lost their power to hold him up and the aircraft turned into a peculiarly shaped brick.

The nose dropped rapidly. In the normal order of things, he would have snapped into a stall-spin and gone into the ground in short order; he was too low to have much prayer of gathering enough speed to pull out. But his gamble paid off. The funny little bone-in-the-nose miniwing, angled differently than the wing, bit into the air almost at once, returning the aerodynamic lift. *Sparrowhawk* snapped into a shallow dive, picking up speed fast.

The middle plane was another top-wing job. Somebody inside it must have spotted him, because it abruptly fell off on the left wing and went scooting away in a serpentine dash.

Casey let off a long burst and missed. Eyes slitted, lips compressed to an angry line, he dove in pursuit, milking short blasts from the jury-rigged guns.

The enemy pulled up in a sharp climb, trying to curve up into the sun. Angie sucked in her breath as Casey pushed the stick forward and *deepened* his dive. Then she was crushed in her seat as he pulled up sharply. She felt the airframe straining at the edge of collapse with the force of the maneuver.

Sparrowhead rose like a rocket toward the other plane. Angie saw its underside, fat and pale as a fish's underbelly, with a pair of green tanks clinging to it like remoras. Casey's thumb pressed the firing button. Angie stuffed her fingers in her ears to cut down the piercing, painful hammering of the guns.

For a moment nothing happened but noise. Then Angie saw sparks dance on the green canisters. A moment later yellow flame spurted in a thin jet from the right side of the enemy plane's nose. At once a pillow-fat cloud of fire engulfed the aircraft. "Oh, God," Angie gasped, and hid her eyes.

She hated the thought of having to shoot people, but self-defense was an absolute right, and if you were attacked you did what you had to. She knew this was self-defense too, that the men in that plane fully intended to murder her friends and neighbors in their homes. But the thought of them burning all the way to the ground was too horrible to bear.

Within arm's reach and yet oblivious to her, Casey cursed and kicked at the makeshift feed box that held the belts of ammo for the guns. Jammed! And there was one plane left —one which Casey had no intention of allowing to escape.

He banked and circled around the thick line of black smoke his ninth victim had drawn at a slant across the sky.

Dreadlock Callahan and his partner, Snake, stood absolutely still. Sam Sloan blinked. Had he really heard Summerill say what he thought he had?

"Search the prisoners," Summerill said as Brothers of Mercy plucked weapons from the hands and persons of the four bikers. "They no doubt are armed as well."

A kick in the ribs lofted Sloan up and onto his side. He moaned and fought for breath while somebody hiked up his camo blouse and the Kevlar vest beneath. "Elder Brother, you're right!" a road gypsy exclaimed. "He's got a gun." At his side, McKay glowered into the muzzle of a Remington auto-loading shotgun as he was relieved of the Ingram hidden under his shirt. Casey liked to carry the vicious little machine pistol as a close-combat weapon. Without its long Sionics silencer—and it was a true silencer, since the .45-caliber bullets it fired moved slower than sound—it wasn't much larger than a Colt Government model autopistol. Given even a hair-breadth of a chance, McKay could have whipped it up and sprayed the pavilion with lead.

"Instinct," Summerill was saying through his nose. "An old intelligence man's instincts tripped you up, Callahan, my friend. I wondered at your nocturnal jaunt night before last. So I had you shadowed when you set out on your reconnaissance patrol this morning. My men saw you meet with the unbelievers."

"In the Lord I see all things," Coffin intoned. He pointed a long, knobby finger at Callahan. "You sought to deceive me. In vain, in vain."

Just then an airplane careened around the hill to the west of them, one wingtip ruffling the chamisa. Behind it whined a white arrowhead, its snout practically pressed against the other aircraft's rudder.

The final aircraft was a sleek green and white low-wing Beechcraft. Casey intended to scare it to death.

It was bound for the heart of Freehold territory, and such was the training of the New Dispensation's air crew that nobody had bothered to warn its pilot that the flight was under attack. He got the idea, however, when a trim canard howled right over his head, so close its fixed wheels nearly brushed the canopy.

He broke off the attack at once. He was no Brother Willie, who knew how to take off, follow a flight plan, and land. He was a professional pilot, and he figured he could do the Lord's work a lot better alive than dead.

The first thing he did was use a little device he'd installed himself without telling his superiors or the mechanics at the Gilpin municipal airport. The twin tanks of poison gas broke away from the underside of his plane and fell harmlessly to the ground. Lightened by jettisoning their weight, the aircraft streaked forward like a startled jackrabbit. It curved in a 180-degree turn.

Casey was on its tail at once. Angie gripped her seat until her knuckles felt as if they'd dislocate, determined not to scream or in any way distract him as he drove his quarry right down to the deck.

He glanced at her for the first time in what seemed like hours. Suddenly he was Casey again, smiling at her boyishly. He reached out and patted her hand reassuringly. Then the mask slipped back in place and he closed in on the fleeing plane as it wove from side to side among the hills, impossibly low to the ground. He caught a flash of color like a circus tent on a hilltop. It passed at the level of his cockpit, but he was too intent on the chase to pay it any mind.

He was about to either bring the third plane down or splash himself and Angie all over the San Luis Valley.

The Brothers of Mercy gaped at the airplanes screaming by at the level of their hilltop. Snake moved like her namesake. Her hand plucked the knuckle-duster knife from the hand of the man next to her, plunged it into his side, then ripped his shotgun away from him as he staggered back clutching at the knife's hilt.

A road gypsy Brother of Mercy with a Mohawk like hers swung his M-16 at her. She blew the left side of his chest open. It registered in Sam Sloan's brain that it was the grinning 'hawker who'd clubbed him and McKay. Then he launched himself against the legs of the nearest guard.

The giant zombi called Lobo grinned an immense, slobbering grin and squeezed a short burst from the MP-5 he held in one huge hand. Three bullets slammed into Snake and knocked her sprawling. With blood gushing from her mouth she tried to rise and aim the shotgun. Lobo went hur-hur-hur in imbecile mirth and shot her again.

With a panther scream of rage Dreadlock Callahan launched himself at Lobo. He sent the submachine gun spinning away with a blow of his forearm. Lobo lunged at him and grabbed him around the neck with both hands. He started to squeeze.

Lobo liked this kind of work. He was going to squeeze the black man's neck until his eyes popped out. That was real funny.

Instead, a vice clamped down on his own neck. His eyes goggled in surprise that turned quickly to rage. *Someone was trying to strangle him*.

Billy McKay had whipped his hands free from the phony magician's knot that held them behind his back and bounced to his feet. A bound had carried him behind the giant. Now his hands were locked around that blubbery, greasy pillar of a neck. The strength of fury flowed in his arms.

In an instant the hilltop had become alive with battling figures. Callahan's other two bikers had jumped the nearest guards and were rolling around in the dirt, kneeing and grunting and gouging. A muffled explosion slammed out as Sloan pulled a pistol from the belt of the man he'd body-checked, jammed it into his gut, and fired. The man bellowed like a branded bull calf.

Lobo reached behind him, tried to grab the smartass who was trying to choke him. McKay felt clumsy fingers brush his arms, but he tightened his grip more and still more.

W. Soames Summerill stood thunderstruck. The triumph he had carefully staged before the very eyes of the First Prophet had unraveled into catastrophe. He saw Sam Sloan come up to one knee and pump three slugs into the man with the hook. The ex-trucker dropped like an empty sack.

The First Prophet himself had taken off like a pronghorn in flight, bounding down the flank of the hill, his black-clad elbows working like wings. There was only one thing for the man called Trajan to do.

He kicked the center pole of the tent loose and ran like a son of a bitch.

The hairless, reeking zombi grunted and drooled in panic. He couldn't breathe! He clawed at the fingers buried in his throat.

With a convulsion of effort, McKay caved in his windpipe. The giant fell down and lay kicking, his flabby, knife-scarred face contorting hideously, turning purple.

The tent dropped on Billy McKay's head.

• • •

In the end it was easy, almost painfully so, because though the New Dispensation flier was a professional pilot, he wasn't a *fighter* pilot.

Casey chivied him along, watching the ground ahead. When he saw something he liked, he pulled up in a steep climb. He got a thousand, two thousand feet on the Beechcraft. Then he pushed over and went screaming down.

The other pilot was shitting bricks by this time. Dividing his attention between the ground that rushed by right under his belly and the nemesis bearing down on him from behind, he wasn't able to think too clearly. When a frantic glance backward showed him that his pursuer was diving on him like a hawk on a pigeon, he did the instinctive thing and dove. Hard.

He wasn't much of a tactician, but he was a hell of a pilot, and his reflexes were superb. He actually managed to clear the hill Casey had been herding him into by a whole half meter.

However, he failed to clear the house trailer parked on top of it.

Casey's mask disintegrated in a triumphant shout. He was a double ace now. Grinning in exultation, he banked above the flaming wreckage and headed back for the lines.

For a wild moment Sam Sloan thought he was drowning. Then he realized the tent had fallen in on him. He started crawling blindly. He blundered into someone, punched out, felt his fist sink into a meaty side. The other man grunted and moved away. Sloan scrambled faster, feeling claustrophobia closing in.

His head broke out into daylight. He drank in a deep breath of air and looked around.

On a ridge top two hundred meters away, the unmistakable black stork form of Josiah Coffin was scrambling up on top of a parked van. Sloan hefted the pistol he'd grabbed in his hands. A .45 auto. *I'm not going to pick him off at this range with this,* he thought.

He took another long breath and ducked back under the canvas to see if he could scrounge up a rifle.

• • •

"Casey," Angelina Connoly exclaimed. "Look down there—there's a man on that van!"

Casey frowned and banked. He'd been looking for promising targets for Angie to drop things on. Though the hills he'd flown over while chasing the Beechcraft had been black with Children of the New Dispensation, the hilltop with the circus tent seemed more promising. Anything as silly as the tent had to be there for a reason. Maybe it was important.

By the time he got back the tent had fallen down. However, troops that had moved out to the attack were moving hurriedly back, away from the nerve gas spilled by the first plane Casey had downed. The area around the tent and the windmill was thick with them. Casey wished his machine guns still worked.

He was about to tell Angie to move back and start chucking out grenades when she called to him about the man on the van. He took one look and a voice in his head said, *Coffin*. There was nobody else he could think of who'd be standing on a van in the middle of battle exhorting the faithful.

He bit his lip. Something had obviously happened to McKay and Sloan. Unfortunately, he'd spent most of the battle out of communicator range. It looked as if it was all up to him.

A plan snapped into his mind. He shook it off. It came back. It was insane, impractical, downright silly. But there wasn't anything else he could do.

"Angie," he said, speaking very carefully in hopes she wouldn't think he'd gone berserk and panic, "would you go back and get into the mountain kit—"

"There!" McKay crowed. He'd found a knife on a body and attacked the enveloping tarp. It had been like fighting an octopus, but at last he'd won.

Then he got a look at *what* he'd won, and almost wished he'd kept his head under the covers. Way off in the distance he glimpsed Coffin ranting at his troops from on top of a van. And near at hand, faithful and black-clad Brothers of Mercy were converging on the hilltop like piranhas on a pig's carcass.

He submerged under the torn canvas, groped briefly, found the submachine gun that Callahan had knocked from Lobo's hand. A good thing about SMGs was that they gave you a lot more range than a pistol. He just hoped it'd be enough.

He lay on his belly. The Children were crowding close—be on him anytime now. He snugged the wooden butt of the MP-5 against his shoulder, took a breath, held it, squeezed. The weapon emitted a discreet little fart and punched his shoulder.

He missed. With a roar, the faithful followers of Coffin swarmed over him.

Air whistled in the open door of the Cessna. Holding the grappling hook in hands that wanted to tremble like an aspen leaf in a high wind, Angie wondered if this could possibly work—and if she could bring herself to try. She'd never harmed another human in her life. The thought of starting now filled her throat with sour bile.

You're willing to have others kill to protect you, she told herself bitterly. *And that's no different from doing it yourself.*

This man is attacking your home, your friends, your . . . love. It's up to you to stop him.

She glanced out. The ground was sickeningly close below. From the way the plane bobbed and slipped up and down and sideways, she knew Casey was fighting with every gram of expertise he possessed to keep airborne at such a low speed. Yet the yellow earth beneath sped by so fast she almost felt its passage would suck her from the aircraft.

Ahead—there was the van with the black-clad man on it. Coffin? It had to be.

Dear God, if you're there, please let me do it! She'd almost never prayed, always despised those who prayed for help in hurting their fellow humans. But she did so now.

She raised her arm.

M-16 in hand, Sam eeled back out from under the tent. A mob of faithful washed over him like an incoming tide. He hauled the trigger back, intending to panic-fire the whole clip in hopes of making them pull back. The weapon snarled three shots so quickly they sounded like one and quit, stopped cold by the three-shot regulator. "Where would we be without progress?" Sloan asked aloud, and someone kicked him in the face.

He managed to swat several heads with the butt of the rifle.
It was made out of nylon, and the results were not very
satisfactory. He was hauled upright and the gun wrested from
his grasp. "Hang him!" somebody shouted while dissenting
voices cried, "Burn him!" From the corner of his eye he saw
McKay and Callahan being likewise manhandled.

Then his attackers let out a single, many-throated gasp. He
was free. He turned to see the Reverend Josiah Coffin take off
into the air like a huge black bird.

Angie screamed in sympathetic agony as the three-pronged
hook slammed itself right under Coffin's right shoulder blade.
Sparrowhawk swept by above him—and almost went down
when it hit the end of the slack.

Up and up the canard rose, towing Coffin like a captured
skyhook balloon. "Angie, are you all right?" Casey yelled.

"Yes," she said, then screamed, "Yes!" when she realized
the first word had been a whisper. The airplane's engine
strained behind the rear bulkhead.

With a squealing of tortured metal, the remaining passenger
seat began to tear loose from the floor. It was the only thing in
the cabin Casey could think of to anchor the rope to. "The
hatchet, Angie," he shouted. "Cut us loose!"

She snatched the hand axe up from the open mountaineering kit and attacked the rigid rope.

On the hilltop with the canvas rumpled up around their
knees, McKay, Sloan, and Dreadlock Callahan stood with
their would-be lynchers and gaped into the sky. Coffin soared
upward dizzily. "Look," somebody cried, "the Prophet's
ascendin' into heaven." Sloan realized that many of the faithful actually didn't recognize that he was being towed by the
buzzing white airplane, and not floating up into heaven on his
own.

Coffin was lifting higher into the sky when his ascent
abruptly reversed. The ecstatic cries of the faithful turned to
screams of consternation as he fell straight toward them, arms
outspread as if in benediction.

With a heavy, wet *thump!* the First Prophet Coffin struck

an upright blade of the windmill. The thin metal slid up inside his rib cage like a spoon into pudding. For a moment he poised there, arms still outflung, eyes standing terribly out of his head while blood fountained from him in all directions and fell on the upturned faces of his faithful like red rain.

Then with a groan, the wheel turned and the Prophet was suspended, lifeless, upside down above an awful ringing stillness.

EPILOGUE

Slowly Yevgeny Maximov laid the printout on the vast desk before him. He closed his eyes and pressed spatulate fingertips to his temples. He seldom had headaches. He had one now.

It had taken valuable days, irreplaceable days, for his intelligence network to piece together the events that had led to the disappearance of Trajan. They made sorry reading indeed. The last links to the Blueprint for Renewal had been snapped. Perkins, that miserable rabbit, had committed suicide. And Dr. Marguerite Connoly— They had robbed him again, those filthy, dung-eating Guardians!

He slammed his fist down on the desk so violently that the thick oak top bowed inward with a dangerous creak. Such news as this, coming on the heels of the food riots in Warsaw, Aachen, and Lyons, and the outbreak of widespread resistance in England. He forced himself to draw a deep, calming breath, and promised that the Guardians would pay for the agony they had caused him. Would pay with interest, oh, very much interest.

His hand swept up the surprisingly dainty handset of his telephone like a bear swiping a gilded trout from a stream. "Get Vesensky," he said.

In a moment his chief aide said, "Yes, Yevgeny."

"Ah, Ivan Vissarionovich." He sighed gustily. So easy now to give way to self-pity, yet he must not. "The time has come when I must do what I perceive I should have done all along."

With his usual intuition, Ivan Vesensky said, "Trajan's made a mess of things in America, hasn't he?"

"Yes, Ivan. So I shall bite the bullet, as the Americans are wont to say, and send you to America."

"I hope I'm worthy of this honor," Vesensky said, a trifle sourly.

"So do I. If I don't get the Blueprint soon, all that we've worked for will go up in smoke. Likely, so shall we."

He gazed out the great window at the blue vistas of the Bernese Alps. Vesensky waited patiently. At length Maximov smiled. "If nothing else, it seems that Trajan had the good taste to spare us the trouble of having to discipline him. Though it would have been neater if the body had been found."

"We can't have everything, Excellency."

"No?" Maximov chuckled. "We shall see."

Happy endings, of a sort.

The spectacular exit of the First Prophet utterly broke the will of the faithful to continue the fight. With rebellions sparked by Rogers bursting into wildfire, they withdrew from the San Luis Valley as best they could. It wasn't pretty, especially since the plague was hitting the survivors streaming back toward Denver.

Between the time when the dazed Children of the New Dispensation allowed the two captive Guardians and Dreadlock Callahan to go and the time the last miserable truckload of true believers rolled north through Poncha Pass, word came down through the grapevine that T. Nolan Perkins, unable to bear the knowledge of the tragedy he'd unwittingly helped unleash on Colorado, had killed himself in the Denver Federal Center. At least, the Guardians thought, it saved them from having to go into the pesthole of the DFC after him.

Dreadlock Callahan and the remnants of his Cruisers rode off in pursuit of the horizon.

On a disgustingly bright day in mid-July—McKay and Sloan had both slept through the Fourth, which was probably just as well—the Guardians took their leave of the Freehold. More than fifty of the Freeholders had died in the war. Most of the rest turned out to see them go. In their outlooks they and the Guardians were as unlike as cats and pine trees, but they had fought together, for one another, and that meant much to both sides.

Connoly mother and daughter exchanged hugs and pecks on the cheek. Dr. Connoly had worked tirelessly throughout the crisis as a volunteer nurse. But the shared danger seemed to have done nothing to bring her and Angelina closer together.

Sam Sloan helped Marguerite Connoly into Mobile One. Angie stepped forward and kissed the Guardians one by one: Tom, Sam, Billy. Then she kissed Casey Wilson. The Guardians and the Freeholders found a lot of different directions to look in.

They sealed up and rolled down the road, over the dwindling foothills, past a half-dozen gutted homes, past the twisted black wreckage of an airplane, past parties of men and women going about the dreary, sickening work of policing up the sad organic flotsam of battle—many of them under the guns and watchful eyes of Freeholders. A number of the faithful had surrendered. The Freeholders wouldn't put any of them to death, and none of the wretched survivors of the Church of the New Dispensation would ever have the resources to pay for a fraction of the damage they'd done to the people of the community. Since no reparations they could levy would make sense, the victors insisted only that the prisoners help clean up the mess they'd made. McKay felt that was lenient to the point of idiocy, but he hadn't been asked. Well, no, that wasn't true; he had. He just hadn't been listened to.

They drove past the lonely windmill. None of them looked at it directly.

After a while, Casey said, "Funny thing. When you go through a battle with somebody, you get real close to them."

Sloan looked at him in surprise. "Heck, you know that, Case."

Casey looked thoughtful for a moment. "But I just learned it all over again."

McKay gazed out the viewport. He didn't envy Casey any more. McKay's own leave-taking with Ruby Vasquez had been a fierce and final session between the sheets. They'd both had a hell of a good time with one another, they'd shared pleasure in the teeth of hell, but that was all over and no more expected.

But for Casey, Freehold would fester inside him until he came back. Or died. And much as he hated to admit it, McKay knew the latter was a lot more likely.

They'd made twenty-some klicks when Sloan said, "Message for you, McKay."

McKay roused himself from his dog-tired stupor. Once he sacked out back at Heartland it'd take a crane to get him out of bed. "What."

"Why, His Honor, the Mayor and president of the Northern Rio Grande Federation, of course," Sloan said, a devilish grin on his face, "inviting us all to attend a banquet in honor of the liberation of the San Luis Valley."

McKay pondered. "Patch me through," he said. A moment later Mayor Westlake said, "Lieutenant McKay, I don't know how to thank—"

For the next five minutes McKay told Mayor Westlake exactly who he was, what he was, where he'd come from, and where he was going. It was not, overall, an optimistic assessment. But when Sloan had broken the connection with a speechless Mayor, McKay felt better.

Sitting on her fold-down, Dr. Connoly favored McKay with a scowl of matronly disapproval. "You really shouldn't speak to Mayor Westlake that way," she said primly. "He and his Federation are still the hope of the people of this valley." She gazed out the window, but she wasn't seeing the patchwork of desert and farmland roll itself past like an old-time panorama. Her eyes were fixed on a glowing vision of the future. "When I've finished my work at Heartland, I believe I'll come back here to advise the Mayor. We can set up the perfect benevolent state of this valley, the perfect partnership of government and well-managed economy."

Billy McKay had stopped listening. His eyes fixed on a vision of their own. He heaved himself off his seat, swayed to the rear of the cabin, twitched up a corner of the black, four-mil plastic that covered flat boxes stacked in front of the engine compartment. Yep. There they still were.

Fifteen cases of Coors beer. A final gift from the people of the Freehold.

Not yet, he told himself. He'd savor the anticipation as long as he could stand it. He let the plastic fall back.

Happy endings. Of a sort. He settled into his seat, leaned against the wall, and went to sleep.

And dreamed of beer.

Richard Austin
The Guardians £3.50

The third adventure in the blistering new series

World War III is over . . . and the ultimate battle for
control has begun.

From the blasted ruins of World War III came the Guardians . . .

Armed with awesome combat skills; equipped with the most
devastating weaponry ever devised; trained to hair trigger tautness;
the Guardians have been entrusted with freedom's last hope . . .

The Top Secret Blueprint for Renewal!

Their first task: to get the new President away from a ravaged
Washington to the mid-western fortress known as Heartland.

But between Washington and the impregnable fortress lie a
thousand miles of chaos . . .

All Pan books are available at your local bookshop or newsagent, or can be ordered direct from the publisher. Indicate the number of copies required and fill in the form below.

Send to: **CS Department, Pan Books Ltd., P.O. Box 40,
              Basingstoke, Hants.   RG21 2YT.**

or phone: 0256 469551 (Ansaphone), quoting title, author
              and Credit Card number.

Please enclose a remittance* to the value of the cover price plus: 60p for the first book plus 30p per copy for each additional book ordered to a maximum charge of £2.40 to cover postage and packing.

*Payment may be made in sterling by UK personal cheque, postal order, sterling draft or international money order, made payable to Pan Books Ltd.

Alternatively by Barclaycard/Access:

Card No. | | | | | | | | | | | | | | | | | |

Signature:

Applicable only in the UK and Republic of Ireland.

While every effort is made to keep prices low, it is sometimes necessary to increase prices at short notice. Pan Books reserve the right to show on covers and charge new retail prices which may differ from those advertised in the text or elsewhere.

NAME AND ADDRESS IN BLOCK LETTERS PLEASE:

....

Name ——————————————————————————————

Address ——————————————————————————————

————————————————————————————————

————————————————————————————————

————————————————————————————————

3/87